Reflections of Dawn

Book Three of the Dawn Trilogy

B.J. Young

"To everything there is a season" Ecclesiastes 3:1

BJYoung

B.J. Young

Cover photo by Carissa Kost

Edited by

Lindsey R Pugsley Studio

ISBN-13:9781494994136
ISBN-10: 1494994135

Note from author: This novel is a work of fiction. Names, characters, places and incidents are either products of the author's imagination or used fictitiously. All characters are fictional, and any similarity to people living or dead is purely coincidental.

Printed in the United States of America

For my mother,

gone now, but her light still shines.

And for my dad,

my guide and my anchor when I need one.

I love you both.

B.J. Young

Acknowledgments

There are many who have traveled with me on this journey of publication. To my dear family and friends, you know who you are; I hope you know how much I appreciate you.

As always, I want to thank my Lord and Savior, Jesus Christ. My desire is that any words I write will point others to Him. May they see Him as their Redeemer, their constant companion, and the source of all joy.

But this last book of my Dawn trilogy was written for my readers. Your words of encouragement, your enthusiasm, and your requests for "more" have inspired me to continue the journey. Thank you

The night is dark and heavy,

a cloak of loneliness and sorrow.

Unrelenting, its weight confines me.

Will it ever set me free?

Then I see it…

a bright star in the East.

Long dead, but still it shines,

it promises joy that only dawn can bring.

Chapter 1

Something huge and heavy pressed down on Ben's chest. It was crushing his lungs, making it difficult to breathe. Fighting and clawing his way out of restless sleep, he bolted upright. He gasped for air, gasped again for life. He reached for Katy. Needing her, he called her name.

Through the darkness that hovered over him in the pre-dawn hours, he searched. But Katy wasn't there. Her side of the bed was empty. The darkness could not hide the reality of his life. His bed was empty. His arms ached to hold his wife, but loneliness was his only companion.

She was gone and wouldn't be back. When she left, half his soul was ripped away, leaving what remained, bleeding and damaged forever.

If it hadn't been for Sam, Ben Browning would have died with her. He knew that in every part of his being. Sam, his and Katy's son, was the reason he now lived. He had her dark hair, her joy, and her ability to see only the good in life. But Sam saw the good in the world through dark blue eyes that were a gift from his dad. Katy had said Sam's eyes were his best feature because they looked like his, but Sam was his mother's child. Sam was the miracle that came from the love he and Katy shared. Sam had been Katy's zenith, and according to her, the purpose for her life. Now he was Ben's only salvation.

Ben had waited for love and a family of his own for a long time. The day he looked into Katy's chocolate brown eyes, he knew he had come home. When she told him she was dying, he refused to believe it. Love, for him, was a forever thing.

When Katy died, Ben was sure he would die too...but he couldn't. Sam needed him.

*****

Ben looked at the clock. It wasn't necessary. He knew it was 4:23 a.m., the same time he woke every morning. It was the exact time Katy had died, two years, nine months and twelve days ago. It didn't matter what time he went to bed, he always woke up at the same time.

It was useless to even try to fall back to sleep. Sleep would not come again until he fell, exhausted, into his bed at the end of the day.

But it was okay. Early mornings had become his special time, a time to drink his coffee on the deck and think uninterrupted thoughts of Katy. Mornings had been their special time of the day when she lived. And now that he was alone, it still was for Ben.

Moving to the middle of the bed, he gave the light blue coverlet a shake and pulled it taut. Then he slipped out from under it and placed the four pillows at the top of the bed. During the night, one of them had been used to rest his head, but the other three had been lined up on her side of the bed. Several times, in the darkness of the night, he had reached over and pulled one of them close to him. He wondered at times if he'd ever stop reaching for her.

Katy had always made the bed. The best he did now was make it presentable. It probably wasn't necessary. No one would enter the room until he returned that night. It was a shrine, a sacred place where only he could come to get away from the world and relive the life he had enjoyed with his beautiful Katy.

Ben pulled his jeans on while he went to his dresser. From the top drawer he took a small notebook. Tucking it into his back pocket, he shuffled to the kitchen where he turned on the light above the sink. He had put the coffee and water in the coffee maker the night before; all he needed to do now was turn it on.

While it brewed, he walked soundlessly to Sam's room. The Mickey Mouse nightlight put out just enough light for Ben to see the tousled, dark brown curls that covered his son's head. In the little boy's arm was the stuffed star his mother gave him four nights before she died. She told him to hold it close when he went to bed, and remember that she loved him.

She also told him to look for her among the stars in the sky when he needed to talk to her. She promised to be there, listening to him, and lighting his way. Almost three years later, Sam was still clinging to his star.

"You look just like your momma, Sam," he whispered, wanting to touch him, but fearful of wakening him. "She'd be so proud of you."

Leaving Sam's room and closing the door quietly behind him, he shuffled quietly to the bedroom next to Sam's. Six month old Molly was sound asleep, sucking on her thumb. A dribble of drool was forming on the sheet. Sweet little Molly—she had come into his and Sam's life so unexpectedly. She came, bringing with her a ray of sunlight and unanticipated joy at a time when they needed her most.

Smiling, he turned away from her and closed the door as he left. Both kids would sleep for two more hours.

And Ben had two hours before he had to face his world. Two hours alone—to some it would have been a time of loneliness. To Ben, it was a gift. It was the only two hours of the day he allowed himself to think about Katy, to reminisce about the four years they had been together. He had two hours a day to focus on the only woman he had ever loved. Two hours in which he could have thanked God for the time he had with her, for the son she gave him, and for the way of life her generosity had provided for him.

But Ben didn't want to talk to God. He was still angry at God.

*****

Taking his cup of coffee to the deck with him, he found the swing in the darkness of the pre-dawn hour. It was warm outside already. But then, it was early May in Florida. Looking up into the moonless sky, Ben found his star. Polaris, the North Star was at the end of the handle of the Little Dipper—just like it always was. He had renamed it Katy. It was always such a comfort when he could see it. When it was cloudy, he missed it. That's when he had to take the little book out of his back pocket and hold it in his hands. He didn't have to read the words she had written to him, he had them memorized.

"Ben. I love you so much, and I know without doubt you love me too. But now, it's time for me to go away. You've given me permission…I know it's because you love me and don't want me to suffer any more. Thank you for that. If I could stay, you know I would. I know you want me to, and I would give anything to grow old with you. But since I can't, I need to tell you something. Even though I'll be gone, I'll still be close by. Always. Just like the North Star that never fails to shine, I'll be here. Cling to that, Baby. Even when our star is hidden by the clouds, we still know it's there. Remind Sam too, will you?"

"I remind him all the time, Katy." Ben whispered to his star. "I hope you can see him. He gives me so much joy."

Smiling, Ben remembered the determination in Sam's eyes at dinner the night before. He had just declared he wasn't going to school in the fall.

"And why is that?" Ben asked his son.

"I already know everything I need to know! I know how to count oranges, I know how to ride a horse, and spell my name. So why do I have to go to school any more?"

"You need to learn other things too." At the time, Ben had his eyes on the tough, stringy piece of beef on his plate. He thought he had cooked it long enough in the crockpot—but obviously he hadn't. His jaws were getting tired of chewing.

"If my momma was here, she wouldn't make me go to school!" Ben looked at his son and saw that determined look in his eyes, another gift from his mother.

"Why do you think that?"

"Cause I remember…she told me she bought our orange grove for me, and I could stay here forever and ever."

"You can stay here forever if you want to, Buddy. But you still need to go to school. Your momma would want you to. She always said you were smart, and she knew school would make you even smarter." There was doubt in his son's eyes now.

"And if you want to fly airplanes someday, you have to go to school."

"You can teach me how to fly airplanes." Sam was stabbing at his roast beef too.

"I can teach you, but there are things you have to learn at school first. And you're going to meet a whole bunch of new friends in first grade and you can play kickball with them."

"Yeah, that's cool. Playing with the other kids is the best part of school. I like being here with you and Grandma, but sometimes I miss playin' with other kids." He stopped for a second, and Ben could tell he was thinking about something. "Dad? Do I have to play with girls? They aren't any fun." Sam scrunched up his nose in disgust.

"You have to be nice to the girls. Your momma was a girl, and she was lots of fun." Ben watched his son as this thought registered in his almost six year old mind.

"Remember when we went to Disney World with her?"

"Yep. She loved Disney, didn't she?"

As Sam rattled on about the last time he went to Disney with his mom, Ben wondered if his son really remembered the day, or was he just recalling what he'd seen in the pictures Ben had taken.

It was a day Ben would never forget.

It was Sam's third birthday, and it was the hottest day in July. Katy didn't seem to notice the heat, probably because she was so emaciated and cold all the time.

Ben had loaded her, the wheelchair, the oxygen tank and all of Sam's things into the car for the ninety minute trip. She slept most of the way, and Sam sat in his car seat in the back, watching a DVD. She woke up once, turned her head, and smiled at him. She had on her Disney head scarf and Minnie Mouse sweatshirt.

Taking his hand off the steering wheel, Ben had reached over and squeezed her hand. "You okay?"

"Of course, we're on our way to Disney. I can't wait to watch the two of you climb to the top of the Swiss Family Robinson tree. He's going to love it this year, isn't he?"

"Yeah…he will."

"Maybe when we get back home, the two of you could build him a tree house in the old oak beside the house. That would be a great place for a tree house."

"Mmmm, we'll see. You need anything?"

"Another fifty years?" There was a smile was on her lips, but pain clouded the one he used to see in her eyes.

"Oh, Katie…I would give my own life to give them to you."

"No," she had said, "a boy needs his dad." Ben was sure he would remember that day for as long as he lived. Sam's third birthday at Disney with his mom was unforgettable.

"Dad?"

"What?" It took Ben a couple of seconds to return to the present.

"Why do you always stop listening to me when I talk about my mom?"

"Do I do that, Sam? I didn't know I did."

"Yeah, you do…is it 'cause you're thinkin' about her?"

"I guess so, Buddy. I'm sorry. I'll try not to do that anymore. I always want to hear what you have to say. Are you finished with your supper?" Ben had been done with his food for several minutes, but sat and watched as Sam picked at his food. The boy would rather have peanut butter and jelly.

"Yeah. It was a pretty good supper. I think you're gettin' better at cookin'. But I like when Grandma cooks for us too." Ben started to pick up his dishes and Sam mimicked his dad, picking his up too.

"Yeah. It's a good thing your Grandma lives close by, isn't it? Why don't we do up these dishes while your sister plays with the rest of her food."

"Why is she always so messy when she eats?" Sam crinkled his nose in disgust as he looked at Molly who was propped up with pillows in her highchair. She had been chewing on a hard teething biscuit. Brown mush covered her face, her hands, and the high chair.

"That's how babies learn to eat by themselves. You used to be messy when you were her age. I remember one time when you threw peas at your momma."

Sam grinned. "Did she get mad at me?"

"No. She knew you were learning how to eat." Ben tousled his son's hair as they stood side by side at the sink, rinsing their dishes.

*****

In the darkness, Ben smiled again as he thought about Sam's arguments last evening for not going to school. But this morning he had to get up and go. Ben had a busy day ahead, but with Sam in school, his son's care was one less thing he had to worry about.

As he finished his coffee, he noticed the first streaks of light in the eastern sky. Dawn. Katy had loved dawn and the two of them had seen their share of them together. Her love for that time of the day had been passed on to her by her biological mother, who named her Dawn when she was born. Her adoptive parents had kept it as her middle name.

And before she died, she whispered to him, "Don't forget, Ben. It's always darkest before the dawn."

Chapter 2

"What are you doing today while I'm at school?" Sam was struggling to get his backpack on, but refused to be helped. All Ben could do was stand and watch his son. He was not only stubborn, he was independent.

"Grandpa and I are going to fly a charter."

"Where you goin'?"

"Miami. I should be back by the time you get off the bus. If I'm not, Grandma will be here, okay?"

"What about Jake and Duchess?"

"The horses will be fine till I get home. They'll keep each other company."

"Can we go riding tonight?" The boy looked at his dad with expectation in his eyes.

"Sure, that sounds like a great idea. You can tell me all about school while we're riding. But we need to get you to the end of the drive now. The school bus should be here soon. You only have one more month of kindergarten, then you can ride Jake all summer."

Sam was big for his age and had been riding his horse by himself since his last birthday. The horse was the same age as his master. He had been a birthday gift to Sam on his first birthday. Katy had thought he was too young for a colt, and he was, but Ben wanted the two of them to grow up together. Ben had a horse when he was a kid, and thought every boy should have one.

14

The grove was the perfect place to ride horses. When Katy first told Ben about the orange grove she wanted to buy with the trust fund her dad had given her, Ben had been skeptical—until he saw the sixty acres of land the grove sat on. Most of it was orange trees, but some of the acreage was giant old oak trees that surrounded a small lake on the property. Paths had been cut through the trees, and Ben knew immediately that it would be a perfect place to have horses for his own kids.

He and Katy had worked together and enjoyed the grove for almost three years before she died. She had loved watching things grow.

Ben put Molly in the back pack then struggled to get it on his back. "These things should come with an extra pair of arms," he muttered to himself.

"You need some help, Dad?"

"Yeah, give it a boost, would ya?" When Sam gave the back pack a boost, Ben heard Molly giggle.

"Hey, Dad! She just spit down your neck." Sam's laugh was contagious.

"What on earth are we going to do with this girl, Sam?"

"Maybe you should get married to Miss Henderson, then she could have a mom to take care of her."

"Oh, I think we're doing okay. What's a little bit of spit? Your horse blows snot on you, and you don't seem to mind that. Besides, we have Grandma to help us with Molly."

"Is she staying with Grandma while you go flying today?"

"She is. Now let's get you to the bus. I don't have time to take you to school today if you miss it."

With Molly on his back, his son's hand in his, Ben stepped out into the warm May sun. The lane to the road wasn't a long one, but it was a scenic one. To Ben it was the prettiest place on earth.

On his right were rows and rows of orange trees. Behind them was the warehouse where the oranges were processed and stored until they could be shipped. To his left were the riding paths that meandered through the old oak trees. The Spanish moss that hung from the arms of the trees created a scent of damp, earthy musk. Katy used to laugh and say the moss made the trees mysterious, almost human. But then, Katy was the kind of girl who treasured and found joy in everything life had to offer her.

Oh, God. How I miss her. Why did you have to take her away from us? This was the only conversation Ben ever had with God anymore. And God wasn't giving him any answers.

"Dad? Hey, Dad! Did you hear what I said?"

"I'm sorry, Sam. No I didn't. What did you say?"

"I said," there was some frustration in his voice, "if you aren't home when I get here, will Grandma let me ride Jake?"

"You know the rules, Sam. No riding unless I'm here with you. I already told you, I should be home. Here comes the bus. You gonna give me a hug?"

Ben noticed that his son looked to see how far away the bus was before he stretched out his arms to embrace his dad. Was he already getting to the age where he didn't want his friends to see him hug his dad? And Ben wondered if his son would have felt that way about his mom. He didn't think so. Ben could still remember his own mom's hugs—the ones she gave him before she and his dad were killed in the auto accident when he was ten. After that, Ben went to live with his grandmother; he had memories of a grandmother's hugs too.

"Have a great day, Sam. Behave yourself and listen to your teacher, okay?"

"I know, Dad!"

Ben was so focused on watching the bus drive away that he didn't hear the purr of the golf cart that came up behind him. Linda and John Carter, Katy's adoptive parents lived on the back side of the grove, and there was a path from their house to his that was well-traveled.

They had moved to Florida from Philadelphia almost five years ago, to be closer to Katy. John, a retired banker, had worked his way to the top in the business world and was now reaping the benefits of his labors. When Katy's leukemia returned, he said he would give all the money he had to keep her alive. But money doesn't buy health.

"Hey, Cowboy! You goin' our way?" At almost seventy, Linda was still youthful.

"I believe I am."

"Want a ride?"

"No, I think Molly and I will finish our walk. I'll see you at the house."

In the five minutes it took Ben to walk back to the house, he thought again of how grateful he was for Katy's parents. They were wonderful people, and Katy had loved them so much. Even after she met her birth mother, an equally wonderful lady, she said she was thankful that it was John and Linda who raised her. And now, they were Ben's greatest support system.

"So...how was our Sam today? I wanted to get here earlier so I could see him before he got on the bus, but Grandpa was a little slow." John grinned at his wife and put his arm around her shoulders. They had been married for over forty years and you could tell they still enjoyed each other's company.

"He is doing well today. But last night, he told me he isn't going to first grade next year. He said he already learned everything he needs to know." Ben laughed again as he thought about his son.

"Well, he *is* pretty smart. Does he know I'll be here when he gets home tonight?"

"I told him. I also told him he's not to ride Jake until I get home. If he gives you a hard time about that, you let me know, okay?"

"I'll keep him busy till you get home. And how's our sweet Molly?" Ben had taken the back pack off, and Linda was already reaching for the baby.

"I think she's teething. She was a little cranky yesterday, but she slept all night after I gave her some of that teething medicine. It's in the cupboard if you need more of it for her."

Ben smiled as he watched Linda kiss Molly's chubby cheeks. The baby responded by giggling and pulling Linda's hair.

"Have you heard anything from her mother?"

"Nope. I'm going to give her another six months. If she doesn't show up by then, my lawyer is going to help me find her. I need to know what she wants to do."

"What if she wants Molly back?"

"I really don't think that's going to happen, Linda. And if it does, I'll fight for her. This is her home now, and there are people here who have grown to love her. I think it would break Sam's heart if we had to give her back."

"Well, we'll just have to pray that God will work it out for all of us."

"Sam's suggestion this morning was that I marry Miss Henderson so Molly could have a mom."

Linda laughed. "Like I said, Sam's a pretty smart guy. And you have been seeing Jan for almost a year, haven't you?"

"Yep. It'll be a year next month. But I don't know, Linda. I'm thinking I'm a one woman man. There just aren't any sparks there for me." Ben felt Linda's eyes searching his face.

"Our Katy was pretty special, wasn't she? But you know, as well as I do, that she didn't want you to be alone for the rest of your life." Linda reached out and gave Ben's arm a pat. "It will all work out…it's one more thing to put in God's hands."

Ben turned away from his mother-in-law before she could see the tears that sprang to his eyes. His whole life seemed to be in limbo, and in his opinion, God wasn't helping much.

"You ready to go, John? Our client said he'd meet us at the airport at nine. We better get going."

"I'm ready whenever you are. I was telling Linda this morning, I only need five more training hours and I'll be ready to get my own license."

"Well, you've been working on it for awhile. You should have those hours in by the end of the month."

"I think I'll make it by the end of the month, too. It's going to be great when we can get in our own plane and fly to Philly to see the boys. And we'll be able to fly ourselves to the cabin in the mountains this summer. That commercial flying is too time-consuming. Maybe we'll even go more often after I get my license."

"John! I told you…we aren't going to the mountains this summer. I want to be here to help Ben with Sam and the baby." Linda's tone was as harsh as Ben had ever heard it.

"I know. But it'll still be nice when I can officially fly my own plane."

"Linda…I think we've discussed this. I don't want the two of you to change your life because of me and the kids. You go ahead and make your plans. I can get a sitter on the days I have to do my charters."

"We'll talk about it later. Right now, you guys need to get going."

*****

Ben's chartering service was one of the three jobs he had when he met Katy. He had wanted to fly since he was a little boy and watched the crop dusters fly over the ranches in west Texas where he lived with his parents and older sister, Sage.

To make that dream come true, he joined the Air Force right out of high school. After several tours of duty in Afghanistan, he left active duty and went into the reserves. With the money he earned from that, he bought his own plane and started his charter service.

But his favorite flying job was the third one. That one introduced him to Katy. As an air ambulance pilot, it was his responsibility to fly critically ill people into the trauma unit at Tampa General Hospital where she was a nurse. On the day he met her, he fell in love. He had never believed it was possible to love at first sight, but she proved him wrong.

They were married just six months later. He would have married her sooner, but Katy had been hesitant. She had been diagnosed with leukemia when she was sixteen and was fearful it would come back again, like it did when she was nineteen. At that time, she had a bone marrow transplant.

Her disease was still in remission when Ben met her seven years later. But she was afraid. She said she didn't want anyone falling in love with her. She didn't believe the old saying that says it's better to have loved and lost, than to never love at all.

When Ben told her he was still in the reserves and could be called back into a war zone at any time, they decided the risk of loving and losing was equal for both of them. They would take whatever time God would give them. At the time, Ben believed they had a good fifty years ahead of them.

Sam was born a year after they married, the same year Katy decided she wanted to be a citrus farmer. Ben would never forget the day they "went for a ride to buy oranges," and ended up buying the grove instead. It was a dream-come-true for both of them. Katy could stay home with Sam, and Ben could have his horses. That's when he gave up his job at the hospital. She insisted. She didn't want to be a single mom because her husband worked all the time.

It was when they realized that Katy's disease was terminal that he gave up his reserves position. She begged him to do it, even though she knew he loved it. She said since Sam was already losing one parent, he shouldn't have to worry about losing the other one who was fighting in a war.

Now, the only flying job he had left was his charters. But between them and the orchard, Ben was able to provide for his family.

Someday, when Sam was older, the orchard would be his. When Katy bought the grove, Ben refused to let her put his name on the deed. He didn't want her family thinking he married her for her money. When she died, Sam received an amazing gift from the mother he would not remember. He was only three years old when he became the sole owner of the "Browning Family Farm."

Chapter 3

Ben didn't like the month of May. He wished he did, since it was usually a pleasant month to live in Florida, but Mother's Day was in May. And Ben wasn't fond of that day. When he was ten, his own mom died the week before her special day and he would never forget that first Mother's Day without her.

Because his dad died in the same auto accident that took his mom away from him, Ben went to live with his grandmother. He knew now that his life could have been worse. He could have ended up in foster care instead of going to live with the kindest woman in the world.

Ben's grandmother loved him dearly and did her best to raise him right. She took him to church and taught him how to work hard for the things he needed and wanted in life. She became a mom to him. Then, when he was nineteen, she died too. After that, Mother's Day became like any other day of the year. He usually offered to work for someone and tried to forget.

Then Ben met Katy, who had not just one, but two, mothers. She had a birth mom and an adoptive mom. She loved both of them dearly, and they shared the honor of being her mother. When Ben married Katy, Beth Phillips and Linda Clinton became his mothers too.

But the Mother's Day after Katy became a mom was the one Ben would never forget. Sam was almost ten months old and after weeks of saying "Da-Da," he finally learned to say "Ma-ma." Pictures of her from that day were now framed, and brought smiles to the faces of everyone who looked at them. They were displayed, not only in his own home, but in the homes of both her mothers.

When Ben woke up at 4:23 a.m. on Mother's Day, he wished he could pull the quilt up over his head and stay in bed. But of course he couldn't. This, like every day, was a day when he had to be both mom and dad to Sam. Katy's shoes were too big to fill though. He knew it and he was sure Sam knew it too.

John and Linda had flown to Philadelphia for the week-end, to be with their two sons and their families, but Ben did have an invitation to go to the Phillips' home for the day. And since he felt like Sam needed some loving from a woman, he decided to go. He also knew it would make Momma Beth's day a little better. Katy couldn't be with her, but her son could be.

Beth Phillips became pregnant with Katy when she was just sixteen years old. Because of the abusive home she lived in, she decided to give Katy up for adoption. Linda and John Clinton had suffered with infertility for years and were the answer to the young mom's prayers.

Katy and her birth mom were reunited when Katy was sixteen and the doctors went looking for a bone marrow donor for her. That donor was Katy's half sister, Carly.

Katy had brought her birth mom's family and her adoptive family together. Now they were meshed into one great big family. Until Sam could understand it all, it was decided that Linda and John would be his Grandma and Grandpa, and Katy's birth mom would be his "Momma Beth." It's what Katy had called her, and Ben followed suit. It seemed right that Sam would know her by that name too.

Momma Beth was married to Alex Phillips—a pastor, and one of the nicest guys Ben had ever met. When they married, he had a seven year old daughter, Abby, from his first marriage. Since her own mother had died, Momma Beth became the only mother Abby knew.

The Phillips family unit was not a typical one, but it was a loving one. When Katy was introduced to them, she received a step sister, Abby, who was her own age, a step brother, Jon, and a half sister, Carly. When Ben, who had no immediate family at all met Katy, he was overwhelmed with how large her family was.

But Katy's large family was one of the things Ben loved about her. It had felt good to finally be part of an extended family. His only living relative after his grandmother died was his sister, Sage, who was ten years older than him. She left home when Ben was eight and he'd seen her only once since then.

Ben woke Sam and Molly early. He knew Momma Beth loved having her family in church with her, and since she'd lost Katy at birth, and then again when she died, Ben wanted to be there for her.

"Sam? Come on buddy, it's time to get up." Ben sat on the edge of his son's bed and tousled his hair.

"It's Sunday, Dad. Why do I have to get up so early?" Sam pulled his blanket up over his head.

"We're going to Momma Beth's house, remember?"

The blanket was thrown off, and Sam sat up, eyes wide open. "Will my cousins be there?"

"I think so. You can play all day with them."

"Oh boy! I haven't seen Kyle and Konnor for a long time!" Sam jumped out of his bed and had his pajamas off before Ben could get clean clothes out for him.

"You just saw them two months ago, Sam."

"That was a long time ago."

"Two months isn't a long time." Ben put a pair of khaki shorts and a dark blue cotton shirt on Sam's bed. Katy had said Sam and Ben should always wear blue because it brought out the blue in their matching eyes.

"Is Aunt Carly going to be there too?"

"I'm sure she is." He got Sam's brown sandals out of the closet. He usually put Sam's clothes out the night before, but he had been too exhausted last evening to be organized.

"For a girl, she's kinda nice, isn't she, Dad?"

"She sure is. Your Momma loved her and your Aunt Abby."

"They're mom's sisters, right?"

"Yep. That's why you're so special to them. They think you look and act like your momma."

"So…is Aunt Carly going to come and stay with us again this summer, like she did last year?" Sam was strapping on his own sandals. He was as independent as his dad was organized.

"I don't know, Buddy. We'll have to ask her. She might have plans for the summer. She's going to college soon, and Momma Beth and Papa Alex said she has to get a job to help pay for it."

"But, I like it when she comes and stays with me when you're flying. Who will stay with me this summer when Grandma and Grandpa go to the mountains?"

"We'll figure it out, Sam. Don't worry about it."

Carly had spent the last two summers at Ben's house. She wanted to come, and because she missed her sister so much, her parents had allowed her to do it. She had been a great help with Sam when Ben had to do a charter and his in-laws were at their cabin in the mountains.

But over the past year, Carly had changed. She had grown up and seemed to be healing from the loss of Katy. She was active in school and talked at Christmas about looking for a job to help pay for her college. Ben was happy for her. He was glad she was no longer grieving for Katy—that she was getting on with her life. He sometimes wished he could too.

But Ben was afraid to stop grieving. He was afraid if he stopped, the memories of his Katy would disappear with the grief. And Ben refused to forget her. He couldn't...she was the love of his life. And he had to keep her memory alive for Sam.

He was planning to talk to Carly again today, to see if she had a job yet for the summer. He really needed someone he could count on to baby-sit, especially now that he had Molly. He could take Sam with him on a charter, but not Molly. She had changed everything for him this summer. Not that he regretted it. He had fallen in love with her the minute they put her in his arms last November.

But he would absolutely not allow the Clintons to change their plans for the summer. They had been available to help him constantly since Katy died. He wanted them to have some time to enjoy life this summer. And they needed to go to the mountains to get out of the humidity of Florida. If Carly couldn't come and stay for the summer, he had one other option—Jan Henderson.

Jan had been Sam's pre-school teacher, and he idolized her. She and Ben became close friends during the year she was Sam's teacher, and started seeing each other socially when Sam left her class.

She wouldn't be teaching this summer and had already offered to help him with the kids. But Ben hated to ask her. He wasn't sure where their relationship was going.

They had been seeing each other more often in the past six months, and she was hinting that she would like for their relationship to become more than it was. She really was a wonderful woman; but Ben couldn't see himself with her for the rest of his life. He had hoped she would grow on him, but she hadn't. If he asked her to baby-sit, that would put her in his house in a more intimate role...caretaker for his children. No. He couldn't ask Jan to help him this summer.

"Hey, Dad! You're zoning out on me again!" *Where on earth is that boy learning to talk like that? Zoning out?*

"Sorry, Sam. I was just thinking about visiting with the family today. You did a good job putting your clothes on. But we better take some play clothes along. You always get so dirty at Momma Beth's house."

"Yeah…she lets us play in the sand box and in the tree house. Do you know she has real sea shells from the beach in her sand box? Me and Konnor and Kyle slide down the rope from the tree house right into the sandbox." Ben wondered when he should start correcting Sam's grammar, but knew he was too weary to do it today.

"I know, I've watched you guys. It looks like fun."

Ben was actually surprised that Abby's boys wanted to play with Sam. They were two and three years older than he was. But the three of them always had a good time together. Abby's little girl was just a year younger than Sam. When they were all together, the three boys never wanted to play with four year old Alexandria. But when Molly came into their lives, "Lexie" was in heaven. She loved "mothering" Molly.

"Okay. Let's go get Miss Molly dressed. We'll just eat some cereal for breakfast. Momma Beth will probably have a big lunch waiting for us after church."

"Yeah…and my teacher at their church always brings cookies too."

"Hey. Maybe I'll go to church with you today instead of going to big people church!"

"You can't do that, Dad. You have to listen to Papa Alex preach!"

"Oh, that's right." Ben rumpled his son's already messy hair. Every time he touched it, he thought of Katy. His son's hair was the same color and texture of his mother's.

Before the two of them reached Molly's room, Ben could hear her babbling in her crib. When they opened the door, she rolled over, looked at them and grinned. Once again, Ben was struck with how much she looked like the pictures of his own mother. She was fair and had blond hair. The deep blue eyes were like his own though, and like Sam's. He couldn't help but smile at her.

He had brought her home with him when she was just three days old. Her mother had left the hospital before she was officially discharged, leaving a note. The note said just one thing: "Call Ben. If he doesn't want her, you can put her up for adoption. I can't take care of her."

What else could he do? Molly was his sister's child. And he was the closest blood relative the little girl had.

Chapter Four

Momma Beth and Alex were at the door of the church to welcome them when they got there. They both gave Ben and Sam a big hug. When they told Sam his cousins were already at children's church, he was off to join them.

"Do you want me to take Molly to the nursery for you, Ben?"

"Sure, that would be fine. Are Abby and Carly already in the church?"

"They're in our regular seat."

After giving Molly and her diaper bag to her grandma, Ben walked into the church. His eyes went to the second row, piano side, and he saw them; Abby's dark hair and Carly's blond hair, side by side. He made his way up the side isle until he reached them.

"Hey, you two. Scoot over!"

Both of them looked up at him, smiled, and scooted over to the center of the seat. He sat down beside Carly. "Hey, sis. Nice to see you again."

"You too. I'm glad you could come today. We needed you here." She squeezed his hand.

"You needed me?"

"Yeah…We'll talk later."

*****

Ben was not comfortable during the worship service. But that was nothing new. Every time he went to church (which wasn't often any more) he was reminded of the one way in which he was failing Sam. He was not, and had never been, the spiritual leader of his family.

As a child living in West Texas with his parents, he never went to church. But when he went to live with his grandmother, he started going with her to the small, friendly, church she had gone to her whole life.

The people there were like an extension of his grandmother's family and came to love Ben, and he them. As he looked back on his life, he was sure it was his Grandmother's, and the church's, positive Christian influence on his life that helped him through his teen years.

During his years in the air force, Ben drifted away from spiritual things. It was Katy who brought him back into the church. But Ben knew that just being a part of a church was not enough. Yes, he believed in a God and was a good, moral person, but Ben didn't have a personal relationship with Jesus Christ. He and Katy had talked about it often, and he knew she prayed for him to take that step of faith. He was just about ready to do it when Katy got sick.

After she died, all he could think about was how Katy's relationship with God should have made things turn out different for her. And there were times when He began to doubt the very existence of a God. But he had promised Katy before she died that he would make sure Sam grew up in a church. Ben kept that promise by sending his son to church on Sundays with the Clintons.

On this Mother's Day, Alex's sermon was about the importance of being a Christian parent, and Ben couldn't wait for the sermon to end. In his mind, he was doing the best he could do, considering the circumstances of his life. God had failed to heal his Katy and until he could understand that, Ben couldn't seek God's forgiveness.

When church was over, Carly went with Ben to get Molly from the nursery. Abby said she would get Sam when she picked up her own kids from children's church. They would all meet at Alex and Momma Beth's house for lunch.

It was while he and Carly were on their way to the house that Ben asked how Abby was getting along.

"That's why we needed you here today. She's having a really difficult time. She had to give up her house. She just couldn't afford to keep it."

"What do you mean? Isn't Brett paying the payments?"

"Yes. And the judge said she could stay in the house for as long as she wants to because she has custody of the kids. But even with Brett paying the payments, she doesn't have the resources to keep it up. She said the alimony and child support isn't enough to pay the utilities and take care of the kids' needs."

"But if she sells it in this economy she's going to lose money on it. Then she'll have nothing."

"She knows that and is stressed out about it. I feel bad for her."

"So where are she and the kids living?"

"They've been with us since Easter. She didn't have any place else to go."

"Is that working out okay?"

"It's pretty crowded. The boys are sleeping in Jon's old room, and she and Alexandria are in the guest room. She just seems so depressed. And you know that isn't Abby. She told me it's humiliating to have to move back in with your parents when you're thirty-three years old."

"I still can't believe Brett ran out on her."

"I know. I think we're all still in shock, and it's been nine months."

"When Katy and I first started dating I was a little envious of him. He seemed to have everything a guy could need…a beautiful wife, happy kids, and a good job."

"Well, obviously it wasn't enough for him. I'm so mad at him right now I feel like I could strangle him. And Abby acts like she's lost. Maybe you could talk to her later today?"

"Oh, I wouldn't know what to say to her…except I'm sorry. Besides your parents are the counselors in the family. I'm sure they're being very supportive of her."

"They are. But I really think you could help her, Ben. She's grieving the loss of her life as it once was. You know what that feels like."

"We'll see. So what have you been up to? Are you ready for college next year? " Ben loved this young sister-in-law as much as his late wife had. She had a bubbly personality that was contagious.

"Yep. It's exciting, but it's also kind of scary."

"Did you decide on a college yet?"

"I'm not sure where to go. I got accepted at the three I applied to, but part of me wants to stay home and go to a local college. My friends can't wait to get away from home and be on their own, but I kind of like mine." As the baby of the family, Carly was special to all of them. Katy, Abby, and their brother Jon were all teenagers when she was born.

"Well you do have a good home and great parents. I wouldn't want to leave them either."

"I did do one grown-up thing this week…I got a job." Ben pulled into the driveway at the Phillip's home, then turned to look at Carly. Her eyes were sparkling.

"Good for you! Where? When do you start?"

"I'm going to waitress at that little restaurant down the street. I heard the tips are pretty good there. And I really want to help my parents with my tuition."

"Your big sis would be very proud of you."

"I know she would. But I feel bad that I won't be able to help you with Sam and Molly this summer. It would have been fun to take care of a baby again."

"It's okay. I have a back-up plan, so don't you worry about that. You need to focus on what you need to do for you."

Ben and Carly walked onto the front porch of his in-law's house. *Okay, Browning…you better come up with a back-up plan soon, summer is almost here!*

*****

If it hadn't been for the kids having such a good time together, dinner at the Phillips' house would have been a solemn affair. Even though this was their second Mother's Day without Katy, she was still missed. And now, Brett wasn't there. Jon and his wife weren't there either. They would be over later, after they went to his wife's family dinner.

After dinner, Carly, Alex and Ben did the dishes. It was, after all, Mother's Day, and they decided Momma Beth and Abby should have a few breaks on this day. Later, while Molly was taking a nap, Ben wandered out to the backyard to check on Sam. He found Abby alone in the lawn swing.

"Hey, Abby. Can I sit with you?" He motioned to the seat beside her.

"Sure." She slid over so he could sit down. Ben was grateful it was in the shade. Florida's afternoon sun was already getting hot.

"So, how are you doing?" He was sitting sideways and could look at her while they talked. He saw the muscles in her jaw tense, and she inhaled deeply.

"I've had better days."

"Yeah. Me too." He put his arm around her and pulled her to him. A hug between siblings sometimes helped.

"We both need Katy right now, don't we?" She smiled, but there was sadness in her eyes.

"Yeah, we do. She had a way of making everything better, didn't she? She would be so upset with Brett right now. Are things getting any more civil between the two of you?"

"Not at all, just the opposite. It's so hard to believe he's the same man I married. I can't believe he would leave me and the kids for another woman."

"I know. But maybe you're better off without him. He isn't the man we all thought he was. Where is he now?"

"He's living with her... has been, since after Christmas. I asked him to stay with me and go to counseling, but he said he didn't want to. He said he doesn't love me anymore."

"I'm sorry, Ab. How do these kinds of things happen?"

"I don't know. He said I was preoccupied after Katy died and didn't give him what he needed. I thought Brett and I were strong enough to weather anything together. I guess I was wrong."

"So he's blaming you?"

"I guess. According to the divorce papers, our marriage is irretrievably broken."

"And you would have taken him back, even after he cheated on you?"

"Of course. I believe God's able to fix broken marriages if both parties want it badly enough."

"You really think you could have forgiven him? And learned to trust him again?"

"With God's help, yes." Ben was doubtful, but had always been in awe of the faith of Katy's whole family.

"That would be difficult."

"But for the kids, I could have done it. That's the hardest thing for me right now—what this is doing to our kids. I hate the thought of them being shuffled back and forth between parents and houses."

She stopped and wiped tears from her eyes. "I guess I'm angry about that more than anything." Ben hurt for her as he watched the tears roll down her face.

"Oh, Abby, I'm so sorry. I wish there was something I could do to help. Do you want me to find him and beat him up?"

She smiled through her tears at that. "No. As mean as he's been, he'd put you in jail for it."

"He's being mean on top of being unfaithful? What a jerk. I still can't believe he would do this to you." Ben felt his fists curl and really felt like he could have hit Brett if he'd been present.

"Yeah, me either. But I hear that the girlfriend is young, single, and beautiful. Temptations can be so powerful, especially if we aren't where we're supposed to be with God."

Ben felt that one hit home, but chose to ignore it. "So what are you going to do, Abby?"

"I don't know. Even with alimony and child support, I can't afford to keep that big house. I've been looking for a job. I was going to do that this year anyways since Lexi's going to kindergarten in the fall."

"That sounds like a good plan."

"But in this economy, who's going to hire an art major who hasn't worked for ten years? It's not a very marketable degree right now."

"You'll find something."

"I hope so. In the meantime, the house is for sale. I hope we can get out of it without owing anything on it. But the market is so bad. It's all such a mess, Ben. What if the kids and I end up homeless and penniless?" There was the sound of desperation in her voice.

"That's not going to happen, Abby. You have a lot of people who love you, and we're going to help you. Can you think of anything I can do to help?"

She smiled at him. "You can keep me and my kids supplied with oranges so we don't get scurvy." The fact that she was still able to joke and laugh in the middle of her desperation, was amazing to Ben.

"You've got a deal. But I want you to call me if you need anything else."

"I will. But Mom and Dad are here for me. I think I'll be okay."

Chapter Five

———————————

Ben thought about Abby and the kids all the way home. And he wondered where God was in all the problems of the world. Katy had been a Christian and died. Abby had been a Christian, and her husband left her for another woman. Momma Beth and Alex had faithfully served God for years, but it hadn't prevented bad things from happening to their children. It just didn't seem fair that bad people could continue to prosper, and the good people of the world had to suffer.

He had mentioned that to Katy once, and she had quoted some scripture about it raining on the just and the unjust. Ben needed a better answer than that one.

After he got home and tucked his kids into bed, Ben decided to call Jan. She had been a good friend to him since Katy died, and it looked like he was going to have to break down and ask her for help with the kids this summer.

They had met the first day Ben took Sam to preschool. Sam was four by then, and Katy had been gone for a year. Even though Ben enjoyed Sam's company and Katy's mom was always willing to babysit, he felt like it was time for Sam to learn to play with other kids.

Jan met them at the door of the classroom and welcomed them in. When Sam decided he didn't want to stay, Jan was able to talk him into it by telling him she needed a special helper that day, and she'd like him to be that person. Ben thought it was interesting that she almost knew Sam loved being a "helper."

The two of them had met together several times that year, she as the teacher and Ben as the dad. By the end of the school year, Ben had come to admire her gentle ways with kids and her obvious love of life. She was the breath of fresh air that he and Sam both needed that year.

When Sam graduated from from preschool, she told Ben how much she enjoyed his son, and hoped she could stay in contact with him.

"You've been wonderful for him this year. Besides me and his grandparents, he doesn't have a lot of other people in his life."

"Then the three of us should get together sometime this summer. We could meet at the park and have a picnic." When she smiled at him, he noticed for the first time that she had the prettiest hazel eyes. They were happy eyes that went well with her short curly auburn hair. She looked like a kid herself. Maybe that's why her students loved her so much.

"I think he would like that. I'll give you a call, if you don't mind giving me your phone number."

And that was how he and Jan become friends. Good friends—the kind of friends who shared almost everything going on in their daily lives. They were the kind of friends that had fun together. Most of the time Sam was with them, but she didn't seem to mind. She knew Sam adored her, and she seemed to enjoy his adoration.

But once in a while, just the two of them would meet somewhere. Usually, it was to see a movie together.

It was in January of this past year when she asked him if he ever thought about getting married again.

"Sometimes. But there are other times when I think I'm a one-woman man. Katy was very special. Maybe someday I'll be ready."

"From what you and Sam have told me, it sounds like she was a wonderful woman. Don't you think she'd want you to get married again?"

"Yes, of course. I know she'd want me to marry again. She told me she did, right before she died. She said she didn't want me to be alone."

"It sounds like she was a generous woman too."

"She was, in more ways than one." Ben didn't like to talk about Katy to anyone besides family. He would still get a lump in his throat.

After that evening with Jan, Ben went home and got Katy's little book out of his top drawer. She started writing it when she knew her leukemia was terminal, and it ended three days before she died. It was full of things she thought were important for him to know. But the last entry was a letter to him. He didn't read it often anymore, but after talking to Jan he felt a need to read it again.

July 27
Dear Ben,

If you're reading this, it means I'm gone from your life.

This is the most difficult thing I've ever written because I know it's the last thing I'll ever write. As I sit here today, I feel certain that I have very little time left on this earth. In less than two weeks, it will be my thirtieth birthday, and I wonder if I'll be here to celebrate it. But it's okay if I'm not. I wish I could stay, but I've told God to take me if he can't heal me. This long journey I've traveled with leukemia needs to end. It's time for my family to get on with their lives.

The most important thing was that I was here for Sam's third birthday last week. It was such a bittersweet day, wasn't it? His joy at being three was so sweet. My sorrow that I would never see him celebrate another one was the bitter part.

I have tears today, but I also have peace. I wonder...why me? Then I ask myself...why not me? I have questions, but I know God will give me the answers soon enough. My focus today is getting this letter written to you. If I run out of strength, I'll dictate the rest to my hospice nurse. She's been so good to help me tie up the loose ends of my life.

I can't explain the urgent need I have to write this letter, except, as I face the reality of my own death, I recognize there's so much I want to say to you. Ben, you know you've been my one and only love. If there was time for me to say only one thing, it's this...I'm leaving this earth feeling loved and adored because of you. Please don't ever forget that.

You know I wish I could stay with you forever. But we both know that isn't going to happen. God wants me in my heavenly home even though he knows I want to stay in my earthly one with you. I'm about to find out why He has chosen this for us. You may never know until you meet me in eternity some day. But I do know, with all certainty, that you will trust God's wisdom and go on with the life he's given you with our boy. What a beautiful gift our Sam has been to us. I know you'll take good care of him for me.

There's another reason I write to you today. I want you to know that I'm expecting you to get on with your life after I'm gone. Knowing you the way I do, I know you'll grieve intensely. But at some point, it will be time for you to set that aside and find a new love. You are such a wonderful man and have so much love to give. Don't waste that. As I told you before, I want you to marry again. I hope our love was so good that you'll want to experience it again with someone else. It would be a compliment to me. I know you'll choose well because the one you choose will be the mother our Sam will need throughout his life.

I'm getting tired now. Give our Sam a kiss and a hug for me. Do it everyday, and remind him that I'll always love him. I'll see both of you again, in that place beyond the stars.
With all my love...your Katy.

After almost three years, reading her letter still brought tears to his eyes. He could almost hear her voice as he read it. And he knew she meant every word she had written.

He thought about Jan again. Katy would approve of her. She would be a perfect second mom for Sam. She already loved him and enjoyed his company. And that's what Katy had wanted.

He knew he would never love Jan the way he loved Katy, but maybe he could love her in a different way. He and Katy had once agreed that love chose them, but he could also remember the few difficult times in their marriage when they had to actively choose to love each other by doing loving things. Maybe if he chose to love Jan, he could.

What was most important was that Jan and Sam were good for each other. Jan was the first woman outside his immediate family that Sam had connected with. She could be the only one, and that would make his life easier.

That was the night Ben decided to try to love Jan. She was a good woman. She would make a good wife and a great mother.

He asked her to go out with him on Valentine's Day, and actually picked her up at her house rather than meeting her somewhere. He sent flowers to her at work, took her out to a nice restaurant, and at the end of the date, he kissed her for the first time.

Ben had kissed a lot of girls before he met Katy. Kissing Jan brought those memories back to him. It had been fun, and he knew it could lead to physical satisfaction, but it still didn't feel right. But he decided he would keep trying. It was just going to take some time.

Chapter 6

Ben was in the swing on the deck again. It was the place where he felt most at peace. As a child growing up in West Texas he had spent most of his time outside. The tiny house he, his parents, and his sister lived in was too tiny and stuffy for him. He needed wide open spaces. Perhaps another reason he became a pilot.

He opened his phone and clicked the speed dial button for Jan.

"Jan? It's Ben."

"Hey. I was wondering if you'd get back in time to call me. How was your day with the in-laws?"

"It was okay. No, actually, it wasn't a very good day." Ben looked up into the night sky for his star.

"Why? What happened?"

"Do you have time to talk? I know you need to get up early in the morning." He found the star he was looking for. It wasn't difficult on this clear night.

"It's okay, Ben. What's going on? Do you want me to come over?" That was Jan, always available, always willing to do whatever she could do, to help him.

"You can come over if you want to. Are you sure you have the time tonight?"

"Of course. I'll see you in fifteen minutes."

While he waited for her to get there, he went back into the house and threw a load of clothes in the washer. Molly had messed herself on the way home, and he had all of Sam's dirty play clothes to wash. *Just another day in the life of a single dad.*

He was packing Sam's lunch for the next day when he heard her car in the lane. He realized then that he hadn't seen her since the weekend before. It was good she understood how busy his life was. Even though all the oranges had been harvested for the year, they were still busy in the grove. They had removed and replanted thirty trees this past week. And he had flown a charter on two different days.

They had talked on the phone a couple times. She had offered to come out and help him, but by the end of his day he was too tired to give to her emotionally. Yet, here she was, coming to him when he needed someone to talk to. And Ben could see the unfairness of that.

He met her at the door and gave her a hug and a kiss. After three months, there was still no magic in their relationship for him, but he was comfortable with her. She had told him a month ago that she was falling in love with him. He had held her close and asked her to give him some time. She said she understood.

"Hey…are you okay? You sounded so tired on the phone." She reached up and pulled his head down again. Her lips were soft and moist on his own.

"I am tired. But I'm glad you're here. Can I get you a cup of tea or something else?"

"It's okay. I'll get it myself. Do you want some?"

"If you're fixing it, I'll take it." Ben sat down at the kitchen table Katy had refinished and ran his hand over the top of it. Katy's hands had made the table shine and whenever he touched it he felt like he was touching a part of her.

Jan had only been to his house a half dozen times since February, but she already knew her way around Ben's kitchen. Each time she had been there, Sam was asleep or at his grandparent's house. Ben didn't want him to wonder what Miss Henderson's new role in their lives was. Ben needed to understand it first.

He watched her as she found the tea in the cupboard and fixed it for them.

"It's the chamomile I brought over the last time I came. You liked it, right?"

"Yeah. Sure. It's okay…for tea. But I'll need some sugar in it." He got up from the table and went to get the sugar bowl.

"It's good for you. It'll help you relax and sleep better."

"I sleep okay."

She rolled her eyes at him. "Yeah, right. Then why do you look tired all the time?"

"Maybe it's because I have two kids and two jobs?" He tried to smile when he said it.

"You need to let me help you more, you know." She put his tea in front of him and sat down in the chair next to him

"I may be doing that this coming summer."

"Really? What's going on? Is something wrong with Carly?"

"No. Carly's fine. But she did get a job for the summer. She isn't going to come and stay with the kids like I had planned. I'll figure that out later, though. It's Abby who's having problems."

In the year they'd been seeing each other, Ben had spent a lot of time helping Jan understand the complex nature of his and Sam's relationship with Katy's family. He felt a need to stay close to all of them, not just because he had grown to love them, but because Sam was their tie to Katy. Although Jan had never met any of them, except John and Linda, she felt like she knew them. She knew they were an important part of Sam's and Ben's life.

"What's going on with Abby?"

"Their divorce was finalized and she got the house, but she can't afford to keep it with nothing but alimony and child support. She's been looking for a job but hasn't found one, so she had to move in with her parents. Her house is on the market. She doesn't know what to do next. I feel so bad for her." Ben spent the next few minutes sharing Abby's story with Jan.

"She's going to have to sell the house? That's horrible. What's she going to do?"

"She doesn't know. She acted like she was in the middle of a dark dream. I don't think it's really hit her yet…just how much her life is going to change. I wish there was something I could do to help her."

"Ben, I think your plate's full right now. I'm sure her mom and dad are going to be there for her."

"I know they will. I guess I feel upset . . . because I know Katy would be upset."

Ben saw Jan take in a deep breath, then let it out slowly.

"I'm sorry, Jan. This is stuff I really shouldn't be burdening you with. I know they'll figure it out. Tell me about your day? Was your mother happy with the gift you gave her?"

"It's okay. I know Katy's family is important to you…because of Sam. And yes, my mother loved her gift. It was a nice day. My brother and his wife and kids were home too. He wants to know when he gets to meet you."

"Does big brother have to give his okay?" Ben smiled when he said it, but Jan's answer sounded defensive.

"No. He just wants to meet you—probably because I talk about you all the time."

"Well, you need to tell him I'm not going to hurt his little sis." But even as he said it, Ben wondered if it was true. If Jan really was falling in love with him, and he found it impossible to love her back, wouldn't that hurt her? And really, was it fair for him to keep seeing her when he didn't know if he could ever love again? If he did keep seeing her, would his respect for her, his trust in her, and the affection he knew he could give her, be enough for her?

"Are you sure about that?" She raised her eyebrows, and Ben noticed that her usual bright hazel eyes looked doubtful. She probably knew the answer already.

"Jan…I've been totally honest with you. I don't know if I can give you everything you need. I don't know if more time will make a difference in my feelings. I hope it will, because you're everything a man could want in a wife. But I can't promise you that I can love you the way you deserve to be loved. You have to decide if you want to take that chance."

"Ben. I love you. I can't change that. Sometimes, I just wish you'd let me show you how much."

"Show me? You mean physically?" Ben felt his pulse quicken.

"Yes. You're a man, and I assume your physical needs didn't die with Katy. I think you could learn to love me, if you'd let me get closer to you. You know, spend more time with you."

"Jan." Ben reached across the table and took her hands in his. "I can promise you, my physical needs didn't die with Katy. You're a beautiful and desirable woman, but until I can make some kind of commitment to you, I won't use you for sex. I understand what you're saying, and it's sweet of you to want to love me in that way." He tried to reject her offer in the kindest way he could.

"Ben." There were tears in her eyes, and Ben felt like the biggest jerk on earth. "I'm thirty years old, and I've dated my share of guys. But I've never loved any of them the way I love you. I want you in my life. I do want that commitment from you. If I could get that, I'm yours in any way you want me. I guess I trust that you would make good on a promise of more."

"Jan…I hate seeing you give so much when I'm giving so little to this relationship. It's like you said, I have a lot on my plate right now. Maybe after I have things with Molly finalized, I'll be able to give more and be able to focus more on you."

"So…you're saying that things stay the way they are right now?"

"They have to."

She took in another big breath, and the tears ran down her cheeks.

"I need more, Ben. Until you can give me that, I don't think we should see each other any more."

Ben was speechless for a few seconds.

"Whoa! What just happened here, Jan? Did you come over here with the intention of having this kind of confrontation?"

"No, Ben. I didn't. But when I see how you're still so connected, not just to Katy, but to her family, I wonder if you'll ever have room in your life for me. I guess I just wanted to know. I think I got my answer."

"I really am sorry, Jan. I know how difficult it is to wait on love. I shouldn't have asked you to do that." He tried to hold on to her hands, but she pulled them away.

"It's a chance I was willing to take for awhile, Ben. But I can't wait anymore. We've known each other for almost two years. It seems like you should know by now."

When she turned and walked away, Ben felt so bad for her. He was sure she was kicking herself for wasting a year of her life on him. And he was sure she was stinging from what she probably assumed was his rejection of her.

But as he closed the door of his house, there was also a part of him that felt a sense of relief. He could stop trying to make himself love her.

When he knew she was gone, Ben went out to the deck and looked up to the stars.

I'm sorry, Katy. I tried to find a new mom for your boy, but it didn't work out. I'm gonna have to find one Sam and I can both love.

Chapter Seven

May was coming to an end, and Ben still didn't have child care set up for the summer. His in-laws had once again offered to stay in Florida for the summer to help him, but Ben would not allow them to do that. They had been helping him day and night since Katy's death, and he wanted them to have a break. He also knew how much they enjoyed their summers in the mountains.

Momma Beth had called and said she was more than willing to make the hour drive to his house on Wednesdays, her only day off from the hospital, to help with the kids. He told her he would let her know if he needed her help.

While he was on the phone with her, he asked how Abby was doing.

"Not good, Ben. She finished moving her things out of the house and put them in storage. She's still looking for a job, but doesn't know if she can find one that will pay her bills and childcare for when she works. I'm thinking about taking a leave of absence from my job to babysit for her if she finds a job."

"That's generous of you, Beth. I'm sure she appreciates it."

"But she won't let me do it. She said she knows I love my work, and it's good that someone in the family has a steady job. She feels like her pride is the only thing she has left from her relationship. I don't know what she's going to do."

"I feel so bad for her. And I'm still in shock that Brett just up and left her and the kids like that. I guess he wasn't the person we all thought he was."

"Alex and I are disappointed in him too. Alex even tried to talk to him, but he doesn't want to talk to any of us."

"Do you think it would help if I tried? He and I weren't real close, but we married sisters so that should count for something."

"You could try, Ben. But I think it's too late. Abby said the kids came home from their last visit with him and told her they were going to get another mommy. It sounds like he's planning on marrying this girl he's seeing."

Ben felt the anger rise up inside him. "What a jerk! Doesn't he know how damaging this could be to his kids? I feel so bad for them. They must all be so confused."

"I know, Ben. We're just going to have to pray that God will protect their little hearts from too much damage. Now stop worrying about her. You have enough on your own plate. Have you heard anything from your sister?"

"No. It looks like she's disappeared again. She does that well, you know."

"Well, she knew who would love Molly. That's why she wanted you to have her."

"I know. And Molly is so loveable. You should see her and Sam play together in the evenings. He has taken to his big brother role so well."

"Katy would be proud of him."

"I know. She wanted him to have a sibling. Now he has one….Well, I better let you go. Let me know if you can think of anything I can do to help Abby. And tell Carly I hope she likes her new job this summer."

"I will, Ben. And you let me know if I can help you on Wednesdays."

"I will…and thanks again."

When Ben hung up the phone, he felt like a deflated balloon. Life had turned out so different than what he imagined it would be when he married Katy. At the time, he had been almost overwhelmed, but so excited to be part of her large family. And now, it felt like the family was shrinking, and everyone was going their own way.

It also looked like his income for taking care of his own family was going to shrink. If he had to take the summer off from flying his charter customers, he might be hurting. The income from the grove took care of the grove expenses, with some left over for Sam's college fund, but he needed the charter income to take care of his family.

He had just two weeks until John and Linda left for the summer. He had to find a babysitter for his kids before then. Maybe he should try to mend his relationship with Jan. But that would be unfair to her. He needed to let her go so she could find someone to give her the love she deserved.

It looked like his only option was to find a school girl who could help him out two or three days a week. Maybe Linda would know of a girl from the church who could do it.

*****

Ben and the kids were at the end of the lane waiting on the school bus. It was already hot outside at seven thirty in the morning.

"It's a good thing your school is air-conditioned, Sam. If it wasn't, you'd cook in there today."

"I know. Mrs. Landon said we'll probably have recess inside for the rest of the week. Why is it always hotter at school than at the grove, Dad?"

"Well, the playground is on black asphalt with no shade, Buddy. Our farm is pretty shaded with the orange trees and those big old oaks."

"I'll be glad when school is over so I can stay home with you every day." Sam said, as he wiped the sweat off his head with his shirt sleeve.

"We're going to have a great summer, Sam. You'll be turning six in a few weeks. Do you want to go to Disney again for your birthday?" Katy had insisted that they go to Disney for Sam's birthday the year he was two, and Ben had kept the tradition for her since she died."

"Well, yeah! Can Kyle and Konnor come with us like they did that one year?"

"We'll see. That would be fun, wouldn't it?" Ben readjusted Molly in his arms. She was getting heavy, and he hadn't put her in the back pack this morning.

"Here comes my bus. I'll see you tonight, Dad. Will you be home when I get there?"

"I'm home all day today, Sam. I'll see you when you get off the bus."

Ben leaned over so Sam could give him a hug. Molly giggled when Sam tickled her under the chin. "Bye, Molly. You be good for Dad. Don't poop on him today." Ben was still laughing when Sam got on the bus. *What a boy he is,* Ben thought as he turned to go back up the lane.

"Well, Miss Molly, I guess you got your marching orders for today, didn't you? Your brother says no pooping on dad today." Sam held the little girl out away from his body for a second, then lifted her high into the air. "You want to fly back home, little girl?" She giggled again.

"Hey, I think I see a tooth in there." Ben stopped walking and cradled her in one arm. "Let Dad see, Molly. Did you get a tooth overnight?" When he put his pinky finger into her mouth, she bit down. "Oh yeah....it finally came in. Good girl. We'll have you eating steak before you know it."

"So, what are we gonna do today, Miss Molly? Do you want to go horse back riding?"

The little girl just looked adoringly at Ben. And Ben was struck again at how much she looked like his mother.

"Your Grandma Browning would have loved you, little girl. Do you know that? But she would have been very upset with your Momma for abandoning you. But her loss is my gain. You're my baby now."

*****

Ben would never forget the phone call he received in November of last year. It had been just a week after Thanksgiving. Sam was at school and Ben was at the grove office. He had sent his pickers to the grove and was working on some invoices when his cell phone rang. He looked at the number. It was one he didn't know. *Probably a new customer*, he thought as he answered it.

""Browning Family Farms. How can I help you?"

There was a pause on the other end of the line. "Mr. Browning?"

"Yes? How can I help you this morning?"

"Mr. Browning…this is Nancy Anderson from the Las Vegas Women's Health Center. I'm calling about your sister."

Ben felt a sense of panic. Sage was in trouble. He hadn't seen her for years, but he knew in his heart that at some time in his life, he would probably be getting a phone call like this.

"My sister?"

"Yes. Can you tell me her name?"

"Her name is Sage. Why are you calling me? Is she hurt? What's wrong with her?"

"Mr. Browning, I'm a social worker here at the Center, and I'm calling to tell you that your sister came to us two days ago and gave birth to a little girl. She left yesterday before the doctor could discharge her and left her baby here. When the nurse went to her room to check on her, she found a note Sage had written. It says we're supposed to call you. She wants you to come and get the baby." Ben felt like he had been hit by a truck. He didn't think Sage even knew where he lived.

"Did she give you my phone number?"

"No. The number she gave us was a Texas number. It was your Aunt Joyce's number. She was the one who gave us your number. We're wondering if you could come out here and get the baby?"

"Wait a minute. Can you read the note to me?"

"Sure. It's right here. It says, "To whom it may concern. At this time in my life, I'm unable to care for my baby. Would you please call my brother, Ben Browning, and ask him to come and get her. I don't have his number, but if you call my Aunt Joyce, she'll know it. If he doesn't want the baby, could you find a good Christian home for her?" Ben closed his eyes and took a deep breath.

"Are you still there, Ben?"

"Yes…I am."

"Are you going to be able to come out and get the baby?"

"Do you know where my sister is? Do you have an address or phone number for her? How about her doctor? Does he have any information on her?"

"Mr. Browning. Your sister came to us in active labor two days ago. She told us she didn't have a doctor, and she gave us a fictitious address. She had no insurance and told us she had no money to pay us. Right now, our primary focus is her baby, who is a ward of the state of Nevada. We're calling to see if you want her."

"Yes. Of course I want her." Ben didn't even stop to think about it. He just followed his heart. This was his niece, his parent's grandchild. This was Sam's cousin. "Can you give me a little bit of time to get there?"

"We can give you until tomorrow at noon. If you aren't here by then, we'll place her in a foster home."

"I'll be there."

When Ben hung up the phone, he was trembling. *Oh, Sage! What have you done? Oh God, I wish Katy was here. What am I going to do with a baby?*

Ben's thoughts began to whirl around in his head. He hadn't seen his sister for twenty-three years. She left home at the age of eighteen, an angry, rebellious girl, and returned to Texas only once—when their parents died in the auto accident. After the funeral, ten year old Ben went to live with his maternal grandmother, and Sage disappeared from his life.

Ben did keep in touch with his aunt and learned from her that Sage came back to Texas for a visit soon after he and Katy married. Katy had wanted Ben to try to find her then, but he knew in his heart that Sage didn't want to be found.

Getting up from his desk, Ben saddled his horse and went for a ride through the massive oaks that grew around the small lake on his and Katy's farm. He felt so overwhelmed. How was he going to take care of Sam, a baby, and do two jobs? The tears came to his eyes then. He hadn't really cried since Katy died; and after that, he didn't think he'd ever cry again. Her death had been the worst of all tragedies.

But this…it was bringing back all the memories from his childhood, the death of his parents when he was ten and the death of his grandmother when he was nineteen. It seemed to him like everyone he had ever loved, left him. Did he really want to bring one more person into his life? What if he brought her home, learned to love her, then Sage came back and took her away? The thought crossed his mind that maybe he should just let the state of Nevada take care of the baby.

But Ben Browning could not do that. This baby was his niece. She was Sam's cousin.

From the back of his horse that day, he looked around. His ride had taken him to the other side of the property, to the house where Katy's parents lived. He knew what he had to do.

Linda was out in the yard working in her flower garden. When she heard the sound of the horse's hooves in the lane, she stood up and watched as Ben approached her.

"Ben. What are you doing here? Is something wrong? Is John okay?"

Ben slid off his horse and tied the reins around a fence post. "John's okay. He's in the grove with the pickers. But I have a bit of a problem, and I need your help."

It seemed to Ben like he was always going to John and Linda for help. But they had insisted he do that since Katy died.

"That's why I'm here, Ben. What's going on? Come inside. We'll have something to drink. You look like you could use some nourishment."

Ben followed his mother-in-law into the modest home they had built when they moved to Florida to take care of Katy. "Here, drink this." She put a tall glass of lemonade in front of him. Ben drank half of it, and his throat still felt dry.

"What is it, Ben? What's wrong?"

"I got a phone call a little while ago…" The whole story came rushing out of him.

"Oh, Ben. What are you going to do?" Linda's eyes were full of concern.

"I have to go get her, Linda! She's Sam's cousin. She's my niece, my only sister's child. I can't let her go into foster care."

"What can I do to help?" The two of them were sitting at her kitchen table. Linda reached over, took his hand, and held on to it.

"Linda…it seems like I'm constantly coming to you for help with something. Don't you ever get sick of me?"

"No, Ben. When you married my daughter, you became my son. We moved here so we could be close to Katy, and you, and Sam. Katy isn't here anymore, but you're still my son."

"If I go get her, I'm going to need your help with her. I know you don't mind helping with Sam, he's your grandchild. But do you really want to help me with a child who isn't even related to you?" Ben felt almost guilty for asking the dear woman to give him more help.

"Ben…did you forget that Katy didn't have our blood either? But when her Momma Beth put her into my arms that day at the hospital, she became my child. This little girl needs a home, just like Katy did. She needs a Dad, a brother and some grandparents who will love her and shelter her. Go get her, Ben. I'll help you with her."

"If I go this evening, can you take care of Sam?"

"Of course. But if you fly your own plane, shouldn't someone go with you? What if the baby needs something on the way home?"

"I'll go commercial. I'll see if I can get on the last flight out of Tampa tonight. I need to be here when Sam gets home from school so I can talk to him about it."

*****

"But I want to go with you!"

"Sam…I know you do, Buddy. But I need you to stay here. I told Grandma you could stay home from school tomorrow, and help her find a baby bed and some clothes for the baby. You can go stay at her house tonight, and I'll be home tomorrow night. I really do need your help with this, okay?"

"O-kaaay. Can I buy her some toys too?"

"Sure. But remember, little girls don't like boy toys. Grandma will show you what kind of toys to buy for baby girls. But, I really think she's going to like you more than toys."

"I really don't know how to play with baby girls."

"Me either. We'll learn together, okay?" Ben pulled his boy close and gave him a hug. "But we need to go. I have to get on the plane at eight."

"Why aren't you flying your own plane?"

"I'll need to hold your little sister on the way home. I can't fly and hold a baby at the same time."

"I could go with you and hold her while you fly."

"We'll do that someday, okay? But, not this time. I think you'll get really bored out there. I'm going to have to meet with people and sign a lot of papers. I'm wondering… when you and Grandma go looking for clothes for her tomorrow, could you find something special she can wear for Christmas? She's kind of like an early Christmas present for us."

"Sure. But can I still have that train set for Christmas too?" Ben had to smile. Sam was getting a new sister, but right now, a train set was at the top of his priority list.

Chapter Eight

The trip to Vegas was one that changed Ben's life.

On the way to the airport, he stopped at a Walmart and bought an infant car seat, a newborn outfit, and some disposable diapers. He hoped the hospital would supply him with enough formula to get his niece back home with him.

He arrived in Las Vegas at midnight and stayed at the airport hotel. It was four a.m., Florida time, when he finally went to bed. But his sleep was a restless one. He woke up several times in a state of panic with the same thoughts going through his head. *What am I doing? I already have more responsibilities than I know what to do with.*

It was a dream about Katy that woke him for the last time and kept him awake. She was flying away in his plane, and he was left behind, begging her not to go because she didn't know how to fly. It was a strange dream. In real life, he was the one left behind, and he didn't know how he was going to parent, not only Sam, but now a baby girl.

He called a taxi and left the hotel at eleven. The baby's things were in his backpack and he had to carry the car seat into the hospital with him.

The social worker had told him to have her paged when he arrived. As he sat in the lobby, watching the throngs of people go in and out, he thought again about his sister. The last time she had called his grandmother, she said she was in Las Vegas working as a dancer. She was twenty one years old then. She was forty-five now. Was it possible that she was still doing the same kind of work? And why was she having a baby at her age? Where was the father of this baby? Did he not want this child either? There were so many unanswered questions.

Nancy, the social worker, found him and told him they would go to her office before they went to see the baby.

"Can I get you some coffee, Ben? This may take awhile."

"That would be great. I didn't sleep much last night, and I have a long day ahead of me."

After they were settled in her office, Nancy informed him that she had already run a criminal background check on him, and it had come back clean. "Since this is a family adoption, we aren't going to have to involve the Interstate Compact on the Placement of Children, but if I were you, Mr. Browning, I'd hire a lawyer."

"Why do you think I need to do that?" Ben had planned on it, but wanted to know the social worker's reason for suggesting it.

"Your sister didn't appear to be emotionally stable when she was here. We think that's probably why she left before discharge. We told her we were going to bring social services in on her case. Does she have any psychiatric problems that you know of?"

"Not that I know of. I was a little boy when she left home, and the only person she's ever reached out to is my aunt. I've been wondering, did you ask her about the father of the baby?"

"We did. She said she didn't know who the father was."

Ben's heart felt like it was going to break for his sister. What kind of life did she lead? And how would she eventually end up?

"Can you tell me anything else about her? Do you think she was a drug user?"

"She did admit to recreational use of drugs, but said she didn't do any after she found out she was pregnant. That was difficult for us to believe, but her blood was clean. The baby is small, but appears to be healthy."

"How small is she?"

"She weighed five pounds and six ounces when she was born, but she appears to be full term. She hasn't had any breathing problems and is eating well."

"Can I see her?"

"After we finish this paperwork. I need to get a social history from you."

The social history took over an hour. When Nancy learned that Ben was a single parent, she took her glasses off, and rubbed her eyes.

"Ben…do you really think you can handle another child on your own?"

"Yes, I do." And in that moment, when his niece's future was in question, Ben knew he could. "I have the most amazing support system. Even though I have no extended family of my own, my late wife had an amazing one. When I married her, they accepted me as their son, and I'm very close to them."

"Do you have a significant other?"

"I've been seeing a woman who's a teacher. She loves kids, and if things work out between us, I know she will make a great mom."

"It seems to me, that with two jobs, you're going to need all the help you can get."

"They'll be there for me, I'm confident of that."

"Let's go get your little girl then." The social worker stood up and started down the long corridor of the hospital. Ben felt like he was in a dream. *What on earth am I doing? This is going to change my life, and Sam's, forever.* But he continued on down the hall towards the little girl that would once again connect him to his blood family.

Ten minutes later, a nurse placed Molly in Ben's arms, and he fell in love again. She was so tiny, and her head was covered with what looked like peach fuzz. Her eyes were open, and he could tell they were the same eyes as his and Sam's. This tiny little girl was his.

The hospital supplied him with bottles of formula and burp pads, and called a taxi for him. Ben was a dad again. But, this time he wouldn't have Katy to mother his little one.

*****

Six months later, Ben was still in love with Molly. Sam had helped name her and had accepted her into their family without a problem. The first time her big brother held her, he had a look on his face that said this little girl belonged to him.

Ben found a lawyer. The lawyer suggested they wait a year to start legal proceedings. Although Ben had the letter Sage left behind, Molly was still an abandoned child, and there were regulations that had to be followed.

"Oh, Miss Molly. I don't know what I ever did without you. But right now, I need to find someone who can help me take care of you and your brother this summer."

Molly looked at him with her big blue eyes, then took her finger out of her mouth and put it into his.

"I don't want your slobbers…" Her giggles bubbled up from inside her, and he couldn't help but laugh.

"Into the swing you go. I need to call your Grandma and see if she knows any ladies at church who will take in little orphans while their daddy works." Ben had already decided that Sam could go on the charters with him. He just needed someone to take care of Molly three or four days a week. His summer schedule looked pretty heavy.

When he clicked his phone off after talking to Linda, he had the numbers of three ladies who did occasional babysitting. One of the numbers belonged to Jan, so he had only two possibilities left.

After he made the two calls, he had no possibilities. One of the ladies was full for the summer. The other one had changed her mind about doing child care. He had no one to help care for his children, and his in-laws were leaving town in a week.

*****

Ben had the same dream that night. It was the one he had the night before Molly came into their lives. Katy was in his plane and flying away. He was petrified because she didn't know how to fly. But this time someone was beside him as Katy flew away. It was her sisters, Abby and Carly.

Katy had loved her sisters intensely, even though she didn't meet them until she was sixteen years old. She had just been diagnosed with the leukemia, and her doctors were looking for bone marrow donors. John and Linda contacted Katy's birth mother to see if she had other children who could be tested.

Momma Beth was pregnant for Carly at the time, and when she was born, her cord blood was harvested. When Katy relapsed at nineteen, the cord blood saved her life.

Abby was Alex's daughter. Her mother died when she was five. After Beth and Alex married, Beth adopted Abby. When Katy met Abby at the age of sixteen, they instantly became not only step-sisters, but best friends.

When Ben first met Katy's sisters, he was amazed at how close they were. He hadn't seen his own sister for years, and a tight knit family was foreign to him. After he and Katy married, Carly was at their house often. She adored Katy, and the feeling was mutual.

In the years after their wedding, Katy and Ben saw Abby and her husband, Brett, only at family get-togethers. They were busy with their little family and Ben and Katy were busy establishing their own.

After Katy died, Momma Beth came to the house every Wednesday to help with Sam who was just three years old. She said she lost her Katy twice, once at birth, then again through death, and she didn't want to lose Katy's son too. Once in awhile, Abby and Carly would come to the grove with their mother.

Ben seldom dreamed about Katy. When he did, he would wake up with the most euphoric feeling, like he'd just been with her. But once he was fully awake, the emptiness was agonizing. It felt like he had lost her all over again.

When Ben woke from his dream this time, he was more confused than sad though. Why were Katy's sisters in his dreams? Perhaps it was because he was going to miss Carly coming to the house this summer to help him with the kids. And Abby had been on his mind a lot since Mother's Day. He felt so bad about her.

As he got his coffee and went to the deck, he decided he would call Momma Beth later and see if they were all okay. And he would talk to her about coming out on Wednesdays. He could at least do charters that day, although it tended to be his slowest day.

Ben finished his coffee and went to wake Sam. He woke up grouchy, something that rarely happened.

"What's wrong, Sam-my-man? You should be happy today. You only have a few days of school left."

"My ear hurts." Ben felt his son's forehead. He did feel hot.

"Whoa…I think you have a fever. Let me get the thermometer." Ben had to search for it. Sam was rarely sick, and he couldn't remember where he put it the last time. Fortunately, Molly hadn't been sick at all since she had come to live with them.

"Here it is. You want to hold it in your ear till it beeps?"

Sam leaned his head on one hand and held the thermometer is his ear with the other one. He looked miserable, and his cheeks were flushed.

The thermometer beeped and Sam looked at it. "It says one, zero, two, Dad."

"Well, it looks like you'll go to the doctor today instead of going to school. Did your ear hurt last night?"

"A little bit. My throat too."

"You probably have an ear infection. I think you had one when you were about Molly's age. I'll call the doctor in a little while. Maybe they'll do Molly's six month check-up while we're there too." Ben tousled the dark hair that looked so much like his mom's. It was thick and curly.

Ben was supposed to fly to Miami that afternoon and bring one of his regulars back to Tampa. He hoped he could get the kids in to see the doctor this morning, and he hoped Sam didn't have something contagious. He would feel awful if they gave some kind of bug to Linda right before she left for the mountains.

Oh, Katy. On days like this, I need you so much. He gave Sam some Tylenol and clear juice then put him on the couch to watch cartoons while he fed Molly. But Molly didn't want to cooperate either. When he would put a bite of baby cereal in her mouth, she would spit it out then rub it all over her face with her fist. Exasperated, Ben gave up and gave her one of her teething biscuits. She was already a mess and in need of a bath—the biscuit would keep her happy and entertained for awhile.

As he was doing the dishes, the phone rang. He knew it was probably Linda. She called him every morning if she didn't come over. But it wasn't Linda this time, it was Momma Beth.

"Ben? You sound tired today. You okay?"

"Hey. I was going to call you in a little while. You reading my mind now?" He heard her laugh. "Yeah…I'm okay. But I didn't sleep well last night, and Sam woke up with a fever. And Molly is being very uncooperative today."

"Oh, no. Wish I was there to help you. But I'm available tomorrow if you need the help. That's why I'm calling."

"I could sure use you today, but tomorrow will be great too. It will give Linda a break from watching Molly. I have a charter this afternoon, and another one in the morning. She was going to watch the kids both times."

"Good. I'm glad I'm free and can help. It sounds like you've got your hands full."

"Yeah. It's been crazy here. How are things there? How is Abby doing?"

"Not good. She still hasn't found a job. She and her dad are moving the last of her things into storage today. I've never seen her so distraught. You know how she is. She doesn't want to be a burden to us."

"I could use some help this summer. Do you think she would come out here and stay?"

The words were out of Ben's mouth before he had time to think. They must have come out of his feelings of desperation. And in the dream, Abby had been standing by him when Katy flew away.

"You want her and the three kids to come live at your house? Oh, Ben. I don't think that would work. I'm not sure it would even be appropriate."

"Yeah, you're right. I guess I'm just feeling overwhelmed this morning. Tell her I'm thinking about her, will you? And I'll see you tomorrow."

Chapter Nine

Ben was able to get an appointment with the doctor for both kids before noon.

Two years earlier, Dr. Leah Miller had taken over the pediatric practice in town after Laurelville's oldest physician retired. She was part of a bigger network of hospitals out of Tampa, but said she preferred working in a small town. Her office was located in the same building as the small local hospital that was part of the same network.

"Hey, Ben. It sounds like you've had your hands full this morning." Dr. Leah, as she liked to be called, came into the examining room, her usual perky self. The nurse had left them after she took both kids' temperatures and done their weights. Ben was happy there would be no waiting around today.

"Yep, it's been a busy one." He was bouncing Molly on his knee to keep her content.

"So, Sam…I hear you have an earache and your throat hurts." She sat down on the stool in front of him.

"It's hard to swallow, but dad gave me a Popsicle for breakfast. It feels better."

Dr. Leah looked up at Ben and smiled. "Sounds like your dad gave you the right medicine then."

"He gave me some Tylenol too. But I think the Popsicle helped more." Ben couldn't help but smile, and he saw Dr. Leah's lips twitch too.

"I'm sure it did, but I still need to look inside your mouth and ears, okay?"

Ben watched the doctor as she examined his son. Sam had only seen her twice, and that was for his school physicals. But since Molly had come to live with them, Ben had been in her office every two months for her well baby check-ups and immunizations.

The first time Ben saw Dr. Leah he was very impressed with her. Not only was she professional, she was personable. And to Ben, personable meant not just pleasant, but charming. The fact that she was attractive didn't miss his attention either.

"Well, what do you know, Sam. I think you caught that bug that's going around your school this week. Did any of your friends say their throats hurt too?" She threw the tongue depressor away and went to wash her hands.

"Yeah. Henry had a sore throat two days ago."

"Henry's your friend?" She was sitting on a stool, writing what looked like a prescription.

"Yep. Do you know him?"

"I sure do." Dr. Miller looked at Ben again. "Looks like strep. It's going around right now. Has Molly had a temp?"

"No, but she wouldn't eat her cereal this morning."

"Well, then. We may have to look at Molly's throat too. If she has this same bug, we'll put off her immunization until she feels better."

"So, this is contagious?" Ben sighed.

"It will be for the next few hours."

Ben felt his shoulders slump. *Great! That's all I need. Two sick kids and no one to help me with them.*

"You okay, Ben? You know you could catch this too?"

"I'm fine. I have a great immune system."

"Most healthy adults do have good immune systems, until they get run down themselves. And you're looking a little tired." Ben felt uncomfortable. He could feel her examining his health status with her eyes.

"Yeah, well, I didn't sleep very well last night."

"Are you ever getting a break?" She looked at him with a stern look on her face.

"Of course I am. My mother-in-law watches the kids for me when I fly my charters. And flying is my get-away time." He smiled at her in hopes that she would believe him. "I'm suppose to do it this afternoon, but don't know now. I would hate to expose my mother-in-law to this bug. They are headed to the mountains next week."

"Who watches the kids when Linda can't?" She was checking Molly's ears now, while Ben held his baby still by holding her head close to his chest.

He caught the faint scent of strawberries. *Shampoo or soap?* As usual, Leah's long sun-streaked hair was casually pulled back into a low pony-tail.

"Well, right now I don't have a backup sitter. My sister-in-law, Carly, has helped me with Sam the last two summers. But I need to find someone else for this summer. You don't happen to know anyone, do you?"

"I'll ask my nurse for you. She knows about things like that better than I do. But I have the afternoon off. I could watch them for you today, so you can do your charter." Ben wasn't quite sure he heard correctly.

"You could watch them? But…but, you're a doctor." Ben felt totally confused.

Dr. Leah laughed. "You have something against doctors watching your kids?" She was done examining Molly and was at her desk, writing again.

"No. But don't you have something better to do on your day off?"

"Well, I could go shopping, but I don't need anything. Or I could go golfing, but I don't have any clubs. Come on, Ben. Let me watch your kids for you. I've already been exposed to their bugs, and you look like you need a break."

"Is it ethical for you to do that?"

"I don't know. Do you want me to check with the ethics committee to see if I can watch a friend's kids on my time off?" She smiled at him, and he noticed the smile lines around her eyes. Brown eyes, like Katy's. *A brown-eyed blond. That's unusual.*

"Come on, Dad. Dr. Leah knows how to take care of kids." Sam looked from his dad to his doctor. "Can we come to your house?"

"Sure. I live close to the park, and if you promise to take your medicine, I'll take you and your sister there to play." She looked at Ben again. "Looks like Sam and I took care of the details, Dad. So, if you trust me, you can bring them over on your way to the airport."

Ben was speechless. Surely this beautiful, professional woman had something else she could do besides babysit his kids.

"Here are their prescriptions. Get them started on the medicine as soon as you get home. And send it with them when they come over. This third prescription has my address on it. Let's just call it medicine for a weary dad."

"Are you sure about this?"

"I am. I wouldn't have asked if I wasn't. This is one of the reasons I wanted to practice in a small town. As much as I love my career, I also wanted a life. And helping friends is part of my life."

Ben was still shaking his head when he left the office. Sam had told him Dr. Miller went to his church. Linda knew her, and said she was a wonderful person, but Ben still couldn't believe she wanted to watch his kids. It was kind of bizarre. But, he wouldn't analyze it today. He was going to be able to fly his charter, and he needed to do as many as he could before summer came. If he couldn't find a babysitter, he was going to lose some money, and maybe some customers.

*****

Ben called Linda as soon as he got home to tell her the kids were sick, and he wouldn't need her to watch them.

"Aren't you going to fly your charter?"

"Yes, but I don't want you exposed to strep. I got someone else to watch them."

"Ben! I'm a mom. Do you know how many times I was exposed to strep when my three kids were little?" Ben could hear the disappointment in her voice. *Does the woman never get tired of my kids?*

"I know. I just don't want you to be sick when it's time for you to leave for the mountains. It really is okay."

"Who's going to watch them?"

"When I took them to see Dr. Miller, she said she had the afternoon off and could do it."

Silence.

"Linda? Are you still there?"

"I'm sorry, Ben. But did you just say Leah Miller is watching your kids this afternoon?" Ben heard the same confusion in her voice that he felt when he left the office.

"Yeah...kinda weird, isn't it? She insisted, and I didn't know how to tell her no."

"Actually, it sounds like something she'd do. She can't seem to get enough of kids. Did I tell you she teaches the three year olds at church now?"

"Really? You'd think after dealing with kids all week, she'd be sick of them."

"No. Not really. She's one of the most down-to-earth people I know. But you better be careful. If Jan finds out, she might be jealous." Ben saw the smile twitching at the corners of her mouth.

"Linda, I told you... Jan and I aren't dating anymore."

"Ohhh, maybe Leah heard about that. Could be she's more interested in you than your kids, Ben." Now Ben heard humor in his mother-in-law's voice. It reminded him of Katy. His wife had not been a blood child of Linda, but she had acted so much like her.

"Stop it. She's just being nice. Besides, I'm sure she has all kinds of men lined up to date her."

"She might. But I think she's going to be picky about who she marries."

"Linda! The woman offered to watch my kids. There is no marriage proposal in the deal." Ben heard her laugh, and he joined in.

"I need to go, okay? Why don't you do something nice for yourself today since you don't have to watch my kids."

*****

When Ben drove up to the address Leah gave him, the first thing he noticed was how neat her place was. The house was an older ranch style, but it was well-kept and the lawn was beautifully manicured. He could see a privacy fence in the back. She probably needed that with her property next to the public park she had mentioned.

He wondered if it was family that had brought her to their small town of twenty thousand people. Why else would she move here?

By the time he got the kids out of their car seats, and the diaper bag out of the front seat, she was standing at her door, waiting on them. Ben felt uncomfortable as he walked up her front steps.

"I still can't believe you want to do this," he said, when she opened the door.

She smiled. "It's okay, Ben. Sam and I are good buddies from church, and I love cuddling babies. Now stop fretting about it."

"Okay. But if you need anything, my mother-in-law's number is in the bag. I should be back by seven-thirty. Is that okay?"

"Sure. We'll be right here." She took Molly out of his arms.

"She's going to need another nap. The one she had this morning was very short. I brought my pack-n-play. Do you want me to bring it in?"

"You don't need to. I have one of my own."

"You have a pack-n-play? Why?" This woman was a puzzle to him. He knew she didn't have kids of her own.

"I watch my friend's kids sometimes."

"You really do like kids, don't you?"

"I really do, Ben. And I promise you, I'll take good care of yours." She smiled at him again, and took the diaper bag as she held Molly in her other arm.

"I know you will…it's just that I've never had to leave them with anyone besides family."

"Well, Sam and I are family because we go to the same church, right, Sam?"

"Yeah, Dad. I get to see Dr. Leah every Sunday."

"See? Maybe when you get back, we can talk about why you don't come to church with him. I'm curious."

Ben decided not to get sucked into that conversation at the moment. "Sam, you be good for Dr. Leah, okay?"

"Okay, Dad. Have fun on your trip." Sam was already checking out her living room. The three of them turned away from him, and Ben had no choice but to leave.

Chapter Ten

Ben's Cessna 340 was on the tarmac at the small airport on the edge of town. It was two-thirty by the time he got it into the air and headed south towards Miami. He was going to meet his client at one of the smaller airports in Miami at four. He would make it on time.

It was a beautiful day to fly. As Ben settled into his flight, his mind wondered, as it always did, back to his home life. Today had been a strange day. It had started with his recurrent dream of Katy flying his airplane. He wondered again if dreams had any meaning. If they did, he wondered if that was why he had impulsively mentioned to Momma Beth the possibility of Abby and the kids coming to stay with him this summer.

Then, like his life wasn't confusing enough, his kids' beautiful doctor was babysitting for them right now. Was Linda right? Was it possible that she was interested in Ben, and not just the kids? She'd always been friendly when he took the kids to see her. But even as pretty as she was, he never felt any special attraction when he was with her. Maybe it was because he had been with Jan, and never entertained the idea of being attracted to Leah. Or maybe he really was just a one-woman man.

She was nice to look at though, and an interesting person. If he tried, maybe she could become more to him than just the kids' interesting doctor. But, it was also possible that she just liked kids and was a kind person who liked to help people in need. There was a label for people like that, but he couldn't remember what it was. Something about a need to be needed.

Or maybe she felt like it was her Christian duty to help widowers with children. Ben hated that word…widower. It sounded so dark and hopeless. But that's what he was, wasn't he?

Katy, why did you have to leave me? You made me a widower, and I don't want to be one of those. He saw the look in people's eyes when he came around. It was that "oh that poor man, his wife died and left him all alone with a little boy," look.

Since Molly had come into their lives, he had gone out into public even less than he usually did. He didn't want to answer a bunch of questions about her, and he was sure the looks would be even more pathetic.

But Dr. Leah already knew him and his situation with Molly. He had told her Molly's history on her first well-baby visit when she was two weeks old. She had been sympathetic and told him he did the right thing. She also told him it would be good for Sam to have a sibling. Dr. Leah was definitely a good doctor and a nice person…maybe he should ask her out and see where it took them.

By the time Ben had picked his client up in Miami, flown him into Tampa then returned to Laurelville, he had convinced himself that he should definitely ask Dr. Leah to go to dinner with him. What could it hurt? She could always say no.

It was seven-ten when Ben drove back into her driveway. He rang her bell, but had to wait a few seconds before he heard footsteps on the other side of the door. He could only imagine how exhausted she probably was. But she didn't look exhausted when she opened the door for him.

"Ben! You're early. Come on in." She led him through the small living area he had been in earlier, through the dining room, and into a great room at the back of her house. It was beautiful with large windows that looked out onto an in-ground swimming pool. The pool had an illuminated waterfall flowing into it at the other end. Ben had seen a lot of pools in his years of living in Florida, but this one was gorgeous. He wondered if she took care of the tropical plants around it, or if she hired it done.

"Dad! You're back! We're eating popcorn and watching a movie."

Ben glanced at Leah, who had picked Molly up out of the pack-n-play and was holding her close. Molly was usually excited to see him and would hold her arms out to him the minute she saw him. But she seemed quite content in Dr. Leah's arms.

"Hey, Sam. Popcorn and a movie? That sounds like fun. Were you good today?"

"Well, of course he was. We had a great time, didn't we, Sam?"

Sam looked away from his movie for a second. "Yeah. We went to the park after Molly woke up, then we got to go swimming in Dr. Leah's pool!"

"I put some of that ear putty in his ears when he was in the water. I think the medicine is working already, but I didn't want his ear canals to get wet and hurt when he went to bed tonight."

"Thanks. He swims like a fish, doesn't he?" Ben turned back to Leah. "His grandparents have a pool, and he swims there a lot. And how's my Molly doing?" Ben held his hands out to her. She looked at Leah, then at Ben. Then she grinned and threw herself into his arms. Ben felt like his heart was going to burst. His Molly still liked him best.

"Can you stay awhile, just until he finishes his popcorn and the movie?"

"How much of the movie is left?"

"Only about a half hour."

"Please...dad?" Sam was back to watching the movie and eating his popcorn. Ben knew he should get his kids home to bed, but it was so homey at Dr. Leah's house.

"I suppose. But that means you have to go to bed as soon as we get home."

Turning back to Dr. Leah, he noticed that she was watching him closely.

"It looks like his medicine is working. You can't eat popcorn with a sore throat."

"It is working. Why don't you go ahead and sit down? Can I get you something to drink?"

"I'll take a soda if you have one." Ben's eyes followed her as far as the dining area where she turned left into the beautiful kitchen he had seen on his way in.

"I'm sorry." She came back to the door. "I only have water and juice. I preach to my patients all the time about the dangers of too many sugary drinks, so I don't keep it in the house."

"Well, it's good to know you practice what you preach. I'll have the juice." Ben had eaten some snacks on his way to Miami, but hadn't had anything since then, and he was starved.

She seemed to read his mind. "Do you want some popcorn too?"

"Don't go to the trouble of popping any more. I'll be fine."

"It's no trouble." She put his juice in front of him and returned to the kitchen. Within seconds, he heard popping sounds from her microwave.

When he took a drink of his juice, Molly reached out both hands, as if she wanted to take it from him. "Oh no you don't, little lady. You drink formula."

"Here you go. Why don't I take Molly while you eat? I was just getting ready to give her a bottle." She had the bottle in her hand and held it out towards Molly, who of course decided Dr. Leah was her favorite person of the moment.

Ben looked at his two contented children. There was no doubt about it. Dr. Leah Miller knew how to take care of kids. But he doubted if she would take the summer off of her regular job to baby-sit for him.

"So, how was your flight?"

"It was good…beautiful day for flying. Were the kids okay for you?"

"They're great kids, Ben. And I can tell you're doing a wonderful job parenting them. How do you do it all?" He noticed that she looked like a natural with Molly in her arms.

"I have lots of help. And when I work in the grove, I can take both of them with me. We make it work."

"Well, if you ever need help again, let me know. I'll do it if I'm available." She looked down at Molly in her arms and smiled at her.

"I think we'll be okay. Today was kind of an emergency, with both of them getting sick. I really appreciate what you did for us. I was wondering if I could repay you by taking you out to dinner sometime?"

"You don't have to repay me, Ben. But I do think I'd like that dinner." Molly was holding her own bottle now, and Dr. Leah looked up at Ben. When she smiled at him, Ben noticed the brown eyes again. A brown-eyed blond. Katy had threatened to dye her hair blond one day because his favorite country singer was a blond with brown eyes. He felt his heart beating a little faster in his chest.

"Good. I'll check the calendar and give you a call if that's okay with you."

"I'm home most evenings, unless I'm on call or at the church. That reminds me, why haven't I ever seen you at church with Sam?"

"I was at his Christmas program a few months ago. There were a lot of people there. Guess that's why we missed each other."

"Is there a reason why you don't attend regularly?" Now Ben felt his stomach tighten up. This woman had a way of making him aware of feelings. He hadn't felt that since. . . well, since Katy.

He was hoping she'd forgotten about the church thing. Why was his not going to church such a big deal? *If people only knew how lonely I feel there without Katy by my side.*

"That's a long story."

"I'd like to hear it sometime."

"Maybe, someday."

"Whenever you're ready. Maybe we can talk about it when we go out to dinner." Ben groaned on the inside. If he told her the real reason why he didn't go to church, he'd have to talk about Katy. He didn't know if he could tell that story to another person, especially this person with her empathetic personality. What if he cried while he was talking about it?

Maybe he wouldn't be calling her again about dinner.

"I think I better get these kids rounded up for now so I can get them tucked into bed. Again…thank you. You were a lifesaver for me today."

She smiled. "It really was my pleasure, Ben. And I'll look forward to that dinner."

"Yeah, me too."

Chapter Eleven

Ben was at the sink, doing the breakfast dishes when he heard a vehicle coming up the lane to his house. Glancing out the kitchen window, he saw Abby's van. He could see Momma Beth and Carly behind the passenger door windows, and the heads of Abby's three kids in the back. He wondered why Momma Beth hadn't told him she was bringing the whole family.

Taking Molly out of the highchair, he went out to meet them.

"Carly, Abby, I didn't know you girls were coming too. But, it's good to see you." Ben hugged all three women as Abby's three kids spilled out of the car.

"I hope you don't mind, Ben. We decided to make today a family affair." Momma Beth was already reaching for Molly.

"I don't mind at all. You know I love seeing all of you." But his thoughts went to his empty refrigerator. He should have shopped last night.

"Momma said I needed a day off from job hunting, and this is the kids' first day of summer vacation. I wanted to do something special with them. Coming to Uncle Ben's house is always fun for them." Abby looked even more exhausted today than she had on Mother's Day.

"I'm glad all of you could come. But Sam has two more days of school. I just put him on the bus."

"Did you hear that, guys? Sam isn't here." Kyle and Konnor looked disappointed.

"Maybe we can go to the city pool after while, guys. I'll take you, and your momma can take a nap." Carly was still everyone's favorite aunt.

"How'd you get off work, Carly?"

"I have to work the weekend, so when Momma said she was coming here, I requested the day off." At seventeen, Carly was now taller than her mom and her sister. With her blue eyes and blond hair, she looked like her dad. Katy and Abby both had brown hair and brown eyes like their respective mothers.

"I was hoping Sam would be here. I miss that boy so much. Guess I'll have to spoil Molly and these other little monkeys until he gets home." Abby's little four-year-old, Lexie, was hanging on tight to her Aunt Carly.

"Well, make yourselves at home. I should be back from my flight by two. If all of you can stay around, I'll order pizza for supper. Sam would love it if you could be here when he gets off the bus."

"Can we, mom?" The boys were looking expectantly at Abby.

"It's up to your Grandma."

"Can we Grandma? Please?" The boys were joined by their little sister as they crowded around Momma Beth.

"Well, of course we have to stay until Sam gets home. Ben…I don't want to rush you off, but don't you have a flight scheduled?"

"Yeah. I better get going. Linda said she may be over later to visit. She'll be surprised to see a whole house full!"

As Ben left the house, he felt a heaviness in his heart. Katy loved it when her family visited the grove. After she talked Ben into buying it, she wanted it to be a place her family could escape to when they got tired of the city. Since Tampa was only an hour away, her family had visited often, especially after her leukemia came back.

They had all been in the house the night she died.

Ben would never forget that night. Katy had been unresponsive for two days, and the hospice nurse told him to call the family in. They wanted to be there at the end, and Ben couldn't deny them that wish. Abby left her kids at home with their dad, but she, Carly, and their brother, Jon, came with Momma Beth and Alex. They were Katy's birth family.

Her adoptive family was already there. John and Linda had called Katy's two adoptive brothers earlier in the week, and they had flown in from Philadelphia. But Ben was the only one with Katy when she died. He was holding her in his arms when she took that last ragged breath. It had been almost three years ago, and he still felt the pain.

After she died, the hospice nurse told them she would give Katy one last bath before the mortician was called. But Katy's moms asked to do it. They had both loved her for all of her thirty years and wanted to do this one last thing for her.

While they washed her and dressed her in her prettiest gown, Ben went to Sam's bedroom to wake him up. Katy had asked to be cremated, so this would be the last time he would see his mother. It was the most difficult thing Ben had ever done.

After he was awake, Ben tried to explain to his three year old son that he needed to say goodbye to his momma. Sam seemed to understand goodbye, what he didn't understand was that it was to be until eternity.

The family had not felt complete since that day…to any of them. They all tried, but Katy's absence was always felt. Ben was happy though that Katy's family still felt comfortable when they came to her home.

He hadn't changed a thing in the house since she died. He knew he should be getting rid of her clothes, but he just didn't have the heart to do it. Once in a while, he would hold a dress or a blouse next to his face, and he was sure he could still smell her. He still needed her things.

He would clear her things out—someday. It might be the same day he scattered her ashes over the grove she loved. Her wish for him to do that had been written in the little book she left for him.

*****

Ben returned home early enough to pick Sam up at school. It would give him an extra hour to play with the boys. And Sam hated that hour on the bus.

"Hey, Dad! Why are you here? I thought you had to fly today?" Ben was waiting by the door of the school so he wouldn't miss his son.

"I got off early and decided to pick you up. That way you can have more time with the surprise that's waiting for you at home."

"I already know Momma Beth is there. Is Carly there too?" Ben took the heavy back pack from Sam. The teacher must have told them to clean out their desks today.

"Now if I told you that, it wouldn't be a surprise, would it?

"Come on, Dad. Tell me." Sam reached over and socked his dad playfully with his fist.

"Okay, Carly's there. And they're staying for supper. We'll order pizza, okay?'

"I sure wish she could come and stay with us this summer… like she did last year."

"Me too. She's fun to have around, isn't she?" He had his arm around his son as he directed him through the heavy traffic at the school.

"Who's gonna watch me and Molly when you go flyin', Dad? Hey, I know! Maybe Dr. Leah could do it." Sam looked expectantly at his dad.

"She has to do her doctoring, Sam."

"I thought you were going to ask Miss Henderson?" Ben slowed his steps; Sam was running to keep up with him.

"No, I think she's busy too. Don't worry about it, Buddy. I'll find someone, or I just won't go flying." Ben knew he had been wise to keep the nature of his and Jan's relationship a secret from Sam. And he'd do the same thing with Dr. Leah. Sam had already lost the most important female in his life and Ben refused to let him lose another one.

The drive from the school to home was less than ten minutes. No wonder Sam hated that hour on the bus when he had to take it.

"Okay, here we are. Why don't we sneak in, and see if we can scare Aunt Carly?"

They closed the truck doors quietly before they started toward the house. But the boys must have been watching for Sam, and they came running out to the deck before Sam could even get there.

"Konnor, Kyle! I didn't know you were here! Dad…is this the surprise you were telling me about?"

"Yep, it is. What have you guys been doing all day?"

"Aunt Carly was going to take us swimming in town, but Grandma Linda said we should wait till Sam came home and go to her house. Can we, Uncle Ben? Can we go swimming at her house?"

Ben had his arms around all three boys as they went in the back door.

"Well, I suppose so. Where's Lexie? You can't go without your sister, boys."

"She's no fun today. She's just been playing with Molly all day. Why do girls like babies so much, Uncle Ben?"

"I like babies. I even liked you guys when you were babies."

"You're crazy, Uncle Ben." Ben was amazed at how much older Abby's boys seemed.

"Hey, watch who you're callin' crazy or I'll take you all down and rub your heads together." Ben couldn't help but laugh and shake his head. These three boys combined, had enough energy to run a power plant. "Let's go see what your Grandma and aunties are doing."

Carly met all of them at the door. "You guys quiet down. We just got Molly down for her nap." Then her attention turned to her brother-in-law. "Hey, Ben. You've probably heard…we're going swimming. Do you want to take them over to John and Linda's house with Momma, or do you want me to go?"

"Why don't you go? I'll go pick up the pizza when Molly wakes up. Sam, we'll have to feed the horses sometime before bed."

"I wanna help feed the horses too!" Konnor loved coming to the grove in hopes of riding a horse while he was visiting.

"Okay. We'll all feed the horses after supper."

"Goodness…what is all the commotion in here?" Momma Beth joined in on the excitement in the kitchen.

"Granmma! Uncle Ben brought Sam home. We can all go swimming now."

"How was school, Sam?" Sam always went straight into his Grandma Beth's arms and he was hugging her.

"It was good today. We went on a field trip, and I only have two more days to go!"

"Great! Now, go get your swimsuit on. And be quiet. Molly and your Aunt Abby are asleep. The rest of you get out to the van." Carly herded all three of Abby's kids out the door.

"Ben. I'm so glad you picked him up at school. I almost called you to see if I could do it. Those boys have been waiting very impatiently all day for him to get home. Abby's taking a nap. She said you can go swimming with us if you want to, and she'll listen for Molly."

"No. You all go ahead. I have some book work I can do while the house is quiet. Can you and Carly handle those four?"

"Linda will be there. It was so nice of her to offer us the use of her pool. Saved us a trip into town. And this way Sam can go with us. Why don't you take a nap too? You look tired." She was shaking her head as she went out the door, and Ben heard her mutter something about everybody being too busy all the time.

Chapter 12

Ben was tempted. He couldn't remember the last time he took an afternoon nap. But with Sam gone and Molly asleep, he had time to do the paperwork he needed to do. It was the one thing about running two businesses that he hated. He loved the work at the grove and his flying, but he missed Katy so much when he had to sit down and do the paper work. They had always worked on it together.

He checked on Molly before heading to his desk in the living room. The door of the spare bedroom was open, and he noticed Abby stretched out on the bed. *Poor thing, she probably hasn't had an afternoon nap in years either.* He quietly pulled the door closed.

He grabbed a soda from the refrigerator before he went to his desk. *I have to get focused here...I can get a lot done in an hour.* The computer was already on, and Ben pulled up the spreadsheet for his flying business. He had a dozen business men who were his regular customers, and a few who called him sporadically. It was great when he had two or three who wanted to go to the same place on the same day. Tallahassee was their usual destination.

He enjoyed the chartering, but it wasn't exciting like when he flew helicopters in Afghanistan—or when he flew the air ambulance in Tampa. It was okay though. Now he had a family and needed a regular schedule. *Focus, Ben!*

He was so focused that he didn't hear Abby until she was right beside him.

"You look busy."

"Abby. I'm sorry, I didn't hear you. Did you have a good nap?" He pushed his chair back and got up to give her a hug. He had learned, soon after meeting Katy, that her family was a bunch of huggers. It had taken him a while to get used to it, but now he liked it.

"I did. It's so peaceful and quiet out here in the country, and once the kids left, I konked out. Molly isn't awake yet?"

"I haven't heard her, and the baby monitor is right here. She usually plays in her bed for awhile after she wakes up."

"That's nice. She's a little sweetheart, isn't she?"

"I think so. She definitely has a different personality than what her mother had. My sister, Sage, was never content with anything in life."

"Have you heard from her?"

"Nope, not a word. So…how are you doing?"

Ben saw the tears in her eyes and heard them in her voice. "I've had better years."

Ben closed his computer. "Let's go to the kitchen. We can make some coffee, and you can tell me about it."

"Are you sure you want to hear about my disaster of a life? Seems like you have your hands full here."

"I do want to hear about it. Tell me what your plans are."

"Well, we finally have a prospective buyer for the house. But the offer is only for what we still owe on it, so I'll get nothing from it. I would have stayed in it, but I couldn't pay the utilities, and Brett's new girlfriend doesn't want to live in it either. I guess she's more of an uptown condo kind of girl. I did get the furniture, but since I don't have a place to live, it's in storage."

"I'm sorry, Abby. That has to hurt. But maybe you can leave him and the house behind, and start over."

"But I have no home and still haven't found a job. It seems like no one needs an art major in the crappy economy. I thank God everyday for my mom and dad, but I don't want to intrude on them too long. But I have no choice now that school is over. I can't go to work. Who would watch the kids?"

"I hope you got a hunk of alimony and child support from Brett."

"I got enough to feed my kids and buy their necessities. I could probably go into low-income housing." She looked away from him then, probably hoping he wouldn't see the tears in her eyes. "I just can't believe this is happening, Ben. One day, I'm a wife and a mom, living the American dream, and the next minute, I'm homeless. Sin sure does wreck a lot of lives."

"I know it does. Death does too. My life changed so drastically when Katy died. If it hadn't been for her parents, I don't think I could have survived. Just goes to prove that we all need each other."

"So...are you doing okay now?"

"Right now, my biggest problem is finding childcare for the summer. I'm afraid if I can't find someone, I'll lose my customers to another charter service."

Ben put a cup of coffee down in front of Abby. "We need caffeine before those kids get home." They both laughed. It was one of those moments when they both knew if they didn't laugh, they'd cry.

"Abby? Did your mom tell you that I mentioned to her, the possibility of you and the kids coming here for the summer?"

"No...." She looked puzzled. "Why would we do that, Ben?"

"I didn't think she'd tell you. She told me it would be inappropriate. But I've been thinking. Maybe we could help each other this summer. I need someone to help me with the kids and the house until John and Linda come back home from the mountains. And you need a place to live. Right?"

"Ye-es?"

"So, why don't you and the kids come here for the summer? I'll provide a home for you, and you can take care of it and my kids when I have to fly. It sounds like a fair deal to me."

"I don't know, Ben. Momma's right. It might appear wrong to people on the outside. They would probably think we were shacking up together."

"You know what, Abby? I don't care what other people think anymore. It was wrong for Brett to leave you with three kids, and it was wrong for Katy to die. Our lives aren't perfect anymore, and we have to do what we have to do."

"I think you're rushing into this, Ben. You're making decisions out of your desperation."

"Desperate times call for desperate measures, Abby-girl." He laughed and she joined in.

"Do you know how noisy my kids are? And how much food they eat?"

"We could work it out. The two boys could bunk with Sam. He'd love it. Don't you have a set of bunk beds we could move into his room?"

"Yes, I have the ones the boys used at our house."

"Do you have a single bed we could put in Molly's room for Alexandria?"

"Yes."

"So we'd have two bedrooms for the kids, I'd have my room, and you can have the guest room. It could work out for both of us. And I do think the Bible says something about two being better than one, doesn't it?"

"Ben…I don't know; meshing two families, even for a short time, sounds risky. You would hate us by the end of the summer."

"I don't think so. If we set the parameters going into it, I think it could work."

"What kind of parameters?" Ben could see the doubt in Abby's face. Maybe she was right. It probably was a crazy idea.

"I don't know. Help me here." They both burst out laughing.

"Katy would love this, wouldn't she?"

"I think she would. It sounds like something she would do."

"Actually, I've had this recurring dream about her flying away in my airplane. The last time I had it, you and Carly were standing beside me as she flew away. Maybe it means the three of us are supposed to stand together. Carly helped me last summer. This summer can be yours." Abby saw the laughter leave his eyes.

"It sounds like our Katy is behind those dreams of yours, Ben. She's still trying to take care of you." Abby felt the tears come to her eyes. She missed her sister so much. "So, about those parameters?"

"Well, we have the living space worked out. We can make a list of all the chores that need to be done and divide them up. For instance, I'll provide the house and clean it, if you provide the food and cook it."

"You'll clean? I'm sold."

"But you have to do all the laundry. And babysit when I take a pretty doctor out to dinner."

"A pretty doctor, huh? What happened to Jan?"

"Long story. But I promise you, I'll babysit if you want to date, too."

"That's something I'll never do again, Ben."

"What? Date?"

"Date and get married. Obviously, I don't do the marriage thing well, or my husband wouldn't have been tempted by another woman."

"Maybe it wasn't you. He's the one who cheated."

"It doesn't matter whose fault it was. I don't ever want to go through this kind of pain again. And I don't ever want to put my kids through it. I'm done with men."

"Hey, I'm a man. And your dad and your brother are men. We're not all bad."

"I know. But I still won't be dating." Ben saw the pessimism in her eyes and recognized the depth of her hurt. "But, hey. I'm beginning to see how this sharing a house could work for us right now. But you know I'm going to get resistance from my mom and dad?"

"We'll make them understand it. We're just two friends helping each other out." As he was saying that, he heard Molly chattering through the baby monitor. "So, let's start now. Do you want to go get Molly and change her pants, or call and order the pizza?"

"You go get Molly since you haven't seen her all day, and I'll order the pizza. My kids are picky about what they want on it. Is Sam picky about it too?"

"Yep. All he wants is pepperoni."

"Well, all three boys agree then. Hey, Ben?" He turned back to look at her.

"Can we keep this plan under our hats until we've discussed it a little bit more? I'll call you tonight after I have my kids in bed. If we can work it out, when do you want to start?"

"How about Monday? I can drive to Tampa on Saturday, and pick up the beds and anything else you want to bring from storage. Then you and the kids could come Sunday after church."

"You mean four days from now?" Abby looked a little stunned. "Wow. I'm going to have to do some fast talking to mom and dad. But maybe it's better this way. They won't have time to talk me out of it. We'll talk more tonight."

When Ben left the kitchen to get his baby girl, Abby was on the phone to the pizza place in town. He felt a little dazed himself. He had just made plans for a woman and her three kids to move into his house for three months. He was sure of only one thing. His life was going to change drastically, again. But it was only three months, and Sam would love it.

He did have a feeling though, that in his downtime, he was going to be giving horse riding lessons to Abby's three kids.

Chapter 13

Momma Beth, Carly and all four kids came home starving. Abby monitored the clothes changing, while Ben took Molly and went to pick up the pizza. He was only five minutes from town, but none of the pizza places would deliver outside the city limits.

As he drove, he reviewed in his mind what he and Abby had discussed. Although he'd told her he didn't care what other people thought about their arrangement, he didn't want it to reflect poorly on Abby's reputation. And he didn't want Brett to have anything to hold against her as a mother.

But if Ben was dating Leah, it would help make the arrangement look totally harmless to others. They would be able to see that he and Abby were just helping each other out. They would be sharing a house, but not a bed. Ben decided to call Dr. Leah as soon as he could get around to it.

This was going to be an arrangement that would help both him and Abby this summer. He remembered Katy reading a book once about a marriage of convenience and saying she was glad theirs was a marriage of love. Well this was going to be an arrangement of convenience. And he felt good about it. It was always good to share responsibilities with another person.

When Ben returned home with the pizza, it took the kids less than a half hour to devour it. Abby must have ordered the right kind, or they were just too hungry to care.

While they were all eating, Ben looked around him…next week there would be four kids and two adults sitting around his table for every meal. He was sure it would be noisier than he and Sam were used to. And he wondered briefly if he should have asked Sam's opinion about the arrangement before he finalized it with Abby.

But he was pretty sure Sam would love it. He would have other kids to play with all summer. They would almost have enough for a basketball team.

After they all took a quick trip to the barn to feed the horses, Abby loaded her kids into the van. Ben gave her a brotherly hug, and she whispered to him that she would call him after nine. Momma Beth reminded him that she was still available to watch the kids on Wednesdays if he needed her, and Carly told him she wished she could watch the kids this summer instead of working at the restaurant.

Ben could tell Sam was exhausted, so after his bath, Ben made him go to bed a little early. "You only have two more nights to go to bed at eight. When school's out, you can stay up till nine if you want to." He figured since Abby's boys were a little bit older, they would probably be staying up later. Sam wouldn't want to go to bed if they didn't.

He gave Molly a quick bath and tucked her into bed too, thankful that she was now sleeping through the night.

While he was waiting for Abby to call, he remembered he was supposed to call Dr. Leah. He had told her he would call. But when would he be able to go out with her? He decided to wait and call her the next day. He needed to know what he and Abby were doing first—before he brought another woman into his life.

With his cell phone in his pocket, he went out to sit on his deck. It was still warm, but surprisingly, it wasn't muggy. That wouldn't be bad until July. He thought of the last time he and Katy sat outside. He had carried her out and propped her up in the porch swing with pillows. It must have been ninety degrees, but she still wanted a blanket.

Looking to the sky, he was disappointed. He wouldn't see her star tonight; it was too hazy. But, he could still talk to her. Would there ever come a time when he wouldn't need to talk to her? He didn't think so. "Katy? You aren't going to believe what I did today. But I think you'll be okay with it. You loved Abby so much, and I'm pretty sure you'd agree that I'm doing the right thing. You always said we were put on this earth to be used by God to help others. She and I are going to help each other this summer."

His one-sided conversation was interrupted by the ring of his cell phone. He picked up the baby monitor and said hello. When his phone kept ringing, he laughed at himself…was he so nervous that he wasn't thinking straight?

"Hey, Ben. I'm calling to let you out of this arrangement."

"Really? Why?"

"I think we're both being a little impulsive. If we wait, something else will work out for us."

"I don't have time to wait, Abby. I need your help now. But if you really don't want to do it, I understand. You're sure you don't want to do it?" He felt a little panicky. He thought she was as excited about the summer as he was.

"No. I'm not sure. Momma was so tired when we got home tonight. I know our being here all the time is a lot of extra stress for her. She says it isn't, but I can tell it is. My kids are noisy and whiney sometimes, and they need a place where they can go outside and run off some energy."

"It sounds to me like they need to be here. I have sixty acres, remember? We have the play-set and the tree house. And Linda told me I could use their pool this summer while they're gone. I think you should come."

"Are you sure?"

"Yes. The more I think about it, the more I like the idea. It's just for the summer, and it will give you a chance to think about what you want to do with your future."

"It does sound good, and I think we could make it work, especially if you're still going to help clean the house."

"But, that's only if you're cooking and doing the laundry." He heard her laugh.

"I enjoy cooking for hungry people. Brett didn't come home for supper for months. I was so angry after I spent the whole day cooking."

"I may not be home some nights either…"

"But you'll tell me ahead of time, won't you?"

"Sure. But speaking of Brett, this isn't going to be something he can hold against you, is it?"

"After what he did? I don't think so. He hasn't even come to get the kids for the last two weekends. At first he said he wanted them every weekend, now it's like once a month. Sometimes I can't believe he's still the same man I loved."

"I'm sorry, Abby. I can't believe this is Brett we're talking about, either. Maybe you can do some healing while you're here this summer."

He heard her sigh over the phone. "I don't know if I'll ever heal from this."

"But you'll try while you're here?"

"It's going to be a busy summer. Maybe it will at least distract me from my pain."

Ben laughed. "You're so right. We're both going to be busy. So, we're back on? Tell you what. Let's take from now till Saturday morning for you to talk to your mom and dad about our plans. While you're doing that, I'll talk to Sam.

"Okay. Maybe I can leave the kids with Carly tomorrow night, and take my parents out to dinner. Then I'll tell my kids on Friday."

"I can meet you at your storage place on Saturday with my truck. We can get what you need to bring out here. Then you and the kids can come out here Sunday afternoon. Does that sound okay with you?"

"Wow, this is all happening so fast."

"It is. But my in-laws are leaving this weekend, and I have a Monday morning charter."

"And I need to get these noisy kids out of this house so my mom and dad can have their peace and quiet back." Now that it was settled, Ben began to feel peaceful about all of it again.

"Abby?"

"Yes?"

"If you have time, could you start making a list of all the chores that will need to be done? I'll do the same on my end, then we can divide them between us."

"Ben, I think that's being unfair to you. You have two businesses to run."

"But the grove doesn't need much attention during the summer months."

"No. But you do have horses to take care of, all the outside maintenance, and charters to fly."

"We'll work it out, Abby. I'll see you on Saturday. And good luck when you talk to your parents. For some reason, I think they'll be more understanding than you think after they hear our plans."

"You're still going to be dating the doctor, right? I think if they know that, they'll understand our arrangement better."

"Well, I haven't called her yet. I wanted to wait and see if you could watch the kids next Saturday night."

"Gee, let me check my social calendar. Yep. I'm free." He heard her giggle.

"Okay. But you have to promise me something."

"What?"

"If you watch my kids on Saturday night, you'll take a few hours for yourself on Sunday afternoon, or some evening the next week. A time when you can do whatever you want to do."

Now she laughed out loud. "Sure, okay, Ben. I'll do that. Maybe I'll go to some park and paint my toenails." He had to laugh too.

"Come on. You can find something more interesting than that to do. Can you drive back to Tampa and go to lunch with your friends?"

"Most of our friends were Brett's friends. But I'll see. Thanks Ben, that's thoughtful of you."

When he hung up, Ben wondered why any man could purposely hurt a woman the way Brett hurt Abby. Didn't he know that marriage was hard work? And sometimes, when you traded one woman for another, all you got was a new set of problems. He'd seen that happen to one of his buddies in the reserves.

*****

Sam was excited about his last day of school. "My teacher said we're going to have a party today, and we don't have to do any work."

"Sam, I'm sorry I won't be here when you get off the bus. But Grandma will be here, okay?"

"Sure. But I was wondering… are we going to have time to ride Jake and Duchess tonight? We haven't had time for awhile, and I bet they want some exercise."

"That's a good idea. Can you do me a favor too?"

"Sure!"

"When your Grandma's here tonight, can you be extra nice to her? She and your grandpa are leaving for the mountains in the morning."

"Daaaad…I'm always nice to Grandma. But who's going to babysit for us when she goes?" Sam was too young for the worry lines Ben saw between his son's eyes.

"Didn't I tell you not to worry about that? I have a really good idea. Maybe we can talk about it when we go riding tonight, okay? Let's get going now. Your last day of kindergarten is waiting for you."

*****

Ben knew he would have to be a good salesman to sell his summer plans to his in-laws. Up until last evening, they were still insisting they could stay in Florida for the summer.

Linda and John both came over at one to watch Molly. Ben didn't need to be at the airport until three.

He had just put Molly down for her nap when they walked into the house. Linda was bearing her usual plate of cookies.

"It's a good thing I have you around to keep me sweetened up, Linda. Did you just bake these?"

"Fresh out of the oven. Do you have time for a cup of coffee?" She moved toward the kitchen counter where his coffee pot was kept."

"Sure." Ben's mind swept back over the past month. Linda was the fifth woman, if you counted Carly, who had been in his kitchen and felt completely comfortable doing his job. Did all of them think he was that helpless?

"I can make that coffee, Linda. You made the cookies."

"I know you can make coffee, Ben. But you just sit and let me do it. John wants to talk to you about something." Ben looked at John. He was an amazing father-in-law. He helped Ben in the grove, and in return, Ben taught him how to fly his own plane.

"What's going on, John?"

"Linda and I have been talking. Why don't you let us take Sam and Molly to the mountains with us for the next two weeks since you won't let us stay here. We'll bring them back when you find a babysitter for them."

Ben didn't have to think too long about that idea. "That's really nice of the two of you. But I'd miss my kids too much if you took them away."

"But don't you think you need a break from them? It would only be for two weeks."

"Actually, I found a babysitter for them. So, now you can go to the mountains and not worry about it."

Linda came over to the table where John and Ben were sitting and sat down. "Who did you find? Is it someone who will be dependable?"

"She's going to be very dependable." Ben paused for a second. He knew he had to present his plan in a positive way. "I asked Abby to bring her kids out for the summer. She can take care of Sam and Molly while I'm doing my charters, and it will give her parents a few months to rest up from everything they've been through."

"Did she find a place in town to rent?"

"No, she and the kids are going to stay here. We've worked out all the details, and I think it's going to be nice for both of us. Her kids love it here."

"She's moving in?" Ben saw the expected surprise on his mother-in-law's face. "Are you sure that's a good thing to do?"

"It will be fine. The boys will move into Sam's room and Alexandria can sleep in Molly's room. Abby will have the guest room. I think we can manage it for the summer."

"But, what will people say? It just seems inappropriate."

Ben had to smile. "Actually the only opinion I care about is Dr. Leah's."

"Dr. Leah? You're confusing me, Ben."

"I think you'll be happy to know that the two of us are going out to dinner next week. Now that Abby will be here to watch the kids for me, I'll have time to date."

"You're going out with Leah? Oh, Ben. That's wonderful news. She's such a sweet woman." And just like that, Linda was beyond the inappropriateness of Abby's stay at Ben's house.

Ben smiled at his mother-in-law. "I think she's pretty sweet too. After she watched the kids this week, I asked her if I could repay her with dinner, and she agreed."

"Oh my. You have to call me and let me know how it goes. When are you going out?"

"I hope next weekend." Ben breathed a sigh of relief. He hoped Abby's parents would be as understanding as John and Linda were.

But Abby's parents were not as easily convinced that her new arrangement for the summer was a good thing.

Chapter 14

"It's unnecessary, Abby. You and the kids are more than welcome to stay here." The three of them were out on the deck that overlooked the backyard. Alex and Beth were both gardeners and their yard looked like a tropical park. Abby was always afraid the kids were going to knock over one of their prized plants when they played out there.

"He needs my help, Mom. And think of all the room the kids will have to play in this summer. I need this time, too; it will be a good place to just take care of my kids and Ben's kids. The grove can be a healing place for me. Maybe, by the end of the summer, I'll be thinking more clearly."

"But what will people say?"

"Anyone who loves me will understand. Those who don't love me, won't be any more shocked than when I got a divorce. And really, Mom...does it matter? We know this is just two friends helping each other. Family taking care of family. I don't really care anymore about the opinions of others." She saw her parents look at each other, so she went on. "Ben needs a baby sitter, and I need to get out of this town and do some healing. I think I can do that when I'm there. You know how peaceful it is at the grove. It's why Katy loved it so much."

"How do you think Brett is going to react to this? He isn't going to be happy if he has to drive all that way to get his kids for a visit."

"If he wants to see them, I'll drive them here. But you know how infrequent that's becoming. Ben will be a good role model for the boys. Their dad hasn't been that good at it, lately."

"Abby, we're going to trust you on this. We have no choice if your mind is made up. But if it doesn't work, promise us you'll call. Carly will be going to college in the fall, and we'll have plenty of room for you at the end of summer."

Abby could always count on her dad to support her. They had bonded well in the years after her mom died. And Momma Beth had been a good stepmom, too. She had loved Abby from the first time they met in a grief support group for little kids. Momma Beth had been the facilitator of that group.

"I will. And thank you. I'll send out some resumes this summer, and hopefully I can find a place for me and the kids. By the way…did Ben tell you he's interested in dating the kids' doctor?"

"Really? Well that's nice. I was hoping the thing with the teacher would work out, but maybe this is the one for him."

"Yeah. He wanted to know if I could watch the kids next weekend. When I told him yes, he said I had to take a day off the next week. So I was wondering, Mom, would you like to meet me at the mall some evening that week?"

"Of course. You just let me know when. So are you going to need any help getting your things moved?"

"Ben's coming into town tomorrow to get some things for me."

"You certainly do have the details worked out well, don't you? Are you sure you haven't been planning this longer than a day?" Abby could tell her dad was still a little wary of her plans, even though he said he'd be supportive. She could only hope that her daughter's dad would be as supportive of Lexie in the years ahead.

*****

When Ben got home from his flight on Friday evening, Sam was waiting for him.

"Say goodbye to your grandparents, Sam. They're going to be gone for three months."

"Unless you need us before then, Ben." Linda was holding Molly tightly in her arms.

"We're going to be okay. You two just enjoy your time. Stick your feet in that cold mountain river for me, okay?"

"We sure will. They say it's going to be a hot one here this summer. Why don't you and the kids fly up for a weekend in July?"

"We'll see. Did these kiddos have their supper yet?"

"They did, and there are left-overs for you in the fridge." Linda came over to give Ben a hug. "Promise me you'll call if you need anything."

"I promise. Now go . . . and have fun."

Before they were at the end of the drive, Sam was half way to the barn. Ben put Molly in the backpack and took off after him. Sam loved his horse. When Ben bought it for him for his first birthday, the colt was just a year old. Katy hadn't been so sure it was a wise thing to buy, but Sam and his Jake had grown up together.

Duchess was Jake's mom, and Ben's horse. Ben and Sam had spent a lot of time on their horses after Katy died. It seemed to be the one thing that brought peace to both of them. Riding was their grief therapy. And for some reason, they could talk more freely when they were in their saddles.

When Ben was coming home from Vegas with Molly, he wondered how riding was going to work with a baby. But Molly hadn't slowed them down. She usually fell asleep in the backpack. It must have been the rhythm of the ride.

Ben did have a pack-n-play in the barn for Molly. He would put her in it when he was working with the horses. She was usually content, as long as she could see her dad and her brother. Ben put her there as he helped Sam put the saddles on the horses. In another year or two, Sam would probably be big enough to do it by himself. But for now, he knew his dad always had to be around. Ben trusted the two animals, but knew accidents could happen.

When they left the barn, they turned right. They would follow the path around and through the grove so they could check the trees. The path would then take them around the lake, before it began to twist and turn through the old oak trees. The horses seemed to know the way as Ben and Sam rode side by side.

"So, tell me about your last day of school, Sam. Was it fun?"

"Yeah. We didn't have to do any work at all. We just had a party and watched a movie."

"That's pretty nice. Did you find out who's going to be your teacher next year?"

"No. But it's okay. Did you forget I'm not going next year?" Sam leaned over and patted Jake's neck. "I'm just gonna stay home with you and Molly and Jake."

"Well, we have the whole summer to talk about that. Do you want to know who I found to babysit for you and Molly this summer?"

"Yeah, sure. Is it someone nice? I don't like crabby babysitters." Ben had to hide his smile.

"When did you ever have a crabby babysitter?"

"I didn't, but Henry has one. He wanted to keep going to school cause he doesn't want to be home with her all summer."

"Well, I think you're going to like this one. It's your Aunt Abby."

"Aunt Abby? Is she gonna bring my cousins when she comes?"

"She sure is. And guess what?"

"What?" Sam looked at his dad, excitement making his eyes dance.

"They're going to stay at our house the whole summer."

"You mean they get to sleep at our house too?" Sam looked puzzled.

"Yep. If you don't mind the boys sleeping in your room with you."

The crooked grin that spread over Sam's face was all Ben needed. "That's cool, Dad. Are they just gonna camp out on the floor? I don't think we can all fit in my bed."

"No. They're going to bring some bunk-beds. We're going to drive to Tampa tomorrow and pick them up. Do you think that will be okay?"

"Bunk beds? That's so cool." "Cool" was obviously Sam's new word of the day. "Are they going to live with us forever?"

"No. Just for the summer . . . just until Grandma and Grandpa get home from the mountains."

"I wish they could stay forever and go to school with me. They could ride the bus with me then it wouldn't be so boring." The two horses had picked up their pace a little bit. They knew Ben and Sam would dismount soon so they could get a drink from the lake.

"Well, we won't worry about school for now. Let's just have a nice summer with your cousins, okay?"

"That's the best news you ever told me, Dad."

"Yeah? I thought you might like it." Ben took in a deep breath. There was the scent of citrus in the air, and it reminded him of the first day he and Katy had come to the grove to buy some fruit. What she really wanted was the whole grove and a whole new way of life with her husband and her son. She got the grove, but not the whole life.

*****

By the time Sam and Ben were finished riding, feeding the horses, and cleaning out their stalls, it was dark. Ben thought for sure Sam would remember that he didn't have school the next day, and argue to stay up late. But he didn't. He took his bath and went straight to bed. The fresh air must have made Molly sleepy too. She went to sleep while Ben was giving her a bottle.

After they were asleep, Ben wondered what he and Abby would do in the evenings after all the kids were asleep. It was probably a good thing Ben had a TV in his bedroom now. That way, Abby could have the one in the family room. Not that he watched TV that much. After getting up at 4:23 every morning for years, Ben was usually asleep by ten.

And he imagined after a day of watching five kids, Abby would be ready for bed too.

But tonight, Ben had too much on his mind to sleep. He felt a need to talk to someone, and thought about calling Abby. But she had told him she'd call the next morning to tell him what time to meet her. If he hadn't been an idiot and chased Jan off, he could have called her. He wondered if she would be willing to get back together if he asked her to. Probably not without the commitment she wanted.

He wandered out to the deck. He could always find Katy's star and talk to it. But tonight he wanted to talk to a real person. One who would talk back to him. He looked at his phone. Dr. Leah's number was on speed dial. Who didn't keep the phone number of their kids' doctor on speed dial? But it might be too late to call her. Or maybe she was on call or at the hospital.

He hit the two numbers that would make her phone ring, then hit the end button. What was he doing? But when else would he have time to ask her out to dinner? He decided he better do it now, or she would think he was one of those guys who said he would call, then didn't. He hit the numbers again.

He'd hang up if she didn't answer after three rings. She answered in two, and he panicked. He didn't know whether to call her Dr. Leah or just Leah.

"Hello? Hello? This is Dr. Leah. Can I help you?"

"Leah? This is Ben."

"Hey, Ben. Is everything okay? Are the kids sick again?" He could hear the concern in her voice.

"No, they're fine. The medicine you gave them worked."

"That's good. I was hoping it would." She sounded even nicer than he remembered.

"I'm calling to see if we can set up that dinner date I owe you."

"You don't owe me anything, Ben. You paid for the visit to the doctor."

"No. I mean the dinner I owe you for watching my kids for me."

"You don't owe me for that either. That was fun for me." Her voice was soft, smooth, like honey. It was a voice that sounded like it could bring comfort to sick kids and their parents.

"Well, can I take you out just so I can get to know you better?"

"That sounds like a perfect reason for a dinner date. What did you have in mind?"

"Do you have any free time next weekend?" Now Ben felt nervous again. What was wrong with him? He was acting like a nervous high school guy who was going on his first date.

"It's supposed to be my weekend off, but I'm taking call for someone else on Sunday. I'm on call Friday night till midnight, but I have Saturday open. Would that work?"

"That would be perfect. Is there somewhere in particular you'd like to go?"

"Not really. I'm fine with wherever you want to go. Just let me know what I need to wear. I wouldn't want to wear my jeans into some place formal. "

"Is a jeans kind of place okay?"

"Sure." He could tell by the enthusiasm in her voice that she was telling the truth.

"Okay. But don't wear your jeans."

"What? You're confusing me. You just asked me if a jeans kind of place was okay."

"I just wanted to know if you were okay with a jeans kind of place. I like girls who are okay with that. But on Saturday, I think we should go some place nice and quiet where we can talk, and get to know each other." Ben knew he was rambling, and he couldn't seem to stop it.

"I like the way you think, Ben."

"You do?"

"I do. I'll see you Saturday evening. What time?"

"Is eight too late? I like to eat with my kids and get them ready for bed."

"Eight is fine…I'll see you then."

Ben pushed the end button again. This time he felt breathless. He had just made a date with a fascinating woman. He really hoped she turned out to be as nice as he thought she was. Ben looked at Katy's star again. It seemed to be twinkling. Was she giving him her blessing?

Chapter 15

Abby woke up at six on Saturday and looked around her. *I'm thirty three years old and I'm still sleeping in the same bedroom I slept in when I was six. Thank you, Ben, for giving me a way out of here.*

She went to the kitchen to start the coffee. Her parents would be up soon. The least she could do to repay them for their hospitality was make their coffee. A shower was next on her agenda. With any luck, she would be ready for this day before her kids got out of bed.

Abby had taken them to a park yesterday afternoon, and told them about her plans to take them to the grove for the summer. They had been so excited. It wasn't that they didn't love their grandparents and enjoy their time with them, they just needed more space. And Abby knew she had been more strict with them since they'd been at her parents. She needed her own space too.

It was while she was drying her hair that the phone rang. She hurried to answer it before it woke up the kids. *Who on earth is calling me at this hour of the day?* She looked at the phone. It was Brett's number. She hadn't talked to him since he had canceled out on the kids last week-end.

"Hello Brett."

"Hey, Abby. I hope I didn't wake you up. But I wanted to catch you before you guys got busy. I'm wondering if I can have the kids this afternoon...since I haven't seen them for three weeks."

"No, Brett. You can't. This is my weekend, and it's your own fault you didn't see them last weekend."

"Abby. You're going to have to be more flexible. I have to arrange my schedule around my job and Lisa now."

"Oh…did Lisa have something more important than you today?" Abby hated the way he made her feel. She had never been a mean, vindictive person, and didn't want to be one now. But Brett could bring out the worst in her.

"It's none of your business what Lisa does. Can I have the kids or not?"

"No. It's. Not. Your. Weekend! I've already made plans with them for today."

"So, when can I see them?"

"Next weekend is your scheduled time. Did you forget we've already been to court twice to get this arrangement figured out. The first time was because you couldn't take them on your Tuesday nights; the last time, it was to change it from every weekend to every other weekend."

"Can't you be more flexible? I mean, what else do you have to do?"

"Goodbye Brett. You can pick the kids up next Friday evening at my parent's house."

She could still hear him talking when she clicked her phone shut. *I can't believe I ever loved that man!* But she knew in her heart that he wasn't the same man she married. His sin had turned him into someone different. Her challenge now was to make sure her anger didn't turn her into someone different.

The boys were downstairs by the time she got done dressing. They had been sleeping in Jon's old room since they moved in, and she told them to stay there until she came to get them. She didn't want her parents to have to feed them and listen to their morning squabbling.

"Boys! What did I tell you about staying in your room till it was time to get up?"

"We weren't tired anymore, and we were hungry."

"And I was going to come in and get you at seven. Mom, thank you for getting their breakfast, but they could have waited." Dad was at the stove flipping pancakes, and her mom was helping the boys with syrup. She obviously knew they would have the sticky stuff all over her kitchen if she let them do it themselves.

"I thought I heard you talking on the phone so I went ahead and helped them. Do you want me to wake up Alexandria?"

"No. I'll do it." Abby started back up the stairs to where her daughter was now sharing a room with Carly. Thankfully, Lexie was a good sleeper and didn't wake up when Carly's alarm went off at 5:30.

"Abby, wait." Her mother followed her up the stairs. "Honey, I wasn't eavesdropping, but when I went by your room a little while ago, I could tell by the tone of your voice that you were talking to Brett. Is there a problem?"

"Not now. He wanted the kids today, and I told him no. If he calls your house phone later on, would you tell him the kids and I are out?"

"When are you going to tell him about your living arrangements this summer?"

"I'll tell him before the kids go with him next weekend…if they do. You never know, Lisa might want him to do something with her."

"Abby, I hate to see you so angry. You know it's hurting you more than it's hurting him."

"I know, Mom. I'm trying to let go of it. Just keep praying for me, okay?"

"I will. I know it's hard. I had to go through the whole forgiveness thing with my dad, remember? I found that once I forgave him, he had no power over me anymore."

"I know, Mom. I'm trying, okay?" She gave her mom a hug. "I better get Lexie now."

*****

Abby met Ben at the storage unit at two that afternoon. Both of them had their kids with them, of course. Who else would the kids be with? They both laughed about all the help they had while the three boys climbed all over the furniture in the unit. Alexandria stayed in Ben's truck to entertain Molly, who woke up the minute Ben turned the engine off.

"I don't know, Ben. You had to be pretty desperate for a babysitter when you signed me and my kids up for the summer."

"And you must have been desperate when you signed up to take care of my kids for the summer. So, where are these beds we're here for? Tell me they aren't all the way in the back."

"I really don't know. Dad and Jon moved the stuff for me. Dad was going to come with me, but he got called to the hospital at the last minute. One of his parishioners was in an accident."

"That's one job I could not do. How long has he been pastoring?"

"Almost forty years and all of them at the same church. I don't know how he does it either. But he and mom both love taking care of other people. Do you want me to call Jon and ask him if he remembers where they put the beds?"

"No. It's okay. We'll just look around. We have these three energetic boys to help me if I need to move anything." He laughed when he said it. He knew, as well as Abby did, that the three boys altogether wouldn't be able to pick up one end of a couch.

"Yeah, right. I think I see the end of Lexie's single bed over here."

It took the two of them three hours to find everything Abby thought she needed and get it loaded in the back of the truck. In that time, Molly had to be fed once and changed twice. Then Lexie got bored and decided to play with the boys who didn't want "a girl" to join them so she cried. Fortunately, Abby had planned ahead and brought a portable DVD player that kept Lexie entertained. In the three hours, the boys only suffered two minor injuries.

"What a circus, Ben. I'm giving you one more chance to back out of this deal."

"It's too late now. Let's go hit the drive thru at Mickey D's and take these monkeys and their food to the park down the street."

"I think we should stay there and eat. It's air-conditioned, and it must be ninety degrees out here."

"Is there a playground in that one?"

"I hope not. When there's a playground, I can't get my kids to sit still long enough to eat."

"You said it, sister! We're thinking alike already."

The heat and the play must have worn the kids out, or they were hungry. The minute they sat down to eat, they were manageable. Ben and Abby actually got to exchange their to-do lists.

"Okay, I'll take yours home with me, and you take mine home with you. Between now and tomorrow night we can both sort out which chores we want to do. After the kids go to bed tomorrow night, we'll sit down and write down a new list for both of us."

"What if there's a chore neither one of us wants to do?" Abby grinned at him.

"We'll flip for it!"

"Deal! You know what? I think Brett and I would still be together if we'd done this in the beginning of our marriage. He seemed to think I should do everything at home because I didn't work outside our home. He never saw everything I did. I even mowed the grass."

"Well you don't have to worry about that with me. I've been mom and dad for three years now. I know how much work goes into making a home for kids. We're just going to have to make sure we both get a time-out once in awhile."

"So did you set up that date?"

"I did. Next Saturday at eight." Abby smiled. She could hear the excitement in his voice.

"That will work out well. Next weekend is Brett's time with my kids. I can spend the whole weekend spoiling your kids."

"That doesn't seem fair. Why don't you plan on spending Saturday with your mom and Carly? I'm not leaving until eight. Then you can have all of Sunday off too."

"Ben! Don't worry about it. We'll figure it out."

*****

But Ben did worry about it—all the way home. If he had known Brett was taking the kids next weekend, he wouldn't have planned a date. Abby could drive into Tampa Friday evening, and spend the whole weekend with her parents. He would have to postpone the date with Leah until Abby was home.

When they finally arrived home, he and Sam moved the kids' bed frames into their respective rooms. Ben was glad they were in pieces, and none of it was too heavy.

It had been a long day and he was tired. He would put the beds together in the morning while Sam was at church. *Church! Oh, no! John and Linda are gone. They can't take him to church.*

Ben felt a sense of panic. *Maybe if I don't mention it, Sam will forget it's Sunday.* He knew that probably wasn't going to happen though—Sam loved going to church.

That was one thing he and Abby hadn't discussed. He wondered if she would be going back to Tampa to Alex's church every Sunday, or staying here. After this week, maybe she could take Sam to church.

Last summer, when the Clintons went to the mountains, Sam was too little to care if he went to church. But he really liked it now and told his dad about his teacher and the friends he had there. Ben thought maybe he could just drop Sam off in the morning if he wanted to go. At almost six, he could find his way around a church he was familiar with.

I could do that and still keep my promise to Katy.

Katy would understand why Ben couldn't go. He had Molly, and she was too little for church. He had a good excuse. When he made his promise to Katy, he didn't know he would end up with an extra baby in his care.

Molly had slept on the way home from Tampa and was still wide awake when Ben was ready for her to go to sleep. And Sam was full of chatter about the day he had spent with his cousins.

"Dad?" Ben knew that tone in Sam's voice. He wanted something.

"Yeah?"

"I think we should get a couple more horses so Kyle and Konnor can each have one."

"Sam...you need to remember that your cousins are only going to be here for the summer. I don't think we'll be buying a new horse for them. You'll have to share Jake with them."

"But it would be so much fun for all of us to ride together."

"I know it would. But we still aren't going to get two more horses." Ben saw the disappointment on his son's face.

"And while we're speaking of horses, Sam. The rules are still going to be the same when your cousins get here. You and the other boys are not allowed in the barn unless I'm with you. Do you understand?"

"Yeah, I know. But what if Kyle and Konnor want to go there?"

"You tell them no, or tell your Aunt Abby about it, if I'm not here. There's going to be a lot of other things you boys can do together."

"Can we take a little ride tonight, Dad?" Sam looked and sounded resigned to the rules.

"Not tonight, Buddy. I'm really tired. But we need to go out and feed them before you take your bath."

Sam was quiet while they did the chores. And for the first time, Ben thought about how much his son's life was going to change this summer. Sam had been his main focus in the three years after Katy died. And although he had adjusted well to Molly being in their home, he was going to have to share a lot of his things with his three cousins. Ben knew he would have to make sure he spent as much time as possible with his son when the other boys went to see their dad. Sam would need his undivided attention at times.

It was while Ben was tucking him into bed that Sam asked about church. "Who's going to take me to church tomorrow, Dad?"

"I think we'll skip church tomorrow, Sam. We need to get the house ready for your cousins."

"Can't we do that after church? My teacher will miss me if I don't come." Sam's voice sounded small tonight. And for some reason, he even looked smaller to Ben. Maybe it was because he had been with Abby's bigger boys all day. Or maybe it was because Ben knew he couldn't just dump his child off in front of a big church and let him go in by himself.

Chapter 16

When Ben woke at his usual time on Sunday morning, he felt anxious. It wasn't the usual heaviness of not having Katy with him. This was something different. Then he remembered. Abby and her kids were all moving into his house today. *What on earth was I thinking?*

But he'd had no choice. He needed a babysitter for the summer. He had to keep his charter business going, just in case he ever had a bad year at the grove. He knew he had been lucky so far with that. But one damaging frost this coming winter could be bad for his business.

And besides, he liked Abby. She hadn't just been Katy's step-sister, she'd been Katy's best friend. And right now she needed a place to live. He knew it was going to work out okay, even though his house would be hectic for the summer.

As usual, Ben went to the kitchen to start his coffee, then to the bedrooms to check on Sam and Molly. As he watched his son sleep, he felt a sense of gratitude sweep over him. Sam was the son Katy had given him before she died. She told him that she fulfilled her purpose in life by giving him a son. He knew that gave her a sense of peace in the last few days of her life.

Ben was glad for that, then and now. But he really thought God should have let his wife live, so she could have been a mother to the son she gave him. It was the ongoing argument Ben had with God.

And then there was Molly. Whenever Ben watched her sleep, he felt so protective of her. Even though she was the child of his sister and some unknown man, Molly was now his, to love and care for. And he knew if Sage ever came to take her away from him, he would fight for this child he loved with his whole being.

Taking his coffee out to the deck, he noticed the first light of dawn already on the horizon. Summer was almost here, and with the sun rising earlier every morning, Katy's star didn't shine as bright now. But she had promised him it would be there, even if he couldn't see it. Ben hoped she would be pleased that he was providing a home today for Abby and her kids. He knew she would do it herself, if she was here. And in spite of the anxiety he felt when he woke, Ben suddenly felt at peace about it.

He was so deep in thought he didn't hear Sam until the little boy was right beside him.

"Dad? What are you doing out here?"

"Sam…what are you doing up so early?" Ben set his empty coffee cup aside and picked up his son. Sam had always slept until Ben woke him.

"I just woke up, and when I went to your room, you weren't there. I was scared. I didn't know where you were." Ben heard the tears in the little boy's voice.

"Oh, Sam, I'm sorry you were scared. You didn't need to be. I'm always going to be here for you, Buddy."

"Will you be here, even when Aunt Abby is here?" Ben was confused. What was his son asking him?

"Well of course I'll be here, Sam. The only time I'll be gone is when I'm flying. Aunt Abby will watch you while I'm gone, just like Grandma did."

"Is Aunt Abby going to be my new momma?"

"No, Sam. She's going to be your babysitter until Grandma comes back from the mountains."

"Then why is she going to live with us?"

"Sam. We talked about this, remember? Your Uncle Brett moved away, and your Aunt Abby and the kids needed a place to stay this summer. I thought you wanted the cousins to come and stay with you."

"I do...but, sometimes I don't understand it."

Ben hugged the boy to him. *Oh, Sam. Sometimes I don't understand life either.*

"Tell you what, Buddy. Why don't you just have fun with your cousins this summer, and let me and Aunt Abby do the understanding, okay?"

"Okay, Dad. So, do I get to go to church today?" The little boy felt so good in Ben's arms. He knew a day was coming when his son would be too big to sit on his lap.

"Sure. We'll all go, okay?"

"Really? You too? Oh, boy! You're gonna love it, Dad!" Ben wasn't so sure he was going to love it, but he did know one thing—life had already been too hard for his son, and if going to church somehow made his life easier then Ben had to make sure it happened.

*****

The community church in Laurelville was where he and Katy went to church after they moved to the grove. The two of them had become good friends with a few of the other couples in the church. When Katy got sick, those friends had been wonderfully supportive of all of them.

But after Katy died, Ben couldn't make himself go back. Their friends, and even the pastor, told him they understood that it was okay to take some time to heal. But Ben didn't just need time to heal, he needed time to be angry too. And since there was no one else to be angry at, he focused that on God.

When Ben's parents died in the car accident when he was ten, he remembered being terribly lonely and sad. But the love of his grandmother helped him heal. Then when she died, although he was sad, he knew it was the way life was. People became old and died. But when Katy died, Ben was angry. He was still angry. Katy had been good and kind and gentle. She had been a Christian her whole life and God should not have taken her from him and Sam. They loved her and needed her.

In the past three years, Ben had gone back to the church only once. That was for Sam's Christmas program last year. It had been difficult to walk into the church that day without Katy. But Sam was excited, and his in-laws were with him. Even though people were happy to see him and made him feel welcome, Ben knew he was there only because of his son.

Now, Ben was returning to church again today, once again, only to please Sam. And Katy would expect him to. Even though he was only five (soon to be six, as he often reminded Ben) Sam wanted to go to church. And Ben had promised Katy he would make sure their son went to church. That was the only reason Ben was going to church. It wasn't to meet God. God had failed him.

Ben felt uneasy as he walked up the sidewalk. *Maybe I should have let Linda and John stay around this summer. If they were here, I wouldn't have to be doing this. Oh, Sam…the things I do for you, son. I hope you appreciate it.*

Pastor Ellis and his wife were at the door, and welcomed him and the kids. They had been wonderful to him after Katy died, and the pastor had even come to the grove two times to make sure he was doing okay. They weren't the reason Ben felt uncomfortable as he shook their hands. He just didn't want to be here—because Katy wasn't here with him.

"Ben, it's good to see you. I was wondering if Sam would be able to come to church when John and Linda left for the summer. It was good of you to bring him."

"Yeah, well…he likes to come. And I couldn't disappoint him."

"Well, we hope you won't be disappointed with the service either. This must be the little sister that big brother Sam has been telling us about."

It was Sam who made the introductions. "This is Molly, Pastor. She is six months old this week." He sounded so grown up, and Ben felt a sense of pride in his son.

The pastor tousled Sam's hair. "I'm sure glad you brought her and your dad to church with you today, Sam."

"Yeah, I'm glad he came too…I gotta go now, Dad. My teacher is waiting for me."

"Okay, Sam. I'll see you after church. Be good." Now Ben felt abandoned.

"Do you remember where the nursery is, Ben?"

"I think so …."

"It's down the hall and to the left. We have some good people working in there today. They'll take good care of Molly for you."

"Thanks." As Ben walked slowly down the hall, he also remembered where the back door of the church was; and he thought about how easy it would be to walk out it. He could come back for Sam later.

But he was at the nursery door now, and there was a friendly face there to greet him.

"Hi. I'm Emily. And who's this little lady?"

"Hi Emily. This is Molly. Is it okay if she stays with you awhile?"

"Sure. She hasn't been here before, has she?"

"No. This is her first time. But I think she'll be okay."

"I'm sure she will." Emily smiled reassuringly at Ben. "We just need you to fill out a short questionnaire for her." When Ben handed Molly to Emily, she started to cry. *I knew this was a mistake. I come to make one kid happy, and the other one gets mad.*

"Maybe I should just take her with me."

"I think she'll be okay. Let me get her a toy while you do the paperwork."

Paperwork? Good grief. What's this all about? It's not like I'm enrolling her in school or something!

But, after he started it, Ben could see the importance of it. They just wanted to know what Molly's needs would be during her time with them. When he was finished, they put matching stickers on her, her bag, and her bottle so they wouldn't get her things mixed up with the other babies there. Ben actually felt reassured that they were so careful.

And the toy had pacified Molly. When Ben turned to leave, they gave him a buzzer. "If she gets too fussy and needs her dad, we'll buzz you." It looked like the church was a good place for both his kids.

Taking in a deep cleansing breath, Ben entered the sanctuary—the same sanctuary where he and Katy had worshipped. His eyes went about half way up on the left side. That had been their seat. Now it was occupied by another couple. *Another couple. Churches are for couples, for families. Not for widowers with little kids.*

He sank down in a seat in the last row. If he got too uncomfortable, he'd just slip out. And next week, he'd find different arrangements for Sam if Abby couldn't bring him.

Ben focused on the bulletin in his lap. He'd just keep his head down, and maybe no one would recognize that he was even there. It was best that way. He had Sam and Molly, and his memories of his life with Katy. He didn't need church or any friends from it.

"Ben?" the voice was soft, and as gentle as the hand she put on his shoulder. Ben looked up to find Dr. Leah standing beside him. "Can I sit with you?"

"Leah…" Ben stood up and let her move into the seat next to him. "I didn't think you'd be here. Linda said you worked in the children's department."

"I do my part during the first service. It's nice to see you. Linda was worried you wouldn't bring Sam to church." She sat down in the seat next to him.

"Linda was worried? She didn't say anything to me."

"She probably felt like you would do what was best. I'm glad you brought Sam. He loves children's church. I thought about calling you to see if I could bring him, but decided to wait and see if you would come." She was still speaking softly.

"I would have let you bring him. You should have called."

"It's better that you brought him." She smiled at him and opened her bulletin.

Although Ben felt more comfortable sitting with someone he knew, he hoped people wouldn't assume that he and Leah had come together—even though he did have a date with her in six days.

Chapter 17

—————————————

"So, what do you think? Painless, wasn't it?" Leah's brown eyes had flecks of gold in them today. Ben wondered if it was the light in the church that changed their color, or the joy that seemed to radiate from her that caused it.

"It was a good service. I had forgotten what a good speaker Pastor Ellis is."

"He's a good preacher and a wonderful pastor. We're a lucky church."

"Yeah. So, what's on your agenda today?" Ben needed to change the subject. He had survived the church service, but his feelings about God were still a tangled mess.

"I'm going out to eat with some friends."

"Professional friends?" The two of them had moved out of their seats, but she stayed at Ben's side. He was going to get Sam from his class before he picked up Molly at the nursery.

"No. Friends from here at church. Most of us don't have family in the area so we made up our own church family."

"That sounds nice. My wi…" Ben stumbled over the word. "Katy's family used to do a big Sunday dinner every week."

"Sunday dinners with family are nice. Do you have plans for the day?"

"Yes, we have family coming." Ben didn't have the time or the energy to explain to her what was happening at his house. "Is this where I'm going to find Sam?" He knew they were in the children's wing, but he wasn't sure which classroom was Sam's.

"He'll be in the big room with the first and second graders now." She led the way to a huge room buzzing with kids. "There he is. Do you want me to go in and get him for you?"

"Sure." Ben stood back and watched as she made her way through the mass of children. She stopped once to help a little one pick up the papers she had dropped, and again to talk to a little boy who came up to her and hugged her. When she finally made it to Sam, she put her arm around him and pointed toward Ben.

Sam's face broke out into a huge smile. He picked up his papers and walked as fast as he could to where Ben was waiting. "Hey, Dad! I got to go to this class today because I'm going into first grade now."

"Did you like it?" Ben felt a little guilty that he didn't realize this was an important day in his child's life.

"Yeah, it was cool. But I missed my old teacher. Can I go see her and tell her about my new class?"

"We need to get Molly. Can you tell her next week?"

"I guess. Did you like church?" His son was looking at him expectantly.

"Yeah, Buddy. It was really good."

"So can you come with me next week too?" Ben put his arm around Sam's shoulders. "We'll talk about that later, okay? We need to get your sister now."

Leah was still talking with some of the other children, but waved at Ben when he turned to leave the room. He nodded at her and took Sam's hand. He wanted to get Molly and leave before he had to talk to anyone else.

Molly was asleep when he got to the nursery. The attendant took him to a "quiet room" behind the nursery that had several cribs in it. "Why don't you go ahead and wake her. She might cry if she sees a strange face when she wakes up."

"Was she okay for you?"

"Oh, yes. She fell asleep while she was taking her bottle. She's a pleasant little thing, isn't she?"

"She usually is. Thanks for watching her for me." Ben bent over and stroked her little blond head. Her head popped up, and when she saw Sam standing by the crib, she grinned at him.

Ben picked her up, and she buried her head in his shoulder. Once again, Ben felt blessed by the children God had given him. He knew he should focus more on God's goodness. But Katy's dying had not been good.

*****

When Ben arrived home, he knew he was going to have to get busy. He made himself and Sam a sandwich, and fed Molly as quickly as he could. "Sam, we need to get those bunk beds set up in your room. Do you think you can entertain your sister while I do that?"

He spread a blanket out on the bedroom floor and put Molly in the middle of it. He surrounded her with pillows and put some toys in front of her. Sam sat down next to her while Ben got busy on the beds. He had left the mattresses in the living room until he could get the frame put together. Fifteen minutes later, he knew it was going to take longer than he expected. He had no instructions.

"Hey, Dad, I think Molly's pooping her pants again." Ben looked over at his kids. Sure enough, she was red in the face.

"You know what, Sam? I don't think we're going to get this bed together before your aunt and cousins get here. You boys might have to camp out on the living room floor tonight."

"That would be more fun than sleeping in the beds."

"Yeah, but we should at least try to get Alexandria's bed together."

He changed Molly's pants then put her in her own bed while he worked on Alexandria's bed. He hoped Molly's sleep wouldn't be disturbed by another person in the room. If it was, they might have to put Alexandria in with her mom. *Time will tell, can't worry about it now.*

"Dad, they're here!" Sam had been out on the deck waiting for his cousins to arrive. Once again, Ben felt the anxiety crawl into his belly. He knew it was just because his life and his home was about to change in a big way. *But, it'll be a good way.* That was what he was hoping for as he joined Sam in the driveway to welcome four more people into his home.

One look at Abby, and he could tell she was feeling the same way.

"Well, here we go, for better or for worse." Her half-hearted smile made Ben smile too.

"It's going to be a good summer, Abby. We're going to make it one, okay?"

"Deal." The boys were already running into the house to look at the mattresses still on the living room floor. Ben hoped the noise wouldn't wake Molly. He was glad he had turned on the fan in her room. Maybe the noise of that would drown out the noise of three rambunctious boys.

Abby started to haul suitcases and boxes out of her car. Ben thought she had sent everything home with him on Saturday.

"More stuff?"

"Just our clothes that were at Momma's house, and a lot of food she sent along. We won't have to grocery shop for weeks."

Ben carried two boxes into the house. While he was there, he yelled at the three boys to go back outside to help Abby. He had a feeling that the first thing he and Abby would have to do was make a list of chores for the kids.

When the last bag and box had been carried into the house, Ben stopped and looked around him. There wasn't an empty spot on the cupboards or table in the kitchen. The living room was a tangle of mattresses, suitcases and more boxes. It looked like major chaos. He knew then that the neat, orderly life he had grown used to was now gone. The only redeeming thought he had was that he would be leaving in the morning to do a charter. Then he felt guilty. Poor Abby would be left with five kids and a thoroughly trashed house.

"Okay…where do we start, Abby?"

"Let's start by eating. I think we're going to need energy for the rest of this day. Then I think we should all go for a walk."

"A walk?" What was she thinking?

"Why not? We have the rest of the summer to sort this mess out." Ben didn't know if she was talking about his house or their lives.

"That sounds like a plan. Food it is! Did Momma Beth send any of her famous chocolate chip cookies?"

"She sure did." Ben and Abby left the kids in the living room and headed for the kitchen. "Why don't you make us some coffee, and I'll get the cookies. But we won't tell the kids we ate dessert first."

Ben moved the bags of groceries from the table to the floor. Moments later, he and Abby were drinking coffee and eating cookies. He decided if Abby wasn't flustered, he wouldn't be either.

*****

The walk after supper turned out to be a long one. First they went to the barn where all four kids had to have a ride on the horses. Ben was glad Abby had learned to ride and take care of horses when she was a teenager. That was one way she and Katy were different. Ben had offered to buy Katy a horse too, but she preferred the golf cart.

"I already told Sam he couldn't ride while I was gone, Abby. I think it would be too much work for you to bring all five kids to the barn by yourself."

"Thank you. I was hoping you'd do that. Did you hear that guys? Rule number one is that we come to the barn only when Uncle Ben is with us." Ben saw the disappointment on all three boys' faces.

"You guys are going to have plenty of other things to do. But when I'm home, I promise you we'll ride the horses."

After everyone gave a carrot to the horses, Abby wanted to walk down by the lake. It was a beautiful evening, and the sun was setting when they reached the water. There was a glider next to the lake that he and Katy put there soon after they moved to the grove. Ben sat down, with Molly in his lap. Abby and the four older kids went looking for frogs and tadpoles. As Ben watched them near the water's edge, he noticed the reflection of twilight in the water.

Twilight...that time right after sunset or right before dawn. Sunset and dawn, complete opposites, but equally beautiful. It's almost like tonight's sunset is simply a reflection of this morning's dawn. Ben looked up and saw the first star of night, and he wondered if it was the same star he talked to every morning.

Chapter 18

On Monday morning Ben woke up at 4:23, just like he did every morning. But he didn't reach for Katy as he usually did. His mind was still on the night before.

When they all got home from their walk, it was decided that Abby and her kids would use the main bathroom, and Ben and his kids would use the master bathroom in his room.

"Dad?"

"Yeah?

"I kind of like this bathroom. Why didn't I use it before?"

"Probably because the other bathroom is closer to your bedroom. It just made sense for you to use that one."

"Can I use this one forever?"

"No. It'll be just for the summer while we have extra people in our house. I told you we would have to make some changes for awhile."

"Tonight was fun, wasn't it, Dad?"

"Yeah, it was. Now why don't you get out of that tub? The other boys will be waiting for you." Sam didn't waste any time. This was the first time other boys had spent the night with him.

Abby knew how to put the bunk beds together since she'd been the one to take them apart. So the boys slept in their own room after all. Ben's fear about Molly waking up with someone else in her room was put to rest when Alexandria cried to sleep in Abby's bed.

"She's been clingy ever since we moved out of our own house. I don't mind her sleeping with me if it helps her get through this whole transition. I thought the divorce would be harder on the boys than her. But they seem to be okay as long as they have each other. Lexie was her daddy's girl though."

Abby tucked the little girl into her bed then she and Ben went to the boys' room. "Okay, guys. We need to talk." The three of them had exchanged beds for the night, and had decided they would sleep in a different bed every night. That way everyone got a turn in the top bunk.

"What do we have to talk about?"

"Well, if we're all going to live together for the summer, we're going to have some rules." Ben gave Abby a "help me" look.

"That's right, guys. When you get up in the morning, there's going to be a list of chores you have to do every day."

The two older boys groaned, and Sam mimicked their noise. Ben knew his son was going to learn some things from his older cousins this summer.

"What kind of chores? I thought we moved out here so we could have fun with Sam."

Kyle, being the oldest, was obviously going to be the spokesman.

"Well, the first chore of the day will be to make the bed you slept in. You can do your bed by yourself, but it might be more fun, and easier, if you all work on all three beds."

The boys looked at each other. Ben could almost see their minds working, and he was sure they would be able to handle that job together.

"What else, Uncle Ben?" Abby looked at him. Since they hadn't sat down and sorted out their own chores yet, they were flying by the seat of their pants tonight.

"I think everyone should hang their pajamas on the hooks in the closet when they get dressed too."

"That's a good one. Okay, boys. You need to do those two things before breakfast tomorrow. We'll tell you the rest of the rules after breakfast, okay?" All three of them nodded. It occurred to Ben that they were just now realizing that the summer was not going to be all fun and games.

"Now, on your knees, it's time for bedtime prayers." Sam looked at Ben. He didn't know what bedtime prayers were. But when Ben nodded his head at him, he followed the older boys example and knelt beside his bed.

"Come on, Uncle Ben. You too." Konnor took Ben's hand. He looked like his dad, but had Abby's laid-back personality.

Abby was already on her knees at the head of the bed with the three boys beside her. Ben had no choice but to kneel at the foot.

"Sam, when we say bedtime prayers, we say them together. You can listen to Kyle and Konnor until you learn it yourself, okay?" Sam looked at Ben for further directions. Ben could only nod his head. This was something he had not planned on.

"One other thing, Sam. When we say our prayers, we try to remember that we're talking to God. So we don't just say the words, we believe them in our hearts. Do you think you can do that too?"

Sam nodded his head then bowed it, like the other boys were doing. But he closed his eyes and folded his hands before the other boys did. And Ben wondered who had taught his son to pray. In his heart, he was glad someone had, since he hadn't.

As the boys prayed together, their words penetrated Ben's heart.

Father in Heaven,

We thank you for the night and for the morning light. We thank you for rest, and food, and loving care that makes our day so fair. Help us to do the things we should, to be to others, kind and good. Help us in work or play, to grow more loving every day. Amen.

Ben expected the boys to fly into bed the minute their "Amen" was said, but they didn't. Now it was time for their mother to pray for them. As Abby prayed her prayer of love and protection over, not only her own children, but his, Ben was taken back in time to the prayers he heard his grandmother pray over him. And Ben felt certain, that even though he felt God had failed him and Katy, his grandmother's prayers had protected him in Afghanistan and brought him the blessings he was now able to call his own.

But as soon as their mother said "Amen", the boys were in bed. She kissed each one, including Sam, and tucked them all in. Ben held back. Family traditions. Would he and Katy have had them with their kids? He knew they would have.

"Dad? Aren't you going to read to me tonight? You can read to Kyle and Konnor too, right guys?"

"Yeah! We want to hear a story too."

Ben pulled the book of Disney stories off the shelf where Sam kept it. He and Sam had traditions too…they just hadn't included God. "Which one do you want tonight, Sam?"

"The Three Pigs!"

"Yeah, The Three Pigs!" The other two boys now mimicked Sam.

*****

Ben still didn't get out of bed like he usually did. Not only was he afraid he would wake Abby, the memories of the night before stopped him.

After turning off their light and shutting their door, Ben made his way back to the kitchen. Abby had put all the groceries away and had started on the supper dishes that were still sitting on the table.

"I think you're doing my job, lady. You cook and I clean, remember?"

"I didn't cook. Momma sent it all, remember?"

"We both seem to have bad memories tonight. You want to wash and I'll dry?"

"Sounds like a deal. Has today been as exhausting for you as it has been for me?"

"It has. And we still have to go through our list of chores. And make up the kids' lists."

"I think it's more important to make the kids' lists. I think you and I are going to figure ours out as we go."

"That's true. Katy told me before she died that I wasn't allowed to spoil Sam just because his mom died. I've tried really hard to set boundaries and teach him to share the work around here. One of the things he has to do is take his own dishes to the sink and rinse them after he eats."

"I like that idea. Brett told the boys they didn't have to do that because it was women's work. So… they haven't done it. But if they see Sam do it, I think they'll do it too. What else does he do?"

"He's been making his bed and keeping his room picked up by himself too. He also has to brush his teeth after breakfast without being told. If he doesn't, he loses time watching TV. He only gets one hour a day, so that's a huge punishment for him."

"He only watches TV one hour a day? That one may be hard for me to enforce when you are away all day."

"Well, it is summer, and some rules do change during the summer. Do what you need to do with the TV. I know taking care of five kids isn't going to be easy. I'll make sure he brushes his teeth in the mornings, but when I'm not here, you are his disciplinarian."

"And I want you to feel free to tell my kids if they are doing something wrong."

"I won't if you're here, unless I see them do something dangerous. I really don't want any of them near the barn or lake if I'm not with them though. Accidents can happen so quickly."

As the two of them went through the lists of chores that needed to be done to keep a house running smoothly, they found themselves laughing more than once. They decided that Ben would keep the living and family rooms clean, in addition to his own bedroom and bathroom. He also promised to keep the dirt, mold, snakes and other vermin out of the boys' room.

The kitchen would be her domain, plus she would keep her bedroom, the girl's bedroom, and the main bathroom clean. She would also do all the laundry but his.

As Ben lay in his bed, he felt good about what they had accomplished the night before. He felt certain that she would respect his space. He didn't know why, but he felt like he needed to tell her that his room still contained all of Katy's things. When he told her, all she said was, "Oh, Ben. I'm sorry she had to leave us." And they both got tears in their eyes.

Ben stayed in bed until five thirty. He got up and put his chartering uniform on. He didn't know why, but he had always felt like he should dress professionally when he was flying. Probably because he had worn a uniform in the air force and when he flew the air ambulance.

As usual, he went to the kitchen first. He didn't go to the kid's rooms though. He was afraid he would wake them. And he knew if they got up, Abby would too. And she needed all the sleep she could get since he would be gone most of the day.

He didn't have to leave until seven because his client was meeting him at the airport where he kept his plane. There were some mornings when Linda had been at his house at six so he could do a charter. She had been so wonderful on those days, assuring him that Sam would be just fine without his dad getting him on the bus. "Don't worry, Ben," she'd said. "I know how to put children on a school bus."

Ben took his coffee to the deck as usual. But the stars were gone this morning. It was okay though; he had seen the evening star last evening and knew Katy's star would continue to shine, whether he saw it or not.

At six-thirty, Abby shuffled out to the deck in her slippers with a cup of coffee in her hands. She had on an ancient looking, frayed, green robe, and her hair was a mess. He had to smile when he saw her. This was Abby. Katy had told him she was the artistic one in the family and could make anything or anyone look beautiful. But when it came to herself, she was just plain Abby— unpretentious, humble, down-to earth Abby. The fact that Brett had found someone just the opposite of her did not surprise Ben. He was an arrogant man.

"Ben! For heaven sakes…what time did you get up?"

"I guess I forgot to tell you, I'm an early riser."

"But we didn't go to bed till midnight."

"I know. No matter what time I go to bed, I wake up at the same time." He didn't want to tell her what time and why.

"Well, why didn't you tell me. I wouldn't have kept you up so late."

"It's okay. I'll catch up tonight. What time are you going to wake up the kids?"

"My boys will be crawling out anytime now. Alexandria is my sleeping beauty. What time do your kids get up?"

"Sam is usually up by now, and I can hear Molly babbling in her bed." He held up the baby monitor he kept with him whenever she was out of his sight. "I think I'll go get her if it's okay with you."

"Ben…she's your child. Go get her. I know you have to leave at seven. I'll take over then."

By the time Ben had Molly changed and dressed, he could hear the boys rustling around in their room. On his way to the kitchen, he stopped and opened their door. The three of them were dressed and trying to make the top bunk. Ben was impressed. The little speech he and Abby made last night must have made an impression on them. He wondered how long it would last.

"Morning, guys. You need help with that top bunk?"

"Nope. We got it." Ben left the room smiling. He hoped they would continue to be as helpful today.

Abby was setting out the cereal and fruit when he got to the kitchen. "I hope your kids don't expect a cooked breakfast every morning. This momma has learned to preserve her energy for more difficult tasks that pop up during the day."

Ben had to smile again. Plain, down-to-earth Abby. They were going to get along just fine.

"Sam will be fine with cold cereal. You might need to warm a bottle for this one though."

She grinned at him. "I think I can handle that. And I promise, I'll feed her throughout the day."

Ben kissed Molly on the head as he handed her off to Abby. As he was ready to head out the door, the boys joined her in the kitchen.

"Bye, guys. Behave yourselves today." Sam ran to get his hug. "Hey, Buddy. Help your Aunt Abby, okay? If she can't find something, show her where it is."

"Okay, Dad. Love you."

"Love you too, Sam." Ben stopped, and went back to tousle his son's hair.

It was a new day, a new summer. And for Ben, it felt like he was starting a new life.

Chapter 19

———————————

Ben had two charters scheduled. He was taking his local client to Ft. Lauderdale then picking one up in Miami to take to Tallahassee. It was going to be a long day.

When he arrived in Tallahassee, it was almost noon. He wondered how Abby was doing, so decided to call her. She picked up on the fourth ring.

"Are you still alive or did they tie you up and toss you into the lake for the alligators."

"There are alligators in the lake? That's awesome, I can use that for a new disciplinary tool." If there hadn't been laughter in her voice, Ben might have been alarmed. He was really hoping the kids were behaving for her.

"Well, at least you're still laughing. How have they been?"

"Pretty good so far. The boys have been outside all morning, counting the orange trees. They thought you would want to have an accurate tally when you got home."

"They're counting orange trees? That's kind of weird."

"But they're having fun, and I promised them they could watch a movie this afternoon during quiet time if they did it."

Ben smiled. He already knew how many trees he had. But if it got the boys outside in the fresh air and kept them busy, he would take their word as truth, whether they got the number right or not.

"So, what time are you getting home? Or are you calling me to tell me you aren't coming back?" He heard Molly babbling in the background, and knew there was no way he wouldn't be going home. He missed his kids.

"I should be home by three. Do we need anything from the store?"

"No. But I'm glad you'll be home early. The boys want to know if we can go swimming."

"Sure. That would be a good pre-supper activity. But we should probably both go, with four kids to watch."

"That's what I figured. They are all pretty good little swimmers, but four is a lot for one person to watch. I'll get Molly's second nap in a little earlier. She didn't sleep very long this morning. I think she's wondering who I am, and why I'm watching her."

"She'll get used to you. I'll see you at three." Before he hung up, he thought of one other thing. "Abby?"

"Yeah?"

"Don't go to a lot of bother with supper. We can just eat sandwiches when we all get home from swimming."

"Don't worry about supper. I have Italian chicken breasts and rice in the crockpot. I think I forgot to tell you, I'm the crockpot queen."

"Sounds good to me as long as I don't have to cook."

When he closed his cell phone, he wondered if he could make it home before three. He had always wanted to go home to his kids, but today he wanted to go home to the fun that awaited him there. Abby was making a large family sound like fun.

He was in the pilot's seat, checking his instruments when his phone rang again. *Maybe she needs something from the store after all.* But the screen said the phone call was from Leah.

"Hey, Doc. You making house calls now?"

He heard her laugh. Like her voice, it was as smooth as honey too. But the comfort he heard in it at the office and at church, suddenly sounded a little bit sexy.

"House calls only go to my favorite patients' dad who can fly airplanes."

"How many of them do you have?"

"Just one. And I was wondering if you're booked for tomorrow?" Ben was confused. Why would she want to know if he was booked? Did she want to hire him?

"I do have a charter tomorrow. Why do you ask?"

"I've been thinking. You've see me in action at my job, and I'd like to watch you at work in your own element. Tomorrow's my day off and I was wondering if I could ride along, just for the fun of it."

"Well sure…but I'm going to be gone all day. I'm picking my client up in Tampa and taking him to Ft. Myers. I'm going to wait around there all day so I can bring him back in the late afternoon."

"What do you do while you're waiting around all day?"

"Depends. Tomorrow I was just going to hang around at the airport. I'll take my laptop, and do some of my accounting work."

"Oh, okay." There was disappointment in her voice.

"Leah? If you want to ride along, you're more than welcome to. I'll let the work go, and we'll explore Ft. Myers. That sounds like more fun than work."

"Are you sure? I thought maybe you were just going to fly some place and come right back? I just wanted to watch you fly, but spending the day with you sounds much better."

"Let's do it then. Can you meet me at the municipal airport at seven?"

"I can, but only if you're sure." She sounded hesitant again.

"It sounds like it will be a much better day than I had planned. We'll go exploring."

"Okay, see you at seven."

It took Ben an hour and a half to fly from Tallahassee to Laurelville. He couldn't quite figure out what had just happened, but he thought maybe he'd just been asked out on a date. Or maybe it was just a friend wanting to hang out with another friend. Or maybe Leah was just one of those girls who liked new experiences. But she had specifically said she wanted to observe him in his element.

She was right about getting to know someone by watching them do what they loved to do. He felt like he knew a lot about Leah just because he had observed her doing what she obviously loved to do.

Ben landed the Cessna at two forty. He would make it home by three like he'd promised Abby. It would be fun to spend the afternoon at the pool with her and the kids.

*****

Sam had so much fun swimming with his cousins. Ben had never observed his son so outgoing, almost daring. He wondered if he was feeling a little inferior to his older and bigger cousins and was compensating for that. Instead of sibling rivalry, was it possible they would have to deal with cousin rivalry this summer?

Abby got in the pool with Alexandria, and Ben got in with Molly. He put her toes in first, and she kicked her feet. When she splashed water on herself, she caught her breath, then puckered like she was going to cry.

"It's okay, baby girl. Water in Florida is a necessity of life." Ben held her close, and while he was kissing her chubby cheeks, he lowered her slowly into the water until she was in up to her waist. Taking her hands from her Daddy's face, she splashed the water. This time, she giggled and did it again.

"She likes it, Dad!" Sam had stopped playing with his cousins long enough to watch his Dad and sister.

"I think she does, Sam. She'll be swimming as well as you pretty soon!"

"I could teach her how…" Sam held his arms out to Molly. And of course, she wanted to go to him.

"You and I will teach her together, Sam. Right now, you better get out there and show the big boys how you jump off the diving board."

Abby was trying to teach Alexandria how to float but finally gave up and put a kid's life jacket on her. Looking at Ben, she shrugged her shoulders. "The boys learned that way, I guess she can too."

Ben was struck again at how relaxed she was as a parent. He could tell she dearly loved her kids and wanted them to be good, but she wasn't obsessed with the right way to parent like some people were…like he was sometimes. There were times when he was afraid he would fail his kids as a parent. Maybe it was because he was trying to be both mom and dad to them. He wished he could be more relaxed like Abby. Maybe by the end of the summer some of her confidence as a parent would rub off on him.

They let the kids swim for almost two hours, stopping them a couple times to apply more sunscreen, even though the screen pool enclosure offered protection from the hot rays.

When Abby climbed out of the pool, she put on a swim cover that was about as ragged looking as the robe she'd worn that morning. Ben had to wonder if she had let her wardrobe go out of neglect or because she and Brett had been short on money. He knew Brett made a good salary, but he was also learning that it cost a lot of money to take care of a family. Had the stress of that been too much for his brother-in-law? He hoped Abby would trust him enough some day to share what she had been through. It might help her heal.

"So, how was today… really?" He was sitting on a blanket on the concrete trying to keep Molly entertained. Abby was resting in a lounge chair with sunglasses on. Even though Ben couldn't see her eyes, he was sure she was awake, watching the kids in the water.

"The kids were really good today. I think my boys are enjoying the chance to get outside and run again, and I think Sam likes them being here. He's keeping up with them pretty good, even though he's smaller. And Alexandria and Molly are entertaining each other. I always heard, the more kids you have, the easier it is…because they take care of each other."

"I just hope they don't get bored and start driving you crazy."

"Don't worry about it. Momma is coming out on Wednesdays to help me. If you have to fly on those days, we'll take them to the park in town. I just need to know which days you'll be here."

"Well, of course. Why don't we sit down with a calendar tonight? I've been wondering…are you planning on going to your Mom's house on the weekends?"

"I've been thinking about that myself. It depends a lot on Brett. He has been so irresponsible and undependable. It seems like he wants the kids less and less. And from what the kids tell me, the girlfriend disappears when they are around. But I'm thinking, if you don't mind, I'd just as soon stay here on the weekends."

"Whatever's best for you, Abby. This is your home for the summer, to come and go as you please. I just need you here when I fly."

"And when you date pretty doctors?"

"Actually, I've been thinking about that. If the kids are going to be in Tampa with their dad this weekend, you don't have to be here. I'll plan the dates around your schedule. And I really need to find a backup sitter, anyways—to give Linda a break when she gets home."

"Didn't you already make a date for this Saturday?"

"Yes, but I can change it. I'm seeing Leah tomorrow. She called today and wanted to know if she could ride along on my charter."

Abby grinned at him. "Wow, this is getting interesting. She wants to see you in action, huh?"

Ben felt a little bit embarrassed. "Something like that, I guess. I was a little confused when she called. I've never had a woman take the initiative like that before. What do you think it means?"

"I don't know, Ben. If I knew her, I might be able to tell you. It sounds like she wants to spend time with you. That's a good thing, right?"

"We'll see, I guess. Anyways, I can cancel Saturday night if you want to stay in Tampa."

"No. I'm going to call Brett Thursday night and find out what he wants to do for the weekend. I still have to tell him the kids and I are out here. I haven't done that yet, and I need to do it before the kids tell him."

"Is he going to be okay with it?" It was a concern for Ben. Even though he'd told her he didn't care what others thought of their arrangement, he didn't want it to reflect poorly on Abby.

"Actually, I don't think he cares what happens to us anymore. Don't worry about it." She waved her hand like she was trying to get rid of a bug or a bad thought. "So do you want to tell those boys it's time to get out of the pool, or should I?"

Ben couldn't help himself. He reached out and gave her hand a squeeze. "Abby, don't ever let Brett make you feel inferior. You're an amazing mom, and now that he's gone, you have a right to live your life the way you want to." She readjusted her sunglasses. Ben was sure she wiped a tear away when she did it. "I'll be the mean guy and tell the boys it's time to go home. You've had to be the disciplinarian all day."

"Thanks, Ben. For everything."

"No problem, sister." He was still holding her hand, so he gave it another squeeze.

"Hey, boys! It's time to go home. I'm starving."

"Just a little while longer, Uncle Ben?" It was Kyle, the self-elected spokesman for the group.

"Nope! Last one out of the pool has to scoop horse poop tonight."

Sam was the last one out, but Ben could tell he didn't care. He cleaned his horse's stable every night.

Chapter 20

After supper, Ben shared with Abby's kids the rules about rinsing their own plates and helping to clear the table. "Work is more fun when it's shared," he told them. He was surprised that there was no complaining.

Once again, they all took a walk. First they went to the barn to do the chores, and everyone took a ride on the horses. Ben really hoped he would be home every night to have supper with them and help Abby in the evenings.

Ben joined in the bedtimes prayers again. He was in awe of Abby. She could have come through the divorce so angry at God. He knew she'd been hurt and was still angry at Brett, but she was able to push that aside when she was with the kids. He could tell she wanted to teach them how to forgive and be thankful for the blessings they *did* have. When she prayed for the kids, she also prayed for God's protection for their dad. Ben knew she meant it. Brett was the only dad her kids had. She truly did want him to be decent to them.

After they were all tucked in, he and Abby sat down with a calendar and penciled in what they knew for certain about their lives. Ben had many charters scheduled for the summer and once again told Abby how grateful he was that he didn't have to cancel them. He put those on the calendar and noticed that almost every Monday and Friday was scheduled.

"That's the way it usually is. The Tuesday and Thursday flights are not as frequent, but I try to stay open on those days, in case someone calls at the last minute. When Sam was in school, I usually did my bookwork on Wednesdays. I'd like to keep doing that, if you don't mind. Or I can do it in the evenings after the kids go to bed."

"No, you do what you need to do. Momma will be here on Wednesdays to help me with the kids. I'm here for whenever you need me this summer, Ben. You're paying me well, just by letting me and the kids stay. I think they needed a change of scenery as much as I did."

Abby penciled in the weekends that her kids were supposed to go with Brett.

"So, what did you decide about the weekends?"

"If you don't mind, I think we'll plan on staying here. In the past few months, Brett has only wanted the kids during the day on the Saturdays when it's his weekend. When the kids get home, they tell me that his girlfriend usually disappears when they are with him. So if he wants them, I'll have him pick them up at Mom and Dad's house. I'll call him on Thursday to see if he wants them this weekend."

"That has to be so difficult for the kids. What does he usually do with them when he has them?"

"Kyle says they usually go out to eat and to a movie or a park. I think he's only taken them to their condo a couple times."

"Does he know that you're here?"

"Not yet. I'll tell him Thursday when I talk to him. I don't want the kids to have to tell him about it."

"I hope he doesn't give you a hard time." Ben watched her closely. She kept her eyes on the calendar they were working on.

"To be really honest with you, Ben, I don't think he'll care."

"I'm sorry, Abby. I know that must hurt." Ben truly did hurt for her, and found himself reaching across the table to squeeze her hand.

"Thanks, Ben. Hey, we better get back to this calendar. I'm thinking I need to pencil in some time to do a little job hunting this summer. I'll probably do most of that online after the kids are in bed or on Wednesdays when Momma's here."

"Maybe you should look for something around here. I know the city has more opportunities, but the rent is cheaper here." She looked at him with questions in her eyes.

"Ben...I'm not going to be your permanent tenant here. I promise I'll have something figured out by the end of the summer."

"You know, if Katy was here, she'd tell you to put it all in God's hands, and He'd take care of it for you."

Abby smiled. "She had an amazing faith, didn't she?"

"She did. But it didn't do her much good in the end." Ben could hear the anger in his voice.

"Yes it did, Ben. Without her faith, dying would have been so much more difficult for her. She loved you so much and didn't want to leave, but she also knew she was going to a better place. She went peacefully, knowing God would give you the strength to go on without her." Abby was tearful again. "Sometimes though, I wish God would give us a glimpse of heaven. I think if we could see her basking in God's eternal love, it would help our grief."

"I wanted her to stay here and bask in my love."

"She loved basking in your love, Ben. You were a good husband to her."

Chapter 21

On Tuesday morning, Ben found himself too restless to stay in bed after he woke up at his usual time. He would just have to be extra quiet in the mornings.

Slipping into the kitchen, he turned on the coffee pot, then sat at the table until it was finished. He missed looking in on his kids when he got up, but he didn't want to wake the other three. He knew it was a small sacrifice to make in return for having Abby here.

Ben took his coffee and went quietly to the deck. The blanket of humidity was heavy, almost as heavy as his blanket of grief had once been. But when he turned his gaze to the heavens, he was rewarded with a sky full of light. The moon was still bright on the western horizon, and the stars were scattered like a million diamonds in the dark sky.

From the lake he heard the sound of frogs and a blue heron. The music of the morning drew him off the deck, and he began to walk the path he and Katy had shared so many times. The glider at the lake's edge invited him to sit, and as he did, he saw the water become a dance floor where the morning stars could dance. Oh, how Katy would have loved it.

And then with great clarity, he recognized that Katy was not just an observer of the dancing stars, she was a participant. And Ben smiled.

As he retraced his steps, he felt lighter, and he wondered if Abby's arrival at the grove had anything to do with it. He had learned to love her as Katy's beloved sister, but in just two short days, she had become woven into the fabric of his daily life. And his life was not only easier now, but more pleasant.

She was awake and in the swing on the deck when he returned.

"There you are. I thought maybe you got beamed up by an alien space ship."

"Well, I am seeing things this morning I've never seen before." He slid into the swing beside her.

"That sounds interesting. And if my memory serves me right, you are going to be spending time today with someone you've never spent time with before. It must be your day for new adventures."

"It could be. How about you? What do you have planned for yourself and five kids today?"

"Staying sane?" When she laughed it sounded like the music from a merry-go-round.

"Think it will be that bad?"

"No. They're good kids. But I do wish I would have remembered to bring the boy's bikes from the storage unit. They would have a great time riding up and down the lane on them."

"We'll have to see what we can do about that. Until we get them, you might want to take them to the park. There's lots of shade there, and some new play equipment."

"Maybe we'll do that this morning before it gets too hot. Aren't you supposed to leave early today?"

"Yeah. Wish I didn't have to. I miss my kids when I don't get to see then in the mornings."

"They'll be here when you get back. You want me to fix you some breakfast while you get your uniform on?"

"I can fix my own breakfast, Abby. I've been doing it for three years; no reason to quit now."

"If you insist. I think I'll go take my shower while you're still here. Can you listen for the kids?"

"Yeah, sure. Go! Your day is going to be more hectic than mine."

"Hey. If I don't see you before you leave, have a fun day with Doctor Leah. I want to hear all about it when you get home." She grinned at him like she had a secret that he didn't know. Maybe it was a girl thing.

*****

Leah was waiting for him when he got to the airport. She was leaning on the fence, watching another plane take off and didn't hear him as he approached her.

The sun was up and shining on her blond hair, making it look like spun gold. The usual pony tail was gone, and it hung half way down her back. She had on a pair of white capris and a turquoise shirt. Neither were tight, but they still managed to show off her tiny figure. She didn't look like the same woman he saw at her office on a regular basis, or the woman he'd seen three days ago at church.

"Well, aren't you the early bird today."

When she turned around, the smile on her face made Ben catch his breath. *How can one woman be so perfect? She's beautiful, intelligent and good. She has to have a flaw somewhere.*

"I like getting up early. I'm afraid I'll miss something if I don't. You look nice this morning. So professional."

"I think the uniform helps my passengers feel safer, more confident of my ability. They might not feel that way with a pilot dressed in cut-offs and a tee shirt. You ready to go?"

"I am. I've never been in a plane smaller than one of those little commercial ones. Is this going to be different?"

"It is. I think it's more fun. I just hope you won't get bored on the flight. I'm going to be kind of busy."

"You don't need a co-pilot?"

"I think you'd be more of a distraction in the cockpit. You look like a real girl today, instead of a doctor."

"I am a real girl." She smiled, but turned away quickly. Ben was sure she didn't want him to see the blush that tinted her cheeks.

"Well, let's get going, real girl. I have work to do. What do you want to do when we get to Ft. Myers?"

"I was wondering if we could grab a taxi and go to Sanibel Island? I heard there are some nice art galleries and artisan shops there. Have you ever been there?"

"No, I haven't. You're interested in art?"

"A little…but I think the artists are even more interesting. The ones I've met are so introspective. They seem to see the world through eyes that are different from ours. They see beauty that we can't see then bring it to life for the rest of us."

"Art, huh? Do you even like that abstract stuff?"

"I don't see the beauty in that, but when I look at it, I want to know what the artist was thinking when he painted it. But I don't think we're going to see a lot of abstract stuff at Sanibel."

"Sanibel Island it is then. Maybe you can teach me something new today." Ben looked at her walking beside him, and knew in his heart that Leah was a woman he wanted to get to know better. She seemed multifaceted, and he wanted to see and understand every intricate detail of her personality. And looking at her made him want to touch her too.

They were early enough that he was able to show her around his "bird" as he called it. Leah could hear the pride in his voice as he showed her the instruments and how he checked them before each flight. She was impressed with the luxury of the cabin. "Your clients are going first class in this buggy, aren't they?"

Ben laughed. "Well, I've never heard it described as a buggy, but yes, they do seem to enjoy the comfort of it. Did you bring something to do during the flight?"

She pulled a couple of medical journals from the tote she had with her and waved them at him. "Doctors never stop learning. But I think I may just sit back and relax. Let the world float below me."

*****

Their day was perfect in every way.

When they arrived at the airport, they made arrangements to meet Ben's client at four, then the two of them rented a car. It was a day for exploration, and Ben didn't want to do it in a taxi. As they crossed the causeway from Ft. Myers to Sanibel Island, Leah couldn't keep her eyes off the water.

"Isn't it beautiful, Ben?"

"It is. The waters of the Gulf are such a beautiful blue color. Have you never seen them before?"

"Yes, I've seen them, but the color is always so impressive."

"You obviously didn't grow up in Florida. People who have lived here for years don't seem to appreciate it. Where did you grow up?"

"Ohio. Not a whole lot of turquoise water there. Not where I grew up."

"Ohio? That's interesting. My wi…, Sam's grandmother lived in Ohio when she was a girl. Cincinnati, I think. What part of Ohio did you grow up in?"

"North central Ohio. Oh, look, I can see the lighthouse. I'm so excited. A whole day on an island is my idea of perfection." Ben took his eyes off the road, just long enough to see the pink tint on her cheeks again.

When he had first met her in the office, he assumed she was a confident, professional woman with sophisticated tastes. But after seeing her in her home with his kids, at church, and now here, he was seeing something unusual in her. It was a simplicity, an innocence, that one would see in a much younger person.

He knew she was thirty-five; Linda told him that. Linda also told him she had never married. She was a mystery to him, and he hoped this day would solve it for him.

They reached the end of the causeway. "Which way now, my lady? You're the tour director today."

She had her smart phone out, and was looking up the details of the island. "Let's go see the lighthouse first. It isn't far. Then we can go on into the town. I just love beach towns, don't you?"

"Actually, they always seem so crowded to me. I'd rather be flying above them."

"I think you'll like this one. I haven't been here, but I've talked to people who have been, and they say it's rather quaint."

"I think it'll be fun, just because I'm with you." Ben had to turn left and didn't see the shy smile that she would have rewarded him with.

By lunch time they had explored not only the lighthouse, but the town. "Why don't we go to that deli and get some sandwiches to take to the beach?"

"It's a little warm for the beach, isn't it?"

"We'll ask if there's one that has a shelter house and trees. You afraid you're going to melt?"

"Hey, I'm dressed in a navy blue uniform shirt and pants, and you're dressed like a tourist. I do feel like I'm melting. Don't you want to eat where it's air-conditioned?"

"Wait here." She disappeared into the souvenir shop they were standing in front of. Five minutes later she returned with a bag. "When we go into the deli, go to the bathroom and put this on while I buy lunch. Then we'll go to the beach."

"What is it?" He started to open the bag, but she stopped him. "Don't look now. Wait till you put it on." Her eyes had those gold flecks in them that he'd noticed before. This time he was sure they were caused by laughter she was holding in.

"What do you want to eat?"

"Any thing is fine. Surprise me, you seem to like doing that."

"Okay. Now go. Change your shirt."

When Ben came out of the bathroom, she was waiting for him and burst into laughter. The white tee-shirt he had on was something only a tourist would wear. In bold letters across the top, it said, "I love Sanibel Island." There was a picture of huge shell, and the words "shell inspector" under the shell.

"Now, you're ready for the beach. You look like a real tourist."

"Very funny! Maybe I should go buy you a matching one."
He nudged her shoulder as they began to walk again.

They found their way to the beach the deli clerk had told her
about. There were picnic tables under some shade trees where they
ate lunch. Although it was a beautiful beach, and they talked about
walking it, they never left the table. The thought crossed Ben's mind
that if he'd been there with Katy, she would have insisted they walk.
She had loved the beach.

"Thanks for bringing me along today, Ben."

"No. Thank you for keeping me company. Sometimes these
day charters can get kind of long for me. I usually end up hanging
around the airport with my computer, so I can do book work. This is
a lot more fun."

"It's been fun for me too. Your mother-in-law told me you
work too hard and don't take any time off for fun."

"Linda told you that? That surprises me. She isn't one to
gossip about others."

"She wasn't gossiping, Ben. We were at our ladies prayer
group a few months ago, and she asked us to remember you in
prayer. It was right after you got Molly. She said she was worried
about you taking on the extra responsibility. I can tell she loves you
like a son, Ben."

"She does. Did you know all her kids were adopted? When I
married Katy, she told me a child didn't need her own blood to be
loved. I feel like another one of her adopted children. She's a
wonderful woman."

"I know. She's shared her grief about Katy with our group a
few times. I feel like I know who Katy was because of her."

"Well, I don't know anything about you." Ben needed to get
her away from the subject of Katy. He only discussed the love of his
life with other people who had loved her too.

"Not really much to tell. I grew up in Ohio and went to
medical school there. I moved down here to practice a few years
ago."

"Do you have family down here?"

"No. They're all still in Ohio."

"Really? What brought you down here? Must have been someone pretty important to leave family for."

"Hey...I grew up in Ohio. It's cold there and warm here. Isn't that a good enough reason?" Ben thought it was an evasive answer. Maybe she had come down for a man, and he dumped her after they got here. That would be reason enough not to talk about it.

"Well, I'm glad you like warm weather and came to Florida. We'll have to do this again. Do you always have Wednesdays off?"

"Usually, unless I'm covering for another doctor. Do you ever get any days off?"

"Not very often. Between the charters, the grove and the kids, I'm pretty busy. That reminds me, we may have to change our plans for this weekend."

He saw the disappointment on her face. "Why? I was looking forward to it."

"I know. I was too. But my babysitting situation may not work out."

"So, who did you find to watch the kids for you this summer? I asked my nurse if she knew anyone who could help, but she didn't."

"Actually, things worked out pretty good. My sister-in-law is watching them."

"Is that the Aunt Carly Sam talks so much about?"

"No. This is his Aunt Abby."

"Does she live around here?"

"Right now, she and her three kids are at my house for the summer."

Leah looked confused. "You have a woman and three extra kids at your house for the summer? Why? "

"It's a long story. But in a nutshell...she needed a place to live for the summer, and I needed childcare. Her husband divorced her this past year, and she hasn't found a job yet."

"Is it crazy at your house?"

"Well, it's only been three days, but so far it's working out well."

"Why can't she babysit this Saturday?"

"I don't know for sure that she can't. But this is the weekend for her ex to get the kids, and she might have to take them to Tampa. She's going to talk to him tomorrow night. I'll call you after she knows what she's doing."

"You and the kids could come to my house. I'm a really good cook."

That sounded wonderful to Ben. But he knew he couldn't. He didn't want Sam to assume that his relationship with Leah was something it wasn't. At least, not yet.

"I have rules about that. I don't want to involve my kids in my relationships. There's too much potential for them getting hurt."

"Didn't you date that school teacher for about a year?"

"Wow…you do know me pretty well, don't you?" He smiled when she blushed again.

"Hey. It's a small town. You can't hide much here, you know? So Sam didn't know you were dating her?"

"She was his preschool teacher, and he knew we were good friends. She never came to my house while he was there, though. I didn't want him to get too close to her. He's already been hurt by loss."

"You're a good man, Ben…and a good dad. Just let me know about Saturday."

"I will. I do want to see you again."

"Me too."

At three, the two of them found their way to the rented car and started back to the airport. The drove in silence for awhile, but it wasn't uncomfortable silence. It was as if they were both processing what the day had meant to each of them. As much as Ben enjoyed his time with her, he felt like she was a bigger mystery to him at the end of the day than she was at the beginning. It was like they had both enjoyed each other and the time they spent together, but neither one of them knew anything about the journeys they had each taken to get to this one day.

And Ben wanted to know about her journey.

Chapter 22

_____

Ben didn't get home until after supper that evening. He called Abby from the airport to tell her he would be late.

"Is everything okay?" He felt a little guilty that he spent the whole day with a beautiful woman, and she had been home with five kids.

"We did okay. My dad came with mom today, and they brought the boys' bicycles. Dad brought his bike too, and all four of them spent the day riding the paths in the grove. I think my dad had as much fun as they did. And Momma took care of the girls for me this morning. She told me to go to town and do something for myself."

"So, what did you do for yourself?"

"I went to the salon and got my hair cut."

"But I liked your long hair." Ben didn't know why he said that. It wasn't any of his business how Abby wore her hair.

"But it's cooler when it's short."

"Of course it is. I'm glad you got a break to do something for yourself. Are your parents still there?"

"They just left. They brought us a bunch of food again. The kids and I'll just eat leftovers tonight. Did you have fun?" Ben wondered how long it would take her to ask, and smiled when the question came.

"Yeah. It was a good day. I'll tell you about it later."

When Ben and Leah arrived at the Laurelville airport, there was no one else there. "Do you want me to show you around while we're here?"

"Sure. It's nice you can park the plane so close to home, isn't it?"

"It's great. It takes me about twenty minutes to get home from here. I didn't get to see my kids this morning, so I'm looking forward to seeing them tonight."

"Why don't you go on home then? They'll be anxious to see you too, I'm sure. I'll get the tour next time."

"You promise me there'll be a next time?"

She grinned at him. "I'll make sure there's a next time."

When they reached her car, she turned to face him. "Thanks again, Ben. It was fun." And as if it was the most natural thing in the world, she stood on the tip of her toes to give him a hug. Ben didn't realize he was so much taller than her until he felt her arms around his chest and her head right under his chin. After a whole day in the sun, her hair still smelled like strawberries.

*****

Ben was able to spend the whole day at home on Thursday. He was amazed at how well Abby managed all the kids. As laid back as her personality was, she was still very organized and in control with them. She had made out a daily schedule that included an hour and a half of quiet time for all of them every afternoon.

The older boys read books in the living and family rooms while Sam got to spend time in his room by himself, playing with his lego blocks. "I really think he likes it, Ben. He's been so good about sharing all his things with my boys, but that room has been his own for a lot of years. I don't want him to resent my boys for taking over his space."

"He isn't going to resent them, Abby. I think he loves having them here. He told me all about his day yesterday with your dad and the boys."

"They did have fun." She had just put Molly down for her afternoon nap, and Alexandria was in Abby's room playing with the toys she brought with her from home.

"So this hour and a half is your quiet time, too?"

"Yep. My time to refuel."

They were sitting at the kitchen table, drinking an iced coffee she made for them.

"Don't you want to lie down and rest?"

"No. I just need quiet time." And Ben noticed that she didn't look as exhausted as she did on Sunday when she got there.

"Abby, tell me the truth. Is this going to be too much for you?"

"No, definitely not. I don't know why, but I feel more rested today than I've felt in months. It must be the country air."

"It is peaceful out here. Katy loved it too."

"Do you still think about her all the time, Ben?" Abby rested her chin on her hand and looked at him intently.

"No. I don't let myself. When I wake up early, I allow myself some time to do that, but then I make myself stop. There are times during the day when something will remind me of her, but I don't allow myself to dwell on it. It would consume me."

"I understand. I allow myself some time every day to be angry at Brett too. But I know I have to keep my focus on my kids. They help keep things in perspective."

"Thank goodness for our kids, huh?"

Pushing back from her chair, she took her phone out of her pocket. "Speaking of Brett and the kids, I need to call him about this weekend. If I go outside to talk, can you keep your ears open for our little monkeys?"

"Yeah, sure. Don't let him get the best of you, Abby. You're too good for that."

"Thanks." Her smile was a weak one, and Ben wondered how long it had been since her ex-husband had said anything positive to her.

With the afternoon free, Ben decided it would be a good time to clean his bedroom and bathroom. He grabbed the cleaning bucket from the hall closet and opened the door to his bedroom. It looked dark and dingy. He kept the blinds closed all the time, and the linens on the bed looked faded and dingy. They had been there since Katy died three years ago, and he had washed them frequently. Walking to his dresser with a dusting cloth in hand, he stopped and reached for the wedding picture that sat on top of it. Usually, when he looked at it, the tears would come. He missed the beautiful girl in the picture.

But today he smiled. The picture had been taken during their first dance at the reception. He remembered that first dance well. He had teased her about the slow dance of intimacy she had insisted on when they first met. She wanted their romance to develop slowly and for a sexual relationship to wait until after they were married. She felt like a rushed romance was a shallow one.

As he looked at the picture again, he remembered thinking that they were dancing the last steps of their dance of intimacy. What he knew now was that their courtship had only been the first few steps. The dance didn't end until she died.

He placed the picture back where he found it. Opening the top drawer of the dresser, he picked up the little notebook. He hadn't looked at it all week. But he really didn't need to, he already knew what was in it. With hands that trembled slightly, he touched a night gown that lay on top of the rest of her clothes. He remembered how she looked in it. In the beginning, she had looked like a dark haired goddess to him. In the end, her illness robbed her of her physical beauty. But it never took her inner joy.

Ben closed the drawer. She was gone. And she wasn't coming back. *Promise me, Ben. Promise me you'll love and marry again. Don't let your love go to waste.*

As he stripped the bed, he knew what he had to do. He had to open the blinds of his room, and his soul, and let the sun shine in. He needed to get rid of the old linens of his bed, and his life, and bring some new ones in. He needed to empty the drawers of things she would never use again, and fill them with the necessities of his new life without her. It was time.

He put the linens and his dirty clothes in the basket and went to the laundry room. One last time, before he placed Katy's blanket into the washer, he lifted it to his face. Her scent was gone and had been for years. He had been fooling himself all those times when he thought he could still smell her in them. But did he really need her blanket and her clothes to remind him of her? He had a heart full of the memories of their love, and he had Sam. She had left him with what really mattered in the world.

Abby found him there. "Ben? I wondered where you disappeared to. Do you want me to wash those things with the kids' dirty towels?"

"No. I'm thinking about throwing them away. Look how old and ragged they're looking. Do you think we could go shopping tonight so you could help me find some new ones?"

"I'd love to help you spend your money. What else can we get you?"

"Actually, I'm wondering if you could help me spruce things up around here. The whole house could use a facelift, don't you think?"

"It could use a few new things, but I wouldn't totally change it. Someday, when you get married to Leah, she'll just redo it anyways."

*****

The kids were excited about an evening out. Ben and the boys did the chores in the barn, while Abby made a list of groceries they needed. They promised the kids pizza before their trip to the only big retail store in town.

When they loaded all the kids and car seats into Abby's van, they laughed about whether there would be any room left for the groceries on the way home.

"You may have to do the grocery shopping alone after this, Abby."

"I just need a few things. I'll get everything else I need when I go to Tampa on Saturday."

She handed him her keys. "You want to drive the bus today?"

"Sure. It's been a long time since I've driven anything but my truck." When he got in, he had to laugh. The girls were in the two middle seats, and all three boys had crowded into the back seat. "This does feel like a bus full of kids, doesn't it? It's a good thing neither one of us has any more, or we'd have to buy a bigger van."

It was even more of a circus getting all five kids out of the van and into the pizza place. And the place was full, so they had to wait on a table big enough to seat all of them.

"We might want to call ahead and reserve a whole room next time." Ben was holding Molly and Abby had Alexandria's hand in hers. The three boys were fidgeting impatiently. Ben noticed that they were drawing a lot of attention. "Big families must be a rarity these days."

"Yeah, I think they are." Abby was whispering. "Why is everyone looking at us?"

"It's a small town, did you forget? Do you want to leave?"

"No. I'm good." But if the waitress hadn't come to get them at that moment, Ben knew he could have gone some place else. He hadn't been out to eat in town since Katy died. He had avoided being in public because he couldn't bear the pity stares from others. Now, here he was, the object of curious looks from many people he recognized.

They were half way through their meal when he saw Jan come through the door. She was with a man he didn't recognize. Ben really hoped she wouldn't notice him, but how could she not? She was a school teacher, and the presence of so many children at one table was like sign that said, "Look at us, teacher!"

Ben saw the look of surprise cross her face, then he watched her as she said something to the man she was with. He nodded his head, and Jan started in Ben's direction.

"Hi Ben, I thought that was you over here."

"Miss Henderson! You're here too." Ben could hear the approval in Sam's voice.

"Hi Sam. How are you doing this summer?" Jan moved her eyes from Ben to Sam.

"I'm having a great summer. My cousins are living with us, and we're having lots of fun."

"That's wonderful, Sam." Jan eyes returned to Ben. He saw the questions in them.

He stood up. "Hi Jan. It's nice to see you. This is Abby, my sister-in-law. She's watching the kids for me this summer."

"Abby. Of course." Jan put her hand out to take Abby's. "Ben's told me about you."

"Abby. This is Jan Henderson. Sam's preschool teacher." Abby glanced at Ben while she swallowed a bite of pizza.

"Hi, Jan. It's nice to meet you."

Jan turned back to Ben. The questions were still there, but he had no desire to answer them. Since she had left his home almost a month ago, he hadn't had much time to think about her, let alone miss her. As he looked around him at Abby and all the kids, he knew he had made the right decision in letting her leave his life.

"It was good to see you again, Jan. I hope you're enjoying your summer." He hoped she would recognize his need for her to go back to the man she came with. Ben wasn't even curious to know who he was.

"The summer has been good so far. You enjoy the rest of yours, too."

She turned and left like he'd hoped she would.

"You okay, Ben?" Abby was whispering again.

"Yeah. But next time we go out to eat, let's do it in Tampa."

After the boys devoured the rest of the pizza, Ben and Abby herded them back out to the van. As soon as everyone was strapped in their seats, they both started to laugh. "Well now, that was fun. But, I really need to know, Ben. How many other ex-girlfriends do I have to meet?"

Chapter 23

By the time they returned home from the store, it was time to put the kids to bed. And Ben was glad. All five of them had been restless at the store. Molly had to be held and fed, Alexandria was whiney, and the three boys wouldn't keep their hands off the merchandise. They wanted everything they saw.

Abby did manage to get the few groceries they needed, and Ben hastily picked out a new bedspread and sheets for his bed. That was the reason they had decided to go into town in the first place.

After prayers, Abby and Ben went to the family room and crashed on the couch.

"Tell me again why we decided to take five kids out to eat and to the store?"

"Hey, it was your idea, mister. When you mentioned it, I wondered if you were out of your mind."

The two of them started laughing again. "But it was worth it to see the shocked look on your ex-girlfriend's face. Do you think she thought you got married and had three more kids in the month since she saw you?"

"Poor Jan. You know…I'm really glad she was with another guy. She's a good woman, and will be a wonderful wife for someone. I just never had any feelings for her. Sometimes I wonder if I'll ever find anyone again."

"Give it some time, Ben. It's only been three years, and you loved our Katy an awful lot."

"I know. But maybe I'm a one-woman man."

"No, I don't think you are. You loved being married. But I know I'm never going to try the marriage thing again."

"You just need some time to heal. Brett hurt you big-time."

"No. I'm serious. I'm never going to do it again. I'm just going to focus on what's best for my kids and for me. I'm going to find a job, and raise my kids to be decent, respectable human beings."

"I'll tell you what. If neither one of us ever find someone else, we'll help each other with all five of our kids. How does that sound?"

"I think it sounds like a great deal, Ben. Katy would like that, wouldn't she?"

"Yep. When I married her, I got the family I never had. I think if she's watching us right now, she's happy that we're helping each other out. And we'll stick together, okay?"

"I like that idea, Ben. And I liked that idea about looking for a job here in Laurelville. This is a nice town, even if we can't go out for pizza without drawing a crowd of curious neighbors." She giggled again.

"You never told me what you and Brett decided for the weekend."

"He wants the kids Saturday morning and for lunch. I guess his girlfriend has plans for Saturday night. I told him I'd meet him at Mom and Dad's house at nine."

"Did you tell him you're living out here this summer?"

"Yeah. He really didn't seem to care as long as he didn't have to drive out here to get the kids. I told him I'd meet him in town every other weekend, and he should call me if he wants to see the kids any other time. As big of a jerk as he is, he's still their dad."

"You're a good woman, Abby. So, are you going to stay at your parents' house all weekend?"

"No. I'll be back here by four on Saturday. You have a date, don't you?"

"If you're sure you don't mind. I can have supper ready for all of you when you get home. I'm not meeting her until eight."

"You're taking her out for a late dinner?"

"Yeah. There's a little Italian place between here and Tampa. One of my clients told me about it. I guess the food is good and it's quiet. I'm hoping I can get her to open up a little bit. She's really a very nice person, but I feel like she's a little mysterious."

"Mysterious? In what way?"

"I can't explain it…she just wasn't very open about her past, and why she came here from Ohio. She doesn't have any family here…says her church family is making up for the family she left behind. Does that sound weird to you?"

"A little bit. But maybe it's just because we are so close to our family members. That reminds me. Could you tell me a little bit more about your sister? I had this spooky feeling the other day about her. What if you're gone, and she shows up and wants to see Molly? What would I do?"

"I don't think she's going to show up, Abby. She lives in a different world, one that doesn't include family and kids."

"But she's also a mother, Ben. I can't imagine giving birth to a child, then never wanting to see her again. Momma said she ached for Katy every day after she gave her to the Clintons."

Ben had heard the story of his wife's birth many times. He had heard Momma Beth's side, and he had heard Linda's side. His wife had one mother who placed her child for adoption out of love, and another one who took her into her heart and life as if Katy was born to her.

"But Sage isn't like Momma Beth. She was wild as a child, rebellious as a teen, and has been unloving to her family as an adult. She doesn't want Molly, I'm sure of it."

"So, you don't think I have to worry about her showing up on your doorstep some day?"

"No. But if she would, you lock her out, and call the police. I have legal custody of her."

"Okay, if you say so. Hey, don't you have to get those new linens washed before you go to bed? You threw the other ones away, didn't you?"

"I guess I better." Ben got up to retrieve the packages he brought from the store, and Abby followed him.

"You want some decaf coffee while you're waiting for them to wash and dry?"

"Sure. And I'm hungry again. I don't think I digested that pizza very well with all those people staring at us tonight. Didn't we get some ice cream at the store?"

"Yeah. I'll get the coffee started while you do your wash."

*****

The two of them sat at the table and talked for the next two hours. They talked about the kids, their past, and their futures. And they talked about Katy. She had been wife to Ben and sister to Abby.

Abby had been able to talk about her grief with their parents, but Ben hadn't really been able to talk to anyone about his. He had kept it inside. But, knowing that Abby loved and missed Katy as much as he did seemed to open the floodgates of his broken heart.

There were a couple times when he got tears in his eyes, but it didn't bother him that Abby saw them. She understood—she had loved Katy too.

"I don't know why, Abby, but taking those old linens off the bed I shared with her was something I didn't think I'd ever be able to do. But I've come to the realization that I don't need them anymore. I have something far more precious than some tattered linens. She'll always be a part of who I am. I have my memories, and I have Sam. I'm even thinking it might be time to get rid of her clothes in the closet and in the dresser."

"That's a huge step, Ben." He saw the tears in Abby's eyes now.

"I know. But, she's gone...and she doesn't need them anymore. I thought about taking them up to the used clothes store; they're too nice to just throw away."

"But what if you'd go to the store someday and see someone wearing something she used to wear. Wouldn't that hurt?"

"Probably. But what else would I do with them?"

"Why don't you put them in a mission box? Dad's church is always sending boxes to places that have had some kind of natural disaster. Katy would like knowing her things went to someone who really needed them."

"That would be a good idea, wouldn't it? Do you think you could help me pack them up some day? And take them to your mom and dad's house?"

"If you think you're ready, I will." She looked at him intently. There had been the hint of resignation in his voice. This had to be so hard for him. But Abby knew enough about grief that she also knew he needed to do it if he was going to heal completely. He wouldn't be able to fully love again, until he had healed completely.

"Maybe we could do it some Wednesday when I'm home, and your mom and dad come again to watch the kids. Do you think your mom would want anything of Katy's?"

"She might. But I've got a feeling she will think she already got the best of Katy when she got you and Sam."

"Yeah. Things really don't matter that much, do they? In the end, it's family that's most important."

"Are you going to keep anything, Ben?"

"Yeah, I'll keep a few things that Sam might want someday. You know that shawl that you and I bought her for the weekend I proposed to her? Maybe I'll keep that, and her wedding dress. And I have her diamond and wedding ring in the safe. He might have a wife and a daughter someday who would like to see two of the things that were important to his mother."

Abby laughed. "Do you remember the day you and I bought that shawl for her? She called me when you guys got back from the mountains, and I think she was half mad that I knew she was getting engaged before she knew."

"She didn't stay mad for very long though, did she?"

"Nope. She was too much in love with you." Abby got up from the table, walked over to him, and gave him a hug. "Thanks, Ben—for making my sister so happy the last five years of her life."

"The pleasure was all mine, Abby." His voice caught, and Abby heard a sob escape from deep inside him. His grief was being resolved, and Abby felt certain of one thing, unlike herself, Ben would love again.

Chapter 24

Abby and the kids left the grove at seven thirty Saturday morning.

"Now what are we going to do, Dad?" Sam had asked to go with Abby to see his grandparents, but Ben told him no.

"You, Molly, and I are going to spend the whole day together Sam. I've kind of missed the three of us hanging out together. Why don't we go riding this morning, then we can go swimming at Grandma and Grandpa's pool this afternoon?"

"It won't be as much fun swimming without Kyle and Konnor."

"Hey! We used to have all kinds of fun without them." Ben grabbed his son and ruffled his hair. "We'll put Molly in the pack-n-play at Grandma's for her nap, and the two of us can swim while she sleeps. But right now, I think Duchess and Jake are calling our names."

"Can we ride all morning, Dad?"

"Sure." Ben put Molly in the backpack and strapped her in. She felt like she'd gained a little weight this week. Abby must be feeding her well.

"Da-da-da" Ben stopped. Had his little girl just called him "Da-da?"

"Hey, Sam. Did you hear that? Molly just called mc dad."

"Yeah. Aunt Abby practiced with her all week. She kept saying...'Molly, your da-da is coming home.'"

"Really? So Aunt Abby taught Molly to say my name?"

"Yeah. I think she likes taking care of babies. She and Alexandria play with Molly all the time."

"Does Aunt Abby play with you guys too?"

"Sometimes during quiet time, she'll play games with us. She's pretty cool, Dad. Maybe you should marry her."

"How come you keep trying to marry me off, Sam? I told you, the three of us are doing okay together, aren't we?"

"Yeah. But it's more fun when there's a mom around."

Ben felt the sting. He had thought he was a good enough parent to make up for the loss of Sam's mom. But he had to agree. Their home had come to life with Abby's arrival. A woman brought a warmth to a home that could be felt, even by a baby. Katy told him once that she believed men and women were equal in their worth to a family, but each brought their own strengths to it. Their home had lost Katy's strengths in the past few years, and Ben knew it.

"Well, let's go have some fun riding the horses today. We need to check the Valencia orange trees, and I'm thinking we should take the fishing poles. We haven't caught that old catfish for awhile."

"Cool! Kyle and Konnor wanted to go fishing this week, but I told them we had to wait till you can take us. I bet they're gonna be mad when they find out we went without them."

"Sam, I'm really proud that you told them to wait till I was home. Maybe we can take them fishing tomorrow."

"Tomorrow is church. You going with me again, Dad?"

"We'll see, Sam. I'm not sure what your Aunt Abby wants to do yet." After the circus they had created at the pizza place this week, Ben wasn't sure he wanted to do it again at church. Just the thought of sitting between Abby and Leah at church made him cringe. That was attention he could do without.

*****

It was three in the afternoon before Ben and the kids got back to the house after swimming, and he had told Abby he'd have supper ready for all of them when she returned. Molly had napped already, so Ben put her in the high chair with some toys while he began to search the kitchen for something to cook.

In the week Abby had been there, she had rearranged his kitchen and his life. It looked like the cupboards had been cleaned and restocked. And for some reason, Ben felt like he was invading her space. If they hadn't just had pizza two days ago, he would have ordered it for tonight.

Then he saw the sloppy joe mix in the cupboard and knew he could handle that. Hopefully they had hamburger and buns in the freezer. Some potato chips and ice cream with the meal would make him a hero in the kids' eyes.

By the time Abby and the kids got back home, it was close to five and Ben had everything ready. She put her bags down, and looked around. Then she burst into laughter.

"What? What's so funny?"

"What's so funny? Look at my kitchen! It looks like a tornado hit it." Ben looked around. She was right. He had cooked one thing and made a mess. What had happened to him? He didn't used to be this messy. But then, he wasn't used to cooking for seven people either.

"Sorry. I'll clean it up after we eat."

"I think your main job after supper is washing the tomato sauce off your face. Dr. Leah won't be impressed." She grinned at him, but cut it short when he frowned at her and shook his head. He nodded toward Sam and put his finger to his lips. He really didn't want Sam to know who he was going out with tonight. Abby looked chastised and mouthed the word, "sorry."

"Hey, kiddos, let's eat. Uncle Ben made supper for us."

"Potato chips! Good job, Uncle Ben. They're my favorite kind of vegetable." Now it was Ben's turn to laugh.

"Yeah, mine too." He just shrugged his shoulders when Abby scowled at him.

The talk at supper was about the morning the kids spent with their dad. Brett had taken them shopping and bought all three of them an expensive toy. Ben could see the muscles in Abby's jaws moving as she tightened them. When she looked at him, her eyes were wet. Ben felt the anger rise up on the inside of him. Abby was the one who cared for and disciplined her kids all week. She was the one who bought the necessities for them out of the meager child support checks, but it was their dad who was the good guy in their eyes tonight.

"What did you do all day, Sam?" Kyle was still stuffing potato chips into his mouth.

"Me and Dad went fishing. We caught four fish."

"Cool. Uncle Ben…can you take us fishing too?"

"Maybe tomorrow, guys. Right now, we need to get these dishes to the sink and all of you into the bathtub. Abby, I'll clean up here if you want to start your kids' baths."

"No. You take care of your two first. I have the rest of the night." Ben could have kissed her. He had a lot to do yet. He probably should have canceled the date with Leah. He was tired, and he still had a long night in front of him.

*****

Abby said she would tuck his kids into bed for him while he got ready. Sam was still awake when he went in to kiss him good-night.

"Where are you going, Dad?"

"I have a meeting with someone tonight, Sam." Ben sat on the edge of his son's bed.

"You flying somewhere?"

"No, I'm just going to go talk to someone. You need to get to sleep now, okay?"

"Are you going to church in the morning? Aunt Abby said I could show Kyle and Konnor where their class is when we go." There was hope in his son's eyes.

"We'll see. I might just stay home with Molly, and let you go with them, okay?"

"But I like it when you go with me." The hope in the blue eyes turned to disappointment.

"I know, Sam. We'll talk about it in the morning. Now get to sleep." He kissed the top of Sam's head then went over to ruffle the hair of the other two boys. "You guys get to sleep too, if you want to go fishing tomorrow."

When he left their room, he heard them whispering. Somehow this summer, he was going to find a way to help Abby's boys understand that it wasn't expensive toys that made them happy, it was time spent doing fun things.

Abby was in the kitchen doing the dishes. "Sorry, I'm leaving you with the mess. I really should have canceled this date tonight. I owe you one, okay?"

"Don't worry about it. You go and have a good time." She seemed tired tonight, like she had been when she arrived last week.

"Did you have a hard day?"

"Yeah. But I'm okay."

"You want me to stay home with you?"

She looked shocked. "No, Ben. I don't want you to stay home. Go...have a good time. I'll be better tomorrow." She picked up a towel to dry her hands and almost pushed him out the door. "I just need some time alone. I'll get it now that the kids are in bed. You just go and have fun."

Ben still had to call Leah when he got in his truck. He was going to be late.

"It's okay, Ben. Kids need their dad to tuck them in at night. I'll be here when you get here."

And she was. When she opened the door, Ben was struck again at how pretty she was. She wasn't drop dead gorgeous. Her beauty was a natural beauty that seemed to radiate from her core. In fact, it looked like she didn't even have much make-up on.

"Hey...you finally made it. Come on in."

"We probably should go. I made reservations."

"Do you think it would be okay if we didn't go out tonight, Ben?"

"Well, yeah, but why?" He stepped inside her house.

"I don't know. I just had a feeling you'd be tired after taking care of the kids all day, and I thought it would be nice if we just stayed in and talked. I have food here we can eat when we get hungry."

"Are you a mind-reader too? I was thinking on the way over here how late it is already, and how I should have planned this better. You sure you're okay with not going out?"

"I'm sure. I think we need to talk tonight. Let me get us something to drink, and we can go out and sit beside the pool. It's not too bad out there, and the enclosure keeps the bugs away."

He followed her to the kitchen and watched as she took glasses out of the freezer and filled them with ice. She was wearing a full skirt that brushed the top of her knees and a delicate white blouse. Her hair was down again, and Ben knew before the night was over he was going to touch it. He wanted to see if it felt as silky as it looked. Katy's hair had been dark and heavy, and he had loved how it felt in his hands. But Leah's hair would feel different, he could tell just by looking at it.

"I bought some soda for you. Is that okay?"

"I thought you didn't believe in sugary drinks."

"I don't believe in them for me. You are more than welcome to a sugar high." She smiled at him as she handed him the glass.

"That was nice of you. Thank you." He took a sip of it. Looking at her made his mouth feel dry.

"No problem...let's go outside, okay?" She led him through the great room he had been in before and out the patio doors to the enclosed pool area. It was more beautiful at night than it had been during the day. The waterfall at the far end of the pool had lights in it, and the bushes and trees had spotlights on them. It looked like a tropical garden.

"Wow. This is beautiful. Did you do this landscaping yourself?

"I designed it, but I hired it done." He walked to the other side of the pool so he could get a better look at the plants that looked so lush they almost looked artificial. She followed him.

"So you must like to swim."

"I do. It's great exercise. When I get home from work, I want a nice place where I can relax. It probably makes me look self-indulgent, but it's a little piece of paradise I felt I deserved after working so hard at med school."

"I'm sure you deserved to do something nice for yourself. Med school must have been tedious."

"It wasn't easy. And my home is where I need to find peace."

"Thank you again for this."

"For what?"

"For not having to go out tonight. I needed peaceful tonight too, and relaxing here with you feels like medicine a doctor would order."

"Very funny. I'm just glad you're okay with it. Do you want to go over and sit?" She led him back to the lounge chairs she had placed side by side.

"So did you work today?"

"Just around here." He noticed that there was a book on one of the chairs, and he wondered if she'd been sitting out here waiting for him. "Tell me about your day. How are Sam and Molly?"

"We had a wonderful day. Abby took her kids into Tampa to see their dad, so the three of us got to hang out by ourselves. Guess what Molly did today."

"What?"

"She called me Da-da today. Sam said Abby's been teaching her all week."

Leah smiled. "It sounds like Abby is doing a good job for you. What about Sam? What did the two of you do today?"

"We rode our horses, then went fishing."

"That sounds wonderful. I miss riding and fishing."

"Really? When did you ever go riding and fishing? For some reason, I picture you growing up in a more sophisticated setting."

She smiled and put her head back on the recliner. Ben looked up too and noticed that the stars could be seen through the pool enclosure.

"You have the picture all wrong, Ben. I grew up in the simplest of homes in Ohio. But we did have horses."

"So you learned to ride? I did too, in Texas, where I grew up. You'll have to come out to the grove sometime and ride Duchess. Sam would love to give you a tour."

"I would like that. How many horses do you have?"

"Just two. My Duchess is the mother of Sam's horse, Jake. I bought them on his first birthday. I wanted him to be able to ride like I did when I was a kid."

"That's sounds wonderful."

"So did you have your own horse growing up?"

"No. We had work horses." She paused for a few seconds.

"Like Clydesdales?"

"No. Draft horses and a few Standardbreds."

"Really? Did your family have a lot of them? What kind of work did they do?"

"They pulled plows and buggies. I grew up in an Amish home."

Ben was speechless for a minute. *Amish? Leah was Amish? But it did explain things. Her gentle ways, her simplicity, and her fascination with the small things in life that he took for granted. It explained her deep faith too.*

Chapter 25

"I know. It's difficult to picture, isn't it?" She was watching his face.

"Actually, no. For some reason, it isn't. I don't know a lot about the Amish culture, but what I do know helps me to understand you a little better. I knew you were different for some reason." She looked away from him, and he felt foolish for calling her different. "Different in a good way, Leah. In all the ways I've come to admire in you. Can you tell me about it? How and why you left?"

"Sure. There aren't a lot of people here who know about it. But I know there are people who are curious about why I don't talk about my family a lot. It's just hard. I miss them, and unless you hear the whole story, it's difficult to understand."

"So, you don't see your family at all?"

"No. So you don't know much about the Amish?"

"I can't say that I do. But I'd like to, if you want to share."

The story she told Ben that night was not only fascinating, it increased his respect and admiration for her.

She was the oldest of ten children. From the time she was a little girl, she'd been in charge of caring for at least one younger sibling. The only time she escaped the difficult work at home was when she went to the small Amish school in her community. But that ended for her after the eighth grade.

"You stopped going to school after the eighth grade? Is that legal?"

"Yes, it is. The Amish in Ohio are exempt from state compulsory attendance beyond the eighth grade due to their religious principles."

"So all Amish children only go to school through the eighth grade? Why?"

"The adults are afraid their children will leave if they become more educated."

"What did you learn in school?"

"We concentrated on the basic reading, writing and math skills. And we learned Amish history and values."

"But you're a doctor. How did that happen?"

"Ben, it's a long story. Are you sure you want to hear it tonight?"

"Yes. Definitely. I want to know how you became the person you are today. It must have been difficult."

"It was. When I gradated from the school, I was fourteen. We were also required to have one year of vocational school when we got done with our formal schooling. That was done by our parents and other adults in the community. The girls learn about what would be expected of them as a wife and mother; the boys learn about the roles of being husbands and fathers, and how to make a living." She stopped, took a deep breath, and looked at him. There were questions in her eyes, and he wondered if she thought he was judging her in some way.

"Go on. Tell me about it."

"Well…for the next year, I got up early every day to learn the chores of an Amish woman. In the morning we took care of the garden while it was still cool. We started the wash that was done by hand. I helped with milking the cows, then we went in and prepared breakfast. I helped get my younger brothers and sisters ready for school and fixed their lunches. Then throughout the day I helped do the cleaning, ironing, baking, canning and cooking. In our down time, we women did a lot of sewing."

She stopped talking and closed her eyes. Ben sat quietly. It was difficult for him to see this beautiful woman beside him working like that.

"Leah? I want to know how you got away from it."

"In all those years, I never once thought about getting away. That was my life and the life of my friends. I don't think we even knew it was a hard life because we had nothing to compare it with. And there were a lot of good times too. When I turned sixteen, I was allowed to start socializing more. There's a tradition in the Amish culture called Rumspringa. It's a time when Amish teenagers are allowed to experience worldly activities."

"Is that when you left?"

"Yes. But I didn't leave for the same reason that some Amish teens leave. During that time, a couple of my friends left because they were looking for an easier life. I've heard they returned to the community when they couldn't function in the outside world."

"Why did you leave?"

"It was during that year that my mother had her tenth and last baby. He was born with some congenital defects and was admitted to a large children's hospital in Akron. When he returned home we had community nurses come into our home to help mother care for him. He had so many problems, and as I watched the nurse care for him, something in my heart changed. I knew I wanted to be like that nurse. I wanted to be a healer. My thoughts then were that I could help my own people."

"Why didn't you stay and do that?"

"I couldn't. They wouldn't let me." Ben heard the grief in her voice.

"When my brother died, one of the nurses who cared for him came to the funeral. I still can't believe I did it, but I asked her to help me leave my home so I could become a nurse like her. For her to help me, I had to leave my family and my faith. It was the most difficult decision I have ever made, but I knew I would never be content with living in an Amish community again. I wanted to do more than just exist in a closed up world."

"That must have been so difficult. Have you had any contact with your family since you were sixteen?"

"I've tried. But being treated like an outcast by the ones you love is difficult to deal with. There were a couple of times when I even thought about going back. I missed my family, and the Amish way of life. I felt safe there."

"I still don't understand how you came out of an Amish community and became a doctor."

"It was my nurse friend who made all the difference in my life. She went with me to talk to my parents about what I wanted to do. When they said I couldn't go, I went with her anyways. Her name is Margie, and when she took me into her home, she vowed to help me in any way she could. She hired tutors for me, and I was able to graduate from an English high school when I was nineteen. She coached me on English culture and helped me adapt to it."

"Where is Margie now?"

"She lives not too far from here, in a community for seniors. That's why I'm here. She helped me when I needed it, and I want to be here for her. She became my second mother. I go see her every Sunday evening."

"Does Margie have any other family?"

"Yes. She has two older sons. They had already left home and were married when she took me in. They both have families and are still in Ohio. They're grateful that I came with her when she decided to retire four years ago."

"So did you go to school to become a nurse like you planned?"

"No. After I graduated from high school, I went into pre-med. It feels like I did nothing in my twenties but go to school."

He had to ask. "No romance?"

She smiled at him. "There've been a couple of guys, but the whole Amish thing kind of freaked them out. I guess they thought I would try to convert them and take them back." She laughed. "I suppose that could be possible, but not probable."

"That's an amazing story, Leah. Do you ever regret becoming English?"

"Only when I think of my family who no longer want me. I'm still glad I was raised the way I was. I learned to work hard, and I learned good values. That training helped me a lot when I was in residency."

"So you settled here in Laurelville to be close to Margie?"

"Yes, I did. And I like it because it's a small country town. I've even driven out by your grove on occasion because it reminds me of the orchard we had at home."

"Well, you're welcome to come out anytime. Can I ask you one more question?"

"Sure."

"Is marriage and motherhood in your plans for the future?" She finished her drink and waited a few seconds before she answered.

"I think I would like to get married if I could find a man who could feel comfortable with my past. But, honestly…I don't see myself having children."

"But you're so good with kids."

"And I love kids. But I feel like I raised my share of children in the first sixteen years of my life. Now I have a career where I get to help children every day. I gave up my family and my community to be a healer, and I need to do that. It seems to be enough for me. Do you think it's selfish of me to not want children of my own?"

"Why would I think it's selfish? You're obviously a very giving person, and you do it every day. I just wonder if you'll ever regret not having the experiences of pregnancy and childbirth. My Katy considered it her greatest contribution to life."

"I don't think I will. Do you know how many Amish babies I cuddled in those years at home? Hundreds! I enjoyed it, but I don't feel like I need it for myself."

Ben was lying back on his lounge chair, looking up into the stars above him. He was in awe of Leah. She was obviously a very strong woman, emotionally. But he could see through that to a heart that was gentle, almost vulnerable. Except for a woman named Margie, she really had no one. And he remembered how that felt before he met Katy. It was lonely.

"Ben?"

"Hmmm?" He turned to look at her. She looked almost angelic in the soft light with her blond hair and white top.

"I hope I haven't scared you off with my story."

"No. You haven't. If anything, I think it makes you more fascinating to me." Their chairs were touching, and he reached over and took her hand. "I think you're a very strong woman, and I like strong women. My life has been full of strong women. My grandmother was one."

"I'd love to hear about her some day, but I'm starving. Are you hungry? For some reason when I think or talk about my Amish family, I get hungry. Those women do know how to cook."

"Can you cook like them?"

"That's one thing I did take away from there that they can't have back. I know how to cook. I have a cherry cobbler in the kitchen. You want some?"

"A real cherry cobbler made from scratch?"

"Of course, is there any other kind?"

He still had her hand in his. It felt tiny and soft. He held on to it while he got up, and pulled her to her feet. For a few second, they stood inches apart and just looked at each other. Then he pulled her close and his hands went to the long hair hanging down her back. It was as soft and silky as it looked.

"Leah?" The top of her head was below his chin again.

"Hmmm?"

"Thanks for sharing your story with me."

"Thank you for listening. It felt good to tell it to you." He kept her hand in his until they got to the kitchen.

When he saw the cherry cobbler, he was really quite happy that she had been raised Amish.

Chapter 26

––––––––––––––––––––

Ben didn't get home until after midnight. But as tired as he was, he couldn't turn his brain off. Dr. Leah Miller had totally captivated him.

When he left her house, she asked him if he would be in church the next morning. He didn't think twice before answering her. If she was going to be there, he wanted to be too.

At one a.m., he was still awake. It was unusual for him to lie awake. After getting up at 4:23 every morning, he was usually asleep before his head hit the pillow. But not tonight, his brain was full of Leah. He was even fascinated with her name. She had told him that the Amish usually name all their children after people in the Bible.

"I don't remember a Leah from the Bible," he told her.

"Leah was the first wife of Jacob. Remember...he worked for seven years for the younger daughter, Rachel...then ended up with the ugly older sister?"

"Oh, right. Well you don't take after the ugly Leah in the Bible."

"But I want to be like Leah. People always talk about the beautiful love story between Jacob and Rachel, but Leah was the one with character. Even though she knew Jacob loved her little sister more, she remained faithful and loyal to him. She had an inner beauty that God loves."

Ben had never been particularly interested in the old Bible stories, but as Leah shared the story with him, he became fascinated by it. She told him that even though Rachel was beautiful and the one Jacob loved, it was Leah who had the honor of giving birth to

Judah. And it was through the descendants of Judah, that Jesus was born.

"My mother named me Leah because she wanted me to have the inner beauty of the Biblical Leah. She told me there are two kinds of beauty. There's the kind that God gives at birth, but mother said it withers like a flower. She wanted me to have the inner beauty that God gives through His grace when we're born again. Mother told me that kind of beauty never vanishes and will bloom eternally."

"I think God blessed you with both kinds of beauty, Leah."

"Thank you, Ben. You know, you could be Amish with a name like Benjamin."

"I could, couldn't I? But I really like to be called Ben. If you start calling me Benjamin, I'll think you're going to drag me back to the Amish farm. And I wouldn't be able to fly my Cessna if I was Amish." Ben's mind flashed back to the day they went flying and she'd called his Cessna a buggy. The memory made him smile now.

They had been in the great room by then. They were both on the couch looking at some pictures she'd taken of her old home. There were no pictures of her family though, just pictures of the house, the barn, the fields, and the horses and buggies.

"You don't have any pictures of your family."

"No. And I never will. They are opposed to pictures being taken of them."

"Leah, I'm so sorry. I can tell you still love them a lot."

"I do, Ben. But, so far, God's love has more than made up for what I don't get from them anymore."

Ben wanted to tell her that he would be more than willing to give her the human love that everyone should experience at least once in a life time. But he didn't, he just put his arm around her and drew her close. He didn't realize he was kissing the top of her silky blond head until he stopped. She looked up at him in surprise. Then he was surprised when she drew his face down to hers and kissed him gently on the lips.

As Ben tossed and turned in his bed, he knew he wanted to kiss, and be kissed by her again.

*****

Ben woke the next morning to the sound of children's voices. *What are those kids doing up this early? It's only 4:23 in the morning.*

But it wasn't 4:23, it was light outside. Ben jumped from his bed. What had he done? Had he really overslept? He never slept in. He always woke every morning at 4:23 so he could have some time to think about Katy.

"Dad? Are you in there?"

"Yeah, Sam. I'll be right out." What would Abby think? He had bailed on her last night, and now here he was sleeping in when he should be up taking care of his kids. He pulled on a shirt and his jeans and opened the door. Sam and his two cousins were waiting for him on the other side.

"Dad. Why are you still in bed? Aunt Abby wants to know if you're sick."

"No, Buddy. I just went to bed late last night and didn't wake up."

When he walked into the kitchen, Abby turned from the stove and smirked at him. When she spoke, there was laughter in her voice. "Long night, Ben?" Her shoulders were still shaking when she returned to her pancakes.

He went to the cupboard to get a cup out for his coffee. The fact that their shoulders were touching when he did it, didn't escape his attention. She nudged him gently. "So, was a good time had by all?"

"Stop it. I can't talk about this now. What do you want me to do?"

"You can get the kids some milk and give them each a banana. I'll finish the pancakes, if you want to go get Molly. I can't believe she's still asleep."

Ben got the kids settled then went to Molly's room. "Hey, baby-girl. It's time to wake up." She popped her head up and grinned at him. She now had two bottom teeth, and they looked like two little pearls when she smiled.

"Da-da-da."

"That's right. Dad's here." He picked her up and flew her through the air to the changing table. "It's a good thing I have you Molly-girl. I may never have any more babies."

While he changed her diaper, Ben thought of Leah and what she'd said about not wanting children of her own. He wondered if he could get her to change her mind. *What am I thinking about? One kiss, and I'm thinking about getting her pregnant already!*

He wanted to talk to Abby about her. Abby would help him think straight.

When he and Molly returned to the kitchen, he stopped at the door for a minute and looked around. He couldn't believe how much his life had changed in one short week. Last Sunday morning, there had been just three people eating breakfast. Today there were seven. The noise level had increased dramatically—and he liked it.

He put Molly in her highchair and went to get her baby cereal out of the cupboard.

"She really likes pancakes and bananas and milk mushed up together. I gave it to her one day and she has refused that cereal ever since."

"Now you're introducing my child to fine cuisine?"

"Have you ever tasted that baby cereal?" She made a nasty face.

"Can't say that I have."

"She also likes scrambled eggs."

"Is she supposed to be eating that kind of food? I thought she was supposed to have just formula and cereal for the first six months."

"She's almost seven months."

"Okay…but eggs? Really?"

"I just gave her a bite. But we need to start her on some vegetable baby food."

"Leah told me I could wait on that."

"You can. But she sees all these other kids eating good stuff, and I can tell she wants to, too." Ben could tell she was arguing with him just for the fun of it.

"You just think you know everything because you're a mom, don't you?"

"No, I'm just in the mood to give you a hard time today, since you stayed up until all hours of the night then slept in like some teenager." She grinned at him again. "I can hardly wait to hear that story."

"Well, it's going to have to wait. Sam says you're going to church with us today."

"You're going? He told me you were staying home with Molly."

"Changed my mind. Women aren't the only ones who can do that."

"Or was it a woman who changed yours? Sam also told me Dr. Leah goes to your church."

"What did you do, give my kid the third degree?"

"Nope, he offered all information willingly." Ben was glad Sam was busy talking to his cousins and didn't hear their whispered conversation as they stood by the stove while she flipped more pancakes.

"Sam also told me your church has two services. I assume, since you slept in, we're going to the second one? Tell me again…why did you have to sleep in today?" She just wouldn't stop, and he heard her soft laugh.

"Abby, I promise I'll tell you all about the date when we have more time. Okay?"

"It's a deal. You want some of these pancakes, or are you too love-sick to eat?"

"Very funny. Actually, I brought home half of a home-made cherry cobbler last night. I think I'll eat some of that."

"Homemade cherry cobbler? Okay, mister…you may have had all the fun last night, but I get some of that." So while the kids finished up the pancakes, Abby and Ben ate cobbler. He was quite sure it was the best thing he had ever eaten in his whole life.

*****

Ben and Abby found an empty seat in the back of the church after taking the kids to their classes. Abby had been there before, for Katy's funeral. She looked at Ben, and when their eyes met he knew she was thinking the same thing. "You okay being here?" he whispered.

"If you can do it, so can I. Is Leah coming?"

"She said she was, but she's also taking call for someone today. Maybe she won't make it."

It was probably a good thing Leah didn't come to church that day. Ben knew he would have been distracted by her sitting beside him. Without her there, he actually listened to the sermon. It was about a young man in the Bible who came to Jesus and asked what he had to do to be a follower. Jesus told the man he needed to leave every thing and every one behind, and follow him.

The pastor told his congregation if they were in church today for any other reason than to follow Jesus, they were there for the wrong reason.

"Some of you are here out of a sense of obligation or because you will feel guilty if you don't come. Others of you came just to see your friends. But I want to tell you, this is a place where you can come to find Jesus, to ask forgiveness, and to begin a personal relation with the one who created you. You can't have that just because you're a good moral person, you must ask for forgiveness. The Bible tells us that all of us have sinned. But that can be fixed through Jesus."

Ben knew he had never had a personal relationship with God. His grandmother had taken him to church as a child, and he had gone to church with Katy from the time he met her. But Ben knew it wasn't enough. Even though he was a good moral person, he had never admitted that he was a sinner and asked for forgiveness. He also knew he wanted to do that. And he knew he would— someday.

Chapter 27

After lunch, Abby told Ben she'd stay home while Molly napped, if he wanted to take the boys fishing. When Alexandria cried to go along, Ben assured Abby it would be fine. He sensed that the little girl missed her dad more than the boys did.

He loaded the excited kids and fishing equipment into the golf cart and took off toward the lake. By the time Ben got four hooks baited and helped Alexandria and Konnor get their lines untangled from the tall grasses, Kyle was pulling in his first fish.

"Look, Uncle Ben. I got one!" Kyle was grinning from ear to ear, and the other three threw down their poles to go inspect the fish that unfortunately died before Ben could get the hook out of it. Alexandria started to cry.

"Lexie...why are you crying, honey?"

"The fish is dead." And she wailed even louder

"Don't cry, Lexie. That just happens sometimes." Sam was doing his best to comfort his cousin, but she wasn't to be comforted.

"Come here, Lex. Come sit on my lap for a minute." Ben took the little girl in his arms and went to sit on the glider. "It's okay, sweetheart. It's just an old fish. I think it was time for him to die anyways."

"B-b-but, what are we going to do with him?"

"We'll just throw him back into the lake where he came from."

"Nooo, Uncle Ben. You have to bury dead things and have a funeral. My Grandma died, and we had to have a funeral."

Ben remembered that Brett's mom died a year ago. Surely, the little girl didn't remember that. "Alexandria, honey…we bury people when they die, not fish."

"No. We have to bury the fish."

Ben didn't know what else to do, but bury the fish. He was glad he brought the shovel to dig worms for bait. "Boys! Bring that fish over here. Alexandria wants to bury it."

Abby found them ten minutes later in a circle around a hole in the ground.

"What's going on?"

"We're having a funeral for a dead fish."

Her lips twitched. "Let me guess. Alexandria's idea?"

"Yep. I don't think she's going to be a very good fisherman." Ben rolled his eyes at Abby.

"Sorry. She's real sensitive these days. I'll talk to her."

"I'll go bait Kyle's hook again." Ben pointed to the boys who had gone back to their fishing poles.

"Don't you think they need to learn to do that themselves if they're going to fish?"

"Then we'll have to deal with fish hooks stuck in their hands."

"They'll be okay. Let them go and come over and sit. I still need to hear about the date last night." She grinned at him as she turned to comfort her daughter.

Ben went to the side of the lake. "Okay, guys, I'm going to show you one more time how to bait your hooks, then you'll have to do it yourself. It's not that hard." He spent a few minutes watching the boys perfect their hook baiting technique, then turned back to Abby.

"I think you're just being nosy."

"You bet I am. I was hoping to meet Leah in church today." She was rocking Molly who acted like she was still tired, and was sucking on her thumb.

"I thought you were going to talk to Alexandria. Where is she?"

"I told her to go pick flowers for the fish's grave. It will be therapeutic for her."

Ben looked around and noticed the little girl happily picking wild flowers to put on the new grave. Once again, he was in awe of Abby.

"How did you learn to be such a good parent? To know what your kids need?"

"My momma taught me how to be a momma. A good example is the best teacher. Who taught you to be a good dad?"

"I'm not sure. I don't remember much about my dad. Maybe I learned by recognizing what I missed. I wanted more for Sam."

"Yeah. I can see that. Now, sit. Tell me the truth about Doctor Leah. Is she as perfect as you thought she'd be?"

Ben felt a little bit embarrassed. He had never had anyone to discuss his love life with. It seemed like something girls did, but not guys. Maybe Abby was just lonely and needed adult conversation. "She's pretty amazing. We ended up spending the whole evening at her house, just talking." Ben spent the next half hour telling Abby about Leah.

"She's Amish?"

"She was. I'm still in awe that she had the courage to follow her heart and do what she felt she needed to do. It sounds like her community has a pretty strong hold on their young. For her give up the safety of her home and family is pretty admirable."

"I can't wait to meet her. I think I'm going to like her. So…is she a good kisser?"

"Now you are getting nosy, sister. But just so you won't worry about it, yes, she is."

"I knew it. You are smitten. Ben, I'm so excited for you. So, does she have any faults?"

"I haven't seen any yet. But let me ask you something. Do you think it's unusual for her not to want any kids?"

"She doesn't want kids? Why?"

"It's part of the whole Amish thing." He explained her reasoning to Abby, hoping it would begin to make more sense to him.

"I understand it, Ben. Not all women need to be mothers to feel fulfilled. Why? Do you think you want more kids?"

"I don't know. Katy wanted me to get married again, so Sam could have siblings."

"He has a sister. I asked you if you wanted more kids."

Ben didn't know how to answer that question. He loved being a dad to Sam and Molly. He assumed he would have more kids if he ever got married again. But, did he have to have more children? It was something he would have to think about if he wanted to have a relationship with Leah, especially if she was really serious about not having children.

*****

Ben called her later that night after the kids were all in bed. He told Abby he was going to walk to the barn and do some work there.

"Okay. Tell Leah I said Hi." It was going to be pretty difficult to keep any relationship he might have with Leah, a secret from his sister-in-law. Not that it needed to be a secret from her. He would need Abby's help with the kids if he was going to spend more time with Leah.

She answered her phone on the second ring.

"Hi, Ben." If she knew it was him who was calling, that meant she had his number on her phone. The thought made Ben smile.

"Hi. How was your day?"

"Very busy. Next time I take call for someone, I'm going to do it on a week day. Weekends are crazy. And I had to miss church. How was it?"

"It was good. The sermon was thought provoking."

"How so?"

"We'll talk about it later. I'm calling to let you know the cobbler is gone, and Abby loved it. She wants to meet you. And I'm wondering…are you off again this Wednesday?"

"I am. Are you flying?"

"No. But I was wondering if I could take you and Abby to lunch. I think she's kind of lonely out here and could use a friend. If I can get her mom to watch the kids for a couple of hours, we can go to the Italian place for lunch."

"Sure. That sounds fine. I'd love to meet her. But when are the two of us going to get together again?"

"Would you like to come out to the grove some evening? We could show you around." Ben was feeling some frustration. He had just been with Leah last evening, and he wanted to see her already. But it was going to be difficult to find the time. He couldn't be leaving his kids with Abby all the time.

"I thought you didn't want Sam to know about me."

"Maybe you could come as Abby's friend."

"I don't know, Ben. Let me think about it. Is there anyway you could come to my house tomorrow evening, maybe after the kids are in bed? I'm not on call, and I usually don't go to bed until about midnight."

"I'll talk to Abby about it. I have a charter in the morning, but should be home in time to help her with supper and spend the evening with them." Ben felt hopeful. Maybe he and Leah could find time to be together in the evenings after the kids were in bed. "I'll call you tomorrow and let you know."

"That sounds good, Ben. I had a really nice time with you last evening. I can't wait to see you again."

Ben felt the pace of his heart quicken. She liked him…at least it sounded like she did. And he knew he liked her. A lot.

"The feeling is mutual, Leah. You have a good day tomorrow, and I'll call you at lunch time…if that's okay."

"That would be perfect. And I really hope you can come over tomorrow evening."

"I'll try."

Chapter 28

_____

When Ben returned to the house, Abby was at the kitchen table with her laptop.

"Did you tell her I said hi?"

"I did. And she wants to meet you too. I suggested that the three of us go out to lunch on Wednesday when your mom is here. Is your dad coming too?"

"He said he was going to try to come with mom on Wednesdays. He usually takes Mondays off from the church work, but says he'll change it for the summer so he can come out and spend time with the kids. Are you sure you want me to go to lunch with the two of you? I'll be kind of a third wheel, won't I?"

"I promise I won't be asking you to go along to chaperone too often. I just want the two of you to meet. And I was wondering if you'd mind if I go over tomorrow evening, after the kids are all in bed."

"Of course not. I'm working on my resume right now and am planning on spending my evenings finding places to send it. You aren't going over tonight?"

"No. I think I'm going to start sorting through some of Katy's things."

She gave him a quizzical look. "Okay. I'll be here if you need any hclp."

Ben checked on all the kids before he went to his room. Alexandria was finally sleeping in the twin bed in Molly's room. By the soft glow of their night light, Ben could see the faces of both little girls. Lexie had her mother's dark hair and complexion, and Molly was just the opposite with her halo of blond hair. It was finally getting longer, and looked like it might have a little bit of curl in it. Ben's own blond hair would get curly if he let it grow too long. He and Molly got that from his mother.

Two precious little girls. Looking at them, Ben felt such a huge sense of responsibility. Neither one of them had his blood running through their veins, but he felt his heart stir with love. He smiled when he thought of Lexie's tears for a dead fish. How vulnerable they seemed to him as he looked at them.

Closing the door, he went to the boys' rooms. They had decided to switch beds every night so all of them would have a turn in the top bunk. Tonight was Sam's night. With the light from the hall shining into their room, Ben could see all of them. They were three little boys, cousins by love, but no common blood. Family…over the years the definition had changed, but the feelings of love didn't. He and Katy had both come from non-traditional families, and now he had another one under his roof.

And he wondered if Leah would ever be a part of it.

*****

Ben had a lot of time to think when he was flying the next morning. He had spent two hours the night before going through Katy's things. More than once, he caught himself wiping away the tears. He realized again that his wife had not been a great collector of possessions.

Although she had the financial resources to have almost anything she wanted, she had collected only the necessities of life. It was like she had known she was just passing through this earth on her way to a better place, and knew she wouldn't be able to take anything with her.

As he went through her closet and the dresser that contained her clothes, the memories of the two of them together came flooding back to him. When he found two pairs of light blue scrubs, it reminded him of the day he met her in the trauma unit where she worked.

He remembered her frustration with him that day when he couldn't tell her what she needed to know about the patient he brought in on the medical helicopter. He had fallen hard for her that day. He wanted to keep one of the scrub shirts to remember that day, but knew it wasn't necessary. He had the memory of her wearing it. But attached to one of the shirts was the badge that said, "Katy, R.N." He kept that for Sam

Tucked away in the back of the closet, he found three of her maternity tops. She had desperately wanted to give Sam a sibling. She kept those tops even though she'd known for months before she died that she'd never have another child. Perhaps she always had hopes of a miracle. He wanted to keep one of them too, just because he remembered her wearing it the day the two of them visited the grove for the first time. But he knew it wasn't necessary. He had the memory.

As he sorted through her things, he began a pile of the few things he wanted to keep. Things he thought Sam might want to see someday. On his way home tonight, he planned to stop and buy a small trunk to put those precious things in. He would put the trunk in the attic and give it to Sam someday.

When he was done with that, he would let Abby and her mom pack up the rest of her things. It was time.

Right before he had turned off his bedside lamp the night before, Ben took the little notebook from the top drawer and began to read it. *Just one more time, in case I missed something.* But over the past three years, Ben had missed nothing in the book. He had read every word Katy had written…had read her words so many times he knew them by heart. And he knew—he needed to put the little notebook in the trunk with the rest of her things. It was time for him to let go of that too.

*****

Ben left the little trunk in the back of his truck when he got home. He would take it into the house at a later time, when no one was around. He didn't want to explain its purpose to anyone.

Abby looked relieved when he walked into the kitchen. "Rough day today?"

"Not that bad. But I do think the summer honeymoon is over for the kids. Today, they wanted to do everything they know they can't do. The boys wanted to go fishing again, they wanted to go horse back riding, and they wanted to go swimming. They know we don't do those things without you."

"I'm sorry, Abby. I'll be here all day tomorrow, and your parents will be here on Wednesday. Is Molly in bed now?"

"Yes. She was the only good one today."

"I have time to take the four older kids to the barn so they can ride the horses. Why don't you sit and rest for awhile?"

"I don't need to rest. I just need a little peace and quiet. Thanks Ben."

"No problem."

The three boys raced ahead while Lexie stayed back and walked with Ben. About half way to the barn she took his hand, and he smiled down at her. And he knew in his heart, at that moment, that asking Abby to come to the grove this summer had been the right thing to do. As difficult as the day had been for her, he knew her kids were happy here. And his own kids were being well-cared for while he worked. Each of their individual shattered lives was somewhat better because of the other.

Ben and the kids spent two hours at the barn. It took that long for each of them to have a ride, and then for him and Sam to clean the stalls. Kyle was now helping Sam with his chores, but Konnor was not ready to help with horse manure. He and Lexie spent their time running off their energy in the lane.

"Okay kiddos. It's time to wrap things up here. Let's go back to the house and see what we're having for supper."

He insisted they take off their shoes on the deck. Then he got the water hose out so they could wash their hands before going inside. The four of them had settled down, and Ben hoped they would be less rambunctious for Abby now.

Molly was in the pack-n-play, and Abby was setting the table when they all trooped in.   "Hey! I thought the whole bunch of you got lost. If you'd stayed in that barn any longer, you would have missed your supper." Ben was grateful that Abby looked rested and back to her normal, in-control self again.

"Something smells good." She was at the stove again, and he went over and peeked around her shoulder. "You need someone to taste-test anything?" He put his arm around her and gave her a hug. "Do you know how nice it is to have someone else cooking in here?"

"I'm glad it's working out, Ben. But I'm so afraid you're going to get sick of all of us."

"Abby. Stop. I'm glad you and the kids are here. But I just don't want them to wear you out. Five kids is a lot of kids to take care of by yourself."

"I just need to get a little more organized. By the end of the summer, I'll have it perfected."

Supper that night was a pleasant affair. None of the kids complained about the food, and they all talked and joked together. When Molly threw a couple of mashed up green beans across the table, the whole bunch of them burst into laughter. And once she knew she had an audience, she did it again. Ben looked at Abby helplessly. "We shouldn't be letting her do that, should we?"

"Probably not. Kids…we can't laugh at her when she does that again, okay?" The kids all agreed they wouldn't, but when she did it again, they almost fell off their chairs from laughing so hard.

Abby looked at Ben helplessly. "Kids. Now stop it. Molly, that's a no-no." Ben tried to be firm, but knew his voice must have been too harsh when poor little Molly looked around the table at the solemn group, puckered up, and burst into tears. Sam jumped up and ran to her. "It's okay, Molly, don't cry." He put his arms around his little sister and held her close until she stopped crying.

Ben and Abby just looked at each other. Meshing these two families into one was definitely becoming a challenge. But Ben felt certain it was all worth it. When he was a little boy, growing up with only a grandmother, this kind of chaos would have been welcome.

And he wondered if he and his two kids would miss the joys of a large family when the summer was over, and Abby and the kids left.

*****

Ben didn't get to Leah's house until almost nine-thirty that evening. After the day of flying, horse back riding with the kids, then getting them ready for bed, he had to take a shower before he left the house.

She was at the opened door before he got to the sidewalk. She had on a sundress, and her hair was pulled back again. It looked like it was wet. "Hey, come on in. I just got home not too long ago, and I went for a swim. Was your day as long as mine?"

"Probably." He followed her into the house. When they reached the kitchen, she turned to him. "Do you want something to drink?"

"In a minute." He reached for her hand. He hadn't seen her for two days, and he had missed her. "First, I need to hold you for a minute."

She came slowly, but willingly, into his arms. "So you missed me as much as I missed you?"

"I think I missed you more."

"I doubt it." She whispered. He took her face in his hands and leaned down to kiss her softly on the forehead. Then he kissed the tip of her nose, and last of all, her sweet soft lips. He could feel her relax in his arms, so he pulled her closer. She felt so good in his arms.

"Ben?" She broke away from him.

"What?" His voice sounded hoarse.

"Do you want something to drink?" She sounded breathless and he sighed.

"Yeah, sure." It had been a long time since he'd felt such a strong need for a woman. What was it about Leah that had attracted him to her so quickly? Less than three weeks earlier she was just his kids' doctor. That was all. The day he had them in her office, he'd felt nothing for her except gratitude that she cared for his children so well. What was it about her that made him want her so desperately? Was it just because it had been so long since he'd been with a woman who stirred him to his very core?

"Soda, again?"

"That's fine. So you had a busy day?" He couldn't keep his eyes off her as she retrieved his iced glass from the freezer and poured his soda into it.

"Very. I got called at four this morning, and I've been on the go ever since. You?"

"Yeah, my day started early too." Although, for the second morning in a row, he didn't wake up at 4:23.

"You want to go out by the pool again?"

Ben really wanted to go to the couch and pull her onto his lap, but decided the lounge chairs on the patio would be safer.

"Sounds good. So you went for a swim? After such a long day, aren't you too tired to swim?"

"My days are more emotionally exhausting. The swim gets rid of stress. So what did you do when got home from your charter?"

"Abby needed a break, so I took the four oldest kids to the barn to ride the horses. They were able to run off some energy."

"It sounds to me like you and Abby are a pretty good team."

"Yeah, it's turning out to be a pretty good deal for both of us this summer."

"What is she doing tonight?" He could hear the curiosity in her voice.

"She's working on her resume. She's desperately trying to find a job by fall. She wanted something where she could use her art major, but I think at this time, she'll take almost anything that pays a decent wage."

"She could be a substitute teacher. That would work well with her kids."

"She needs health insurance. The kids are still on their dad's policy, but she doesn't have any. She's been a stay at home mom for nine years."

"So, are we still going out to lunch on Wednesday?"

"If you want to. She'd really like to meet you." He reached over and took her hand in his.

"Does she need to meet her competition?"

"Competition?" Ben was confused. What was Leah saying?

"You know…the competition for your time and affections."

"She's my sister-in-law, Leah. I love her because she's Katy's sister, that's all."

"Are you sure? You talk about her like she's more than that." Leah turned on her side to face him.

"Leah…I admire her for her strength, and I respect her for who she is. But she's my sister, and a good friend. I can't believe you'd think she's anything more than that to me. Maybe I need to kiss you again…" He had to grin when she blushed and turned away from him.

"Look at me, Leah." She turned back to him. "I'm not quite sure what's happening between us, but I know something's going on, and it's happening really fast. I haven't been able to stop thinking about you since our trip to Sanibel last week."

"I know, me too. It kind of scares me."

"It scares you? Why?"

"I don't know. I guess because I wasn't planning on you. I've been really content with my life, Ben. I've come to terms with my past, and I love my work. My life has been full, and I'm not sure how to fit you into it. Your life is full too. You have six other people in your life right now."

"So…do you want me to go away and leave you in your contentment?"

"That's just it, Ben. I *was* content. For the past week, I've been wondering if what I have now is enough."

"You really never thought about getting married and having a family of your own?"

"Once in a while. But I told you before, I didn't feel like it was something I had to have."

"You don't get lonely? You don't want that one special person in your life? That someone you can come home to at the end of the day?"

"I didn't think I needed that for myself. But you're changing my thoughts on it, I think. But, I'm not sure I'm the kind of woman that would be good for you, Ben. You need someone like Abby. Someone who loves being in a home taking care of her children. Someone who knows that any job she takes outside the home, is just that—a job. I love my job, Ben. It really isn't even a job, it's more of a calling. I feel like God called me to be a healer. I left the only home, the only family, the only security I knew, to follow that calling. Does that make sense to you?"

"Leah, I think it's wonderful that you love what you do. I appreciate that you make such an important contribution to lives. But don't you deserve to be loved?"

"I am loved. God loves me."

"Are you sure you aren't just hiding behind the calling thing because you're afraid of human love?"

"Human love fails. God's love doesn't."

"But it can also be the most wonderful thing in this world. Don't be afraid to allow that to happen to you."

She was still facing him, and he turned slightly in his chair so he was facing her.

"Ben...to me, love is caring more about the needs and feelings of another than what you care about your own. What if I can't do that? Let's just say, that you and I get together. What if you decide you want more children? I don't want to give up my calling to do that. My work takes most of my time and energy. I would feel like my need to be a doctor is greater than your need for more children."

"Lots of women doctors are also mothers. You never know, you may find that being a mother can also be a calling."

"Did you forget? I mothered lots of Amish babies in the first sixteen years of my life. I know how much time and energy it takes. I won't do both, and I've put too much into my career to give it up."

"It sounds like you've made up your mind on the subject."

"I have. And you love being a dad. If you want more kids, I won't be the one that takes that dream away from you."

"I don't know if I want more kids. Maybe I'm blessed just to have the two I have."

"So, you aren't worried about losing Molly someday? What if your sister comes back and wants her."

"Why do you and Abby keep asking me that? Sage isn't coming back. I am sure of that. In her mind, Molly was an accident, a problem that she was more than willing to give to me. And I'm so glad she did. I love that little girl so much, and I'll never give her up."

"I hope it works out for you, Ben. But I do have a favor to ask of you. I need you to think about whether you want any more kids. If you do, we better call this off right now before our feelings for each other deepen."

"Wow. You've made up your mind, haven't you?"

"Yes. I have, and I don't want to mislead you. I want to be a doctor for children. I want to make them better when they're sick. That doesn't leave any time to mother my own."

"Could you mother the two I have?" He had to ask the question. If he chose her over more children, he had to know if she thought she could be a mother to Sam and Molly.

He saw the corners of her mouth begin to turn up. "Now that I think I could do. Because I know they already have a dad that has the desire to spend as much time with them as he can."

The arms on the lounge chairs between them made kissing difficult, but not impossible.

Chapter 29

On Tuesday, Ben and Abby packed a picnic and took the kids to the city park—the one behind Leah's house.

"See that privacy fence over there, Abby?"

"Yeah. Someone wants to keep the kids from the park out of their yard."

"No, she wants to keep the kids from the park from drowning in her swimming pool."

"Who does?" Abby took off her sunglasses and squinted at the fence.

"That's where Leah lives."

"Really? For some reason, I thought she'd be living in one of those big houses on the edge of town. She could afford one, couldn't she?"

"I suppose. But I don't know, I haven't asked about her finances." He grinned at her. "But that one suits her better. It looks like a humble little house from the outside, but it's beautiful on the inside. You should see her pool. It looks like it was built for a resort somewhere."

"Really? The little Amish girl likes to swim? She's learned a lot since she left her community, hasn't she?"

"When you stop to think about it, she really has. She's thirty-five, that means she's only lived in the outside world for less than twenty years. Sometimes when I look at her, it's hard to believe she used to wear dark dresses down to her ankles and a bonnet on her head. She never even rode in a car until she was sixteen." Ben had his eyes glued to the fence.

He heard Abby chuckle. "What? Why are you laughing at me?"

"Because you're a grown man acting like a star struck school boy. You've got it bad, don't you?"

"It feels like it. But guess what?"

"What?"

"She came right out and told me last night that she won't be changing her mind about having kids. She said if I wanted more, we should call things off right now."

"So she's serious about that. You do have to admire her for knowing what she wants, and what she doesn't want in life."

"But she's such a loving, giving person. She would be a great mother."

"From what you've told me about her, she does her loving and giving to her patients, the kids at church, and to desperate dads who need babysitters." They were sitting side by side on a glider, and she pushed him with her shoulder. "Tell you what. Why don't you marry her, then if you feel like you need more kids around, you can come get mine any time you want. That will fix your need for more kids."

"That might work. But it would mean you'd have to stay here in town. I can't be running into Tampa every week just to spend time with my other kids."

Ben pulled his cell phone out of his pocket to look at the time. "Looks like it's time to round up our kids and feed them. You want to take them swimming at John and Linda's house after this?"

"Sure. Why not? I need to take advantage of this summer with my kids. I'll probably be working next summer, and they'll be in daycare. Ben… how am I ever going to manage that? Everything I make will go to daycare."

"You know what Katy would say, right?"

"Yep. She'd say don't worry about it today. Just put it in God's hands, and let him take care of it. That's really difficult to do sometimes, isn't it, Ben?"

"You said it, sister. Hey… did you call your mom yet to see if she can watch the kids while we go to lunch tomorrow? I told Leah I'd call her at noon to let her know for sure."

"Are you sure you still want to do that, Ben? Why don't you just go with Leah. I can meet her some other time. Or better still…why don't you take her to lunch, then bring her out to the grove to meet mom and dad. I'm sure they'd love to meet her too."

"Nooo… that's too much, too fast. Did you forget, I'm supposed to be thinking about whether we even have a future? I think I just want your opinion of her. Getting your opinion is as close to getting Katy's opinion as I'll get."

"Ben. You shouldn't need Katy's or my opinion. This is your future, not ours."

*****

Ben didn't wake up at 4:23 the next morning either, but he did wake up early. He thought about staying in his room to put Katy's things in the trunk he finally managed to get into the house. But he felt too restless. The dawn was calling his name.

Taking his coffee to the deck once again, he looked to the heavens. The morning star was there. "Katy…you wouldn't believe how much my life is changing this summer. I still miss you, still think about you, but life is so full, there isn't much time. Sometimes I feel guilty about that. I haven't even talked to Sam about you. I don't want him to forget you, but I do want him to enjoy his time of being a little boy. He's doing that this summer. I know you're okay with that."

"Dad? Are you talking to God?"

Ben turned around so quickly, he spilled his coffee.

"Sam. What are you doing up already?"

"I just couldn't sleep anymore. Who were you talking to?"

Ben sat down on the edge of the deck. "Come on over here and sit beside your dad." The little boy padded over to where Ben sat. His feet were bare, and his superman pajamas looked like they were getting too small.

"You see that star over there?" Ben pointed to the brightest one in the pre-dawn sky.

"Yeah?" Ben watched Sam squint while he looked towards the heavens.

"Sometimes when I get up in the morning and see that star, I pretend it's your mom. And I talk to it."

"Sometimes when I wake up, I find the stuffed star she gave me and I hug it really tight."

"That's good Sam. I like that we both have a star that reminds us of your mom. As long as we do, we won't forget her, will we?"

"Sometimes I do forget what she looked like. Then I have to look at her picture."

"That's okay. I think she wants us to not think about her all the time. I think she wants us to just enjoy the days we have, and the other people in our lives."

"Yeah, I'm having fun with my cousins and Aunt Abby this summer." He grew quiet for a moment. "Hey, Dad? Do you think you and me could go ride the horses before the other kids get up?"

"I think that sounds like a great idea, Sam. Let me see if you have any clothes in the dryer. If you go back into your room, you might wake the other guys. And I need to leave a note for your Aunt Abby so she knows where we are."

"Cool. I think Duchess and Jake miss us taking them for long rides."

"They probably do."

Ben helped Sam get his clothes on and left a note for Abby. They should be back by the time Molly woke up and needed him.

The sky was getting light by the time Ben had the horses saddled. "You want to go through the grove, and then to the lake?"

"Yeah. Maybe we can see that blue heron again."

The two of them spent about a half hour in the grove. As they rode through the different sections of the grove, Ben noticed that a good number of the orange blossoms from spring had not dropped, but had clung to the trees to form tiny green fruit. The temperatures and moisture levels had been almost perfect during, and after, the flowering. If conditions remained good, he would have a good harvest this year. If Katy was here, the small green oranges he saw on the trees now would be like babies to her. She loved watching her oranges grow.

"Dad? Dad!" Ben heard his son's voice come through the fog in his brain. Thinking of Katy did that to him.

"What, Sam?" He looked back at his son.

"Can we go to the lake now?"

"Sure. Go ahead of me, you lead the way."

Those words would come back to haunt Ben in the hours ahead. If only he had stayed in the lead.

*****

Abby woke to the smell of coffee. *Ben must be back on his early schedule again.* She smiled when she remembered how embarrassed he was on Sunday when he'd slept in. As she stretched out in her bed, she thought of the day ahead of her.

Her mom and dad would be here by nine and were planning on watching the kids while she went out to lunch with Ben and Leah. She still couldn't figure out why Ben was so adamant that she go with them. He had said something about Abby needing girlfriends in Laurelville, but Abby didn't see the need. She was only going to be here for the summer. And she certainly didn't have time to build relationships right now.

She really thought Ben wanted her to become friends with Leah so he could invite her to the grove and tell Sam that Leah was Abby's friend, not his. He was so protective of Sam and his feelings.

Crawling out of bed, she quickly made it, and put a light robe over her skimpy pajamas. The air was on, but Ben insisted it not be cold in the house. She didn't know if it was because he was thrifty or because he knew it was healthier. The kids didn't need a huge variation in temperatures as they ran from the stifling heat of the outside to the inside throughout the day.

When she reached the kitchen, she immediately noticed the note next to the coffee pot. It would have been impossible to miss, it was a huge piece of notebook paper.

Abby, Sam and I are out riding. I wanted to check the grove today, and he woke early so is going with me. Be back before breakfast.

She wondered why Sam woke so early and went in to check on her own boys. They were both still sound asleep. But then, it usually took them longer to get to sleep at night. Sam was one of those kids who was sound asleep, seconds after his head hit the pillow. It was probably what he was used to after living with two parents who had always been early birds.

When she went in to check on the girls, Molly's head bobbed up. Abby picked her up before she could start babbling. Lexie was a good sleeper, but Abby didn't think she'd sleep through Molly's giggles.

Abby held the little girl close as she made her way to the utility room off the kitchen. She had put some diaper changing supplies in there to save herself some steps during the day. When she put Molly down on the towel she had placed on the washer, she felt her phone in her pocket vibrate. *Who on earth is calling at this hour?*

The read-out on the phone said "Ben."

"Hey, Ben. You guys enjoying your ride?"

"Abby. Listen to me." There was something peculiar about Ben's voice. It didn't sound like him, and she heard it break.

"What? What's wrong?"

"Abby! I need you to stay calm. There's been an accident. Sam's hurt."

"Oh, no! Ben...where are you?"

"Abby. I need you to listen to me. I've called the rescue squad. They'll be coming in a few minutes. When they get here, I want you to direct them to the part of the grove that's directly behind the house. They'll have to drive on the lane between the lake and the orchard. I told them that, but you need to go out front when you hear them and show them where the lane is."

"Is Sam okay, Ben? What happened." Abby felt the fear constrict her throat.

"Something spooked his horse, and he was thrown off. He's unconscious. It looks like he hit his head, and his left arm is twisted under him. I don't want to move him. I just need you to go outside and wait for the squad, okay?"

Abby could hear the control in Ben's voice. And she knew he was putting his own fear aside to make sure his son got treatment as quickly as he could.

"Okay, Ben. I will."

"Are the other kids still in bed?"

"All but Molly."

"I told the squad to turn off the sirens when they got to the lane. I don't want the other kids scared to death."

"I want to be with you, Ben."

"Not right now, Abby. I need you to stay in control. Your mom and dad will be here soon. After they get here, you can come to the hospital if I need you. I think I hear the siren. Now go out front. I'll call you as soon as I can."

Chapter 30

Ben wanted to pick Sam up and hold him in his arms, but he knew better. If his son had a neck injury, moving him could injure him further.

There was one thing he could do while he waited for the squad to reach him. He opened his phone one more time and pushed the speed dial button for Leah.

When she answered, she sounded sleepy.

"Ben. You're up early."

"Leah. Listen to me. I know it's your day off, but I need you to meet me at the hospital. Sam's been in an accident. I have the emergency squad on their way out here to the grove."

"What kind of accident, Ben? I need to know so I can have things ready."

"We were riding, and his horse got spooked and threw him. It looks like he hit his head, and his arm is twisted behind him."

"Don't move him, Ben."

"I know, Leah. I just need you to be there when we get to the hospital."

"I'll be there. But we need to pray, Ben. I'll call the pastor on the way to the hospital."

"Okay. We'll see you in a few minutes."

Ben looked at Sam again. He looked so pale. He was still breathing, but he wasn't moving. Ben's hand went to his son's chest. He could feel Sam's heartbeat. It seemed fast, and Ben's training as a medical helicopter pilot had taught him that an elevated pulse and the pallor he saw in his son's face were not good signs. He looked around. Had Sam hit something hard that would cause internal injuries? Ben couldn't see anything. He kept the grove paths free of rocks and tree limbs. But why was Sam so pale? He knew he should pray. But he'd prayed for Katy a million times, and his prayers for her had gone unanswered.

But this was Sam. He had to do something. "God…please. I know I've not allowed you to be part of my life, but I'm asking you to keep my son alive. I know I don't deserve it, but he does. Save him, and I'll do anything to make sure he grows up to be a good Godly man."

Ben could hear the squad coming closer. He got up and ran toward the sound of the engine. "Over here, over here." He jumped into the lane, waving his arms.

The first paramedic was with Ben before the squad even came to a stop.

"Where is he?"

"A couple rows over. Bring a neck stabilizer and the stretcher."

"Is he still unconscious? Is he breathing?"

"Yes to both.

The next five minutes were a nightmare for Ben. He had always been the one to take care of his son. Now he had to stand back and allow others to care for him. That's when Ben felt the tears on his cheeks and breathed one more prayer. "Please, God."

Ben got into the squad. No one could have kept him out of it. When they drove by the house, he didn't see Abby. But he knew what Abby was doing. She was praying, and he knew she would have called her parents already. And he knew they would be praying all the way from Tampa. *God...I know I'm not worthy, but could you at least answer their prayers this time. They've already lost Katy. Don't let them lose her son too.*

*****

Leah was waiting for him in the emergency room. He wanted to hug her, but she went straight to Sam.

"Ben, I'm going to run a few tests, but if at any point I think he's too unstable to be here, I'm going to have him transported by air to the children's hospital. I've called our neuro doc. He said he'd come in and look at him too."

Leah was all business. "How long has he been unresponsive, Ben?"

Ben looked at his phone and pulled up the 9-1-1 call. "It's only been fifteen minutes." *Fifteen minutes? It already seemed like a life time since he'd told Sam to take the lead.*

"We're going to get a CT scan first, then some x-rays. But we really need him to wake up soon. We need to rule out a spinal cord injury and a traumatic brain injury, but from what I can see so far, it may just be a bad concussion. It does look like that arm is broken, though. We'll fix it after we do the other tests."

"Can I go with him?"

"Of course. We'll both go. And we'll put him into the capable hands of the best Healer of all, Ben."

And Ben knew at that moment that he was dependent on God. He had tried to be self-sufficient his whole life. But now he wasn't. He needed God.

It wasn't until after the x-rays that Sam opened his eyes. He tried to move his head, but the neck stabilizer was still on. He tried to raise his arms, but the left one was in an immobilizer, and Ben was holding his other hand.

"Sam. It's dad. I'm right here. Don't move, Sam."

213

Ben was up and looking into the face of his son. The little boy's eyes were open, but they didn't seem to be focused. "Sam. I'm right here. Look at me, Sam." But Sam closed his eyes and began to gag. "Nurse! I think he's going to throw up."

Ben was pushed away from the stretcher his son was still on. He heard the whir of a suction machine. All at once, he felt faint. "Ben. Go sit down." It was Leah's voice. Hands began to push him into a chair that someone else pushed under him. "Get your head down, Ben. You're going to be okay. We'll take care of Sam."

In that instant, Ben had a vision of what life could be like for Sam in the future. He could end up in a wheelchair with brain damage and totally dependent on others for his every need. He would never be able to run and play, or fish, or ride a horse again. Ben couldn't bear the thought of that. And he wondered if Sam would be better off with his mother than living in this world in a vegetative state.

He felt the room begin to spin. *No! I can't faint. I have to be strong...for Sam.*

Lifting his head, he saw a glass of water someone was holding in front of him. He took it with trembling hands. Water. He needed water. Then he'd go back to Sam.

"Ben. We're here now." The voice sounded familiar, but Abby looked different. Her usual happy face was stricken, and her eyes were red. "Dad and I are here now, Ben." Ben moved his eyes to the figure beside Abby. It was Alex. Abby's dad, Katy's step-dad. Alex the pastor. He would pray for Sam.

"We need to pray, Abby."

"I know, Ben. We have been. You know what Katy would say Ben?"

"Leave it in God's hands...He knows best."

"Believe that, Ben. And remember, God loves Sam more than we do. He knows what's best. But He also knows the desires of our hearts and wants to give them to us when He can."

"Ben?" It was Leah again.

"He wants you. Sam's calling your name."

With hands that steadied him, Ben walked toward his son. "I'm here, Buddy."

"Wha…what happened, Dad?"

"You were in an accident, Sam. But you're going to be okay. Dr. Leah is here. She's going to take good care of you."

,   "It hurts, Dad. My arm hurts, and my head hurts too." Tears began to run down the little boy's cheeks. Ben hated when Sam cried. He leaned over him and kissed him on both cheeks. His tears mingled with his son's.

"It will be better, soon. Here hold my hand. I'm right here."

I'm right here too, Ben. He felt the voice, but didn't hear it. *Lean on me, Ben. I'm your heavenly Father, and I love you and Sam more than you can imagine.*

Ben put his head down beside Sam. It was time, and he knew it. It was time to have a relationship with his heavenly Father.

"I'm sorry, God. I'm sorry I've been so stubborn and willful. I'm sorry I ever doubted you. Forgive me." Ben whispered the words into the stretcher Sam was on, but he knew they were heard by the One for whom they were intended.

Chapter 31

Sam stayed at the hospital for two nights. He was drowsy and slept a lot. When he did wake up, he was nauseated and said his head hurt. He had an IV for fluids and medicine. On his second day, Leah came in and told him they were going to get him out of bed.

"I feel dizzy." Sam put his good hand to his head.

"It will pass, Sam. We just want you to sit up in a chair for a few minutes and try to eat something." Sam looked from his dad to Leah.

"Can I go home if I sit up?"

"Maybe tomorrow. We need to make sure you're all well before you go home."

"Okay." There was resignation in his voice. "But I need to see Molly, and the other kids."

"The boys and Lexie sent you some pictures, Sam." Ben pointed to the wall that now looked like an art gallery.

"I know. But I need to go home and see Jake too. Is he okay, Dad?"

"He's fine. I went home and took care of him while you were asleep."

"Who stayed with me?" Sam looked from Ben to Leah.

"Dr. Leah was here with you, Sam. She spent the whole night with you." Ben took Leah's hand and squeezed it. "She's been a really good doctor for you."

"Oh. I thought I had a dream about you. But it was really you?" Sam grinned at Leah.

"It was me, Sam. Can I ask you a question? Do you remember anything about your accident?"

"No. I just remember me and Dad riding the horses, and the next thing I knew, I was here. But now I'm ready to go home."

"Okay. Tomorrow, if you keep getting better."

*****

Sam's homecoming was a huge deal. Momma Beth had stayed at the grove with Abby, but Alex had gone home as soon as he knew Sam was going to be okay. She had been instrumental in making sure there were balloons, ice cream, and cake to welcome Sam home.

Kyle and Konnor were anxious to examine the cast on his arm, and Molly waved her arms and squealed at him. Even shy little Lexie got in on the festivities by welcoming him home with another hand drawn picture.

At the end of the day, when all the kids were in bed, Ben went out to the swing on the deck. But this time when he looked to the stars, his words were not for Katy. They were for the Creator of the stars. "Thank you" was all he could manage to say as the gratitude in his heart threatened to choke him.

"Ben? Momma and I are going to have a cup of decaf coffee and another piece of this cake. Do you want some?"

Ben got up and went back into the house. As he settled into a chair and looked at the women in his kitchen, he felt another sense of gratitude.

"How am I ever going to thank the two of you for all your help this week?"

"You don't have to thank us, Ben. We're family."

"Then I'm thankful for family. Besides her love, you are the best thing Katy gave me."

Momma Beth reached across the table and gripped his hand. "And we're grateful that Katy brought you into our family. We're going to be here for you forever, Ben. We are your family."

He smiled at both of them. "How would you feel about me bringing someone else into the family?" He saw the look that went between the two of them.

"Well...that depends on who this other person is? If it's a pretty blond doctor, I think we could be okay with that."

"I wish the two of you could have seen her when Sam and I got to the hospital Wednesday. I have never seen anyone so efficient and in charge. You could just tell that she was exactly where she was supposed to be."

"She is pretty amazing, but I'm sorry I had to meet her at the hospital instead of at that Italian restaurant we were suppose to go to. Will she be making house calls on her patient?"

"I have a feeling she'll be here. She said she might come tomorrow afternoon."

"I'm glad. I want to meet her before I leave. If it looks like Sam's going to be okay, Alex will come and get me tomorrow afternoon. It's a good thing Abby had some of her bigger old clothes here, but I'm getting a little tired of wearing sweats."

"Thank you for staying, Beth. I would have felt awful if Abby had been here alone with all the responsibility of Molly."

"Ben...we told you, it's okay. This is what family does. And now I get to stay till tomorrow so I can meet the infamous Dr. Leah." He could tell by the smile that flitted across her face that she was teasing him.

"I want you and Alex to meet her too. Do you want me to call her and invite her to Sunday dinner?" Ben had just seen her that morning at the hospital, but he was already missing her.

"Sure. But we'll probably eat late. We have to wait until Alex gets here."

"I'm sure she won't mind."

*****

Ben stayed home from church with Sam and Molly. Sam was upset, but Leah had told Ben to make sure his son rested a lot for at least a week, maybe longer.

"I know you want to go, Sam. But Dr. Leah said you need to stay home today and rest. She's going to come out later to see how you're doing."

"Dr. Leah is coming here to see me?"

"Yes. She was very worried about you this week."

"Can I take her out to meet Jake?"

"We could probably do that. But you'll have to ride to the barn on the golf cart."

"But I want to show her how I ride Jake."

"That will have to wait for some other time, Sam." Ben was actually having doubts about whether he should let Sam get back on his horse at all. He still hadn't figured out what spooked Jake on Wednesday, and Sam had no memory of the accident.

Ben had left Sam at the hospital with Leah the night of the accident, just long enough to come home and feed the horses. The day after the accident, while he was home, he had saddled Jake and ridden him to the same area where Sam had been thrown. The horse seemed fine. All Ben could figure out was that he must have been spooked by a snake, or maybe a bird.

"Why can't I ride him today?"

"Because Dr. Leah said you needed to take it easy. And you have a broken arm and a concussion."

"What's a concussion?"

"It means when you fell off Jake, your brain got bounced around in your head. And it takes awhile for it to feel better. That's why you still have a headache sometimes. In fact, I'm thinking you probably need to go in and rest before the family comes back home from church. It's going to be a busy day."

"Can I watch my Scooby Doo movie?"

"Sure." *Anything to get him to rest.* He wondered how Abby was going to be able to keep him down this week with the other boys wanting him to play.

"I'm going to get the grill ready while you watch TV, okay?" Abby and her mom had made some side dishes to go with the pork chops Ben was going to grill. Leah was going to bring dessert. Ben told her she didn't have to, but she had insisted. His mouth started to water just thinking about the cherry cobbler she made for him last week.

Molly was in the pack-n-play on the deck while Ben worked on the grill. He was just getting ready to pick her up when he heard the whir of a golf cart motor. Puzzled, he looked toward the side of the house where the sound was coming from. Around the corner came John and Linda.

Linda was off the cart the minute John turned the engine off. "Where are my babies?"

"Linda...what are you and John doing home?"

"I couldn't take it, Ben. After you called the other night and told us about the accident, I told John I had to come home and make sure everyone was okay."

"But I told you Sam was okay."

"I know, but I had to come home and see for myself." She took Molly out of Ben's arms and hugged her close. Ben looked at John who just shrugged his shoulders.

"Can't keep a Grandma away from her babies when she's intent on seeing them."

"Well, it's good to see you." Ben took his father-in-law's hand and pulled him close. Katy's dad had become his best friend over the past few years.

"Where's my Sam?"

"He's inside. He's going to be thrilled to see both of you. And he's going to insist that you sign that cast of his."

The three of them walked into the kitchen. Linda stopped when she saw the table set. "What's going on here? You having a party?

"Yep. And you're just in time to join us."

"That's a lot of plates. Who on earth is coming? Looks like you've become more social since we left, Ben."

"It does seem like our family is growing. I'm glad you're here."

Sam heard the commotion and came into the kitchen. "Grandma, Grandpa! You're here." Linda gave Molly back to Ben.

"Sam…my boy. How are you doing, honey?" Within seconds she had the little boy in her arms. "Grandma was so worried about you. Are you okay?" Ben saw the tears in her eyes.

"I'm okay, Grandma. 'Cept Dad won't let me ride Jake. He said I have to wait awhile."

"I think your dad is right. How are you going to hold the reins with your arm in a cast? Let me see that cast. I like the color. I don't think I've ever seen a blue one before."

"You want to sign it? I got a whole bunch of names on it."

"I see. Why don't we go back to the living room so Grandpa and I can sit down and read all those names."

As Ben watched them go, he shook his head. What a crazy week. As horrible as Sam's accident had been, there was good coming out of it. Most of his family would be gathered around his table for lunch today, and he'd been able to see Leah doing what she loved to do, what she was called to do. Most importantly, it had been the week he'd finally made peace with his God.

Chapter 32

There were so many people in Ben's big eat-in kitchen, that a second table had to be set up. The four kids sat at a card table, and the eight adults just fit at the big table. Both sets of Katy's parents, Abby, Carly, Leah and Ben sat for an hour after eating, talking and laughing. For a couple of seconds, Ben thought about Katy and how much she would have loved so many people around the table she had refinished.

Linda and John both knew Leah, but introductions to Momma Beth, Alex and Carly had to be made. Ben noticed Carly watching Leah intently during the meal. Since Katy's death, Carly had often mentioned that she would like to be a doctor. She had been so close to her sister and for a couple years had been devastated by her death. She was thinking about going into pre-med now, and wanted to help find a cure for leukemia.

After lunch, the boys and Lexie finished watching a movie while Molly went to bed for her nap. But as soon as the movie was over, the kids insisted on going to see the horses. All the women, except Carly and Leah, decided it was too hot to go outside, so they stayed inside with Molly.

Ben told Sam he had to ride on the golf cart with his two grandpas and Lexie. The rest of them walked to the barn. Ben had to walk fast to keep up with Kyle and Konnor. That left Carly and Leah bringing up the tail of the procession. Ben turned and looked at the two of them once. They seemed to be in the middle of a serious conversation. He wondered if Carly was more interested in Leah the doctor or Leah the woman who might be taking the place of her sister in Ben's life. Ben wanted Carly to like Leah. Carly had been Katy's special little sister.

*****

Leah left as soon as the visit to the horses came to a conclusion. Ben walked her to her car and asked her if she was too tired for him to see her later that night.

"I can't come until the kids are in bed, but I really need to talk to you."

"Please come. I need to talk to you too." Their eyes met, and he wanted to kiss her, but the rest of the family was gathered outside, and he knew it wasn't time for a public display of affection.

Soon after, the Phillips family left for Tampa. When Ben hugged Carly, she whispered, "I like her. Katy would too." Ben gave her an extra tight squeeze.

"Thanks, little sis. I needed that."

Ben cleaned up his grill before he went inside, where he found Abby and Linda discussing the coming week. He could hear John's voice coming from the living room where he was playing Bingo with the kids.

"Ben...I'm glad you're here. Abby and I are talking about what we need to do with Sam this week. I think I need to take him home with me so he won't be tempted to rough-house with the other boys. What do you think?"

"I was thinking about that this morning. It would probably by easier for Abby if he was with you. But, aren't you going back to the mountains?"

"Linda, I'll be okay with the kids if you want to go back. I'll think of something to keep them all quiet this week." To Ben, keeping five kids quiet for a week sounded like a week of torture. Kids needed to run off energy. But not Sam. Not this week.

"I'm not going back to the mountains until I know Sam is going to be okay. And since I'm here now, I might as well help. Abby, I'll come and get Sam and Molly in the mornings this week, and keep them till Ben gets home. It will give you a chance to spend more time with your own kids."

"It sounds like a good plan to me, Abby. I'm flying four days this week. And maybe it will give you some extra time to send out resumes."

"I guess it would be okay. But I don't think the boys are going to be happy if they are split up. I know it might be good for all of them though. And they'll be together in the evenings."

"Linda... thank you. I was worried that it would be too much for Abby. What would I do without my family?"

"We're only doing for you, what you've done for your sister, Ben. When she needed you to take Molly, you did it. Extended family is a blessing that not everyone has."

*****

Ben tucked his kids into bed early. Sam had slept with him the night before, and Ben was going to insist that his son sleep with him for the rest of the week. Leah had mentioned watching him closely for seizure activity, and Ben couldn't do that if Sam was all the way down the hall. He had even stopped in town and bought a second monitor. Now he had one at the bedside of both his kids.

After all the kids were in bed, Ben dropped himself onto the couch beside Abby. "Hey sis, are you as tired as I am?"

"I am. Big day, wasn't it?" she reached over and patted his knee. "But I think you'll be pleased that Leah passed the family inspection." She was teasing him, and he knew it.

"How do you know? Have you talked to Carly?"

"Just got off the phone with her. She is quite impressed with your Leah. Guess that means you can marry her now."

"We've only been seeing each other for three weeks. And even if I did want to marry her, maybe she doesn't want to marry me.

"You've only dated for three weeks, but how long have you known her? Three years. You only knew my sister for six months before you twisted her arm and insisted she marry you."

"No. Katy and I had a mutual agreement. But, it's kind of weird, Abby. She and Leah are so different. Katy loved being a nurse, but wanted babies more than she wanted a career. Leah wants her career. And their personalities are so different. Even their goals in life are different. How is it possible that I could love two women who are so different?"

"It's good they're different, Ben. And by the way, you just said 'love.' You really think she's the one?"

"How about I go over and find out for sure? Do you mind listening to two monitors for awhile?" If he hadn't wanted to see Leah so much, he would have felt really bad asking Abby to listen for his kids again.

"You know I don't mind. But, I gotta tell you though, if I ever start dating again, I know who owes me."

"Thought you weren't ever going to date again."

"I might be changing my mind about dating. I said I wasn't ever getting married again."

"We'll see about that. Gonna run, okay?"

"Go! But no staying over night." She gave him a gentle push. "You have to marry her before you do that. Those are dad's rules, and they'll be dad's rules no matter how old we get."

She didn't have to tell him to "go" more than once.

*****

As soon as Leah closed the door, Ben lifted her off her feet and kissed her. He just couldn't help himself. In the short time he had been seeing her, the only time he didn't think about her was when he was busy with his kids. The more he saw of her, the more intriguing she became to him. He wanted to know everything there was to know about her. Yet, he felt like he already knew her, because he had seen her heart and knew what was in it.

"Whoa! Slow down, boy."

"Can't help it, Leah. I'm crazy about you. I can't stop thinking about you."

"You're supposed to be thinking about what we talked about the other night. Come on, let's go sit." She took his hand and pulled him toward her great room. For some reason, his eyes were drawn to the crescent window above her patio doors that led to the pool. Why hadn't he noticed it before? Maybe because there hadn't been a full moon shining through it before?

"Want to go outside? It's pretty out there tonight." She had noticed that he stopped and looked up.

"No. I want stay in here. You're prettier than the moon."

She grinned at him. "Wonderful dad, great pilot, successful business man… and a romantic on top of all that. What other amazing qualities do you have?"

"I'm an open book. What you see is what you get."

"Same here…that means we better talk. Let's sit."

Ben made himself comfortable on her couch and pulled her down beside him. "And what exactly is on your mind tonight, pretty lady?"

"I need you to be serious, Ben." He loved watching her eyes. They seemed to change color with her changing emotions.

"Okay. I'm serious."

She picked his hand up off her lap, and ran her fingers over his knuckles. "After today, Ben, I'm feeling like we may not be good for each other."

Her words stopped him cold. "Why would you say that, Leah? I thought today was wonderful. My family loves you."

"I don't know. I think it's because I saw a side of you I hadn't seen before. I saw you with Katy's family. I don't know if I can fit in. You're all so close."

"We are. But, I can promise you, Leah, they are the most open and accepting family I know."

"What will they think when they find out I don't want to have children? It appears to me that they are a family that loves children. I didn't know Katy had three brothers, and they all have kids, too?"

"They are a family that loves children. But if it doesn't bother me that you don't want kids of your own, it won't bother them."

"So, you've thought about it? You'll be happy with no more kids?"

"Leah, look at me." He lifted her chin so he could see her eyes again. "When I saw you waiting for us in that emergency room on Wednesday, I understood. You're a wonderful doctor, and I could tell how important it is for you to do what you know God has called you to do. I understand how torn you'd feel if you got called to take care of an ill child and had to leave your own to do it. You know how much you have to give, and what your limitations are. You and I can work with that."

There were tears in her eyes. "You do understand? Oh…thank you, Ben. But that doesn't mean I don't want to help you raise the kids you already have."

"I know that. And I appreciate it. And I love that Molly is blond like you. You know, the two of you could pass for biological mother and daughter?"

"That's something else I've been wanting to talk to you about. Do you think you could wait until after we're married to file for legal custody of her? I would love for her adoption papers to list me as her mother."

Ben had to smile. In one sentence she was saying she didn't know if they were meant for each other, and in the next, she was planning on, not only marriage, but adopting his child.

"I think that's a wonderful idea, sweetheart. I would love to share custody of her with you. Now, what else did you want to tell me?"

"I guess it isn't important now. It's just that when I saw you surrounded by Katy's family today, I realized that in addition to her love, she also gave you a son, an extended family, and a way of life. All I have to offer you is my love. And that didn't seem like very much."

"That's everything to me right now. I need you, Leah. I want you in my life. I want you to be that one special person to love and be loved by. Even with all the blessings I have, I feel incomplete without that. And I want you to be that person."

"Are you sure? You haven't known me very long, and I'm not Katy."

"I've known you long enough. And, as wonderful as she was, I don't want you to be like Katy. I just want you to be your own kind of wonderful."

"So this is it? We're ready to move forward?"

"I'm so ready. And we'll work out the details as we go, okay?" He brushed the fine strands of golden hair away from her face and lifted her chin so he could look into her eyes. The reflection of the moon shone in them and turned them almost golden. When her arms came up around his neck, what could he do, but kiss her again? It was the kiss that sealed their future.

Chapter 33

By the end of July, Abby and Ben had settled into a routine that worked well for both of them. During the days when he flew, she watched the kids. In the evenings, they shared the responsibilities of not just the kids, but the house. A couple evenings a week, he shooed her out of the house so she could have a break. On those evenings, Leah would come to the grove and spend time with him and the kids.

They all loved her, and as he watched her with them, he could see that her simple affection for them must have come from her years in an Amish home. She loved riding the horses with them and even helped Sam clean out Jake's stall.

There were a couple nights, after the kids went to bed, that the two of them got on the horses and went riding. She loved it and asked him if she could board a horse with him, if she bought one. Ben was thrilled, and told her about one of the memories he had of his parents. They would often leave him and his sister at home in the evenings and go riding into the Texas sunset.

"Did Katy ride with you?"

"No. She wasn't really very fond of the horses. Her love here was growing the oranges. She loved everything about the grove. It was her baby."

"I don't know much about orange growing."

"It's okay. You know about doctoring. Everyone has their own thing. Mine is flying…in case you haven't figured that out yet."

"Really? How did I miss that?" She was turning out to be a little bit of a tease. "When are you going to take me flying again?"

"Anytime you wish, my lady."

Most evenings, after the kids were in bed, Ben went to see Leah, though. He loved being in her home with her. It was so comfortable and he felt at home there. And he loved her pool. The times the two of them spent alone there was so peaceful after the pleasant chaos that existed in his home.

"Maybe after the two of us get married, we could build a pool like this behind our house at the grove."

"We're getting married?" She grinned at him. "I don't remember you asking me to marry you."

"It's coming…so prepare yourself, my dear."

"Maybe that's something else we should talk about."

"You want to talk about getting married?"

"No. I want to talk about where we'll live, if we get married." She hesitated for a minute. "I was wondering how you'd feel about living here."

"Here? But my work is at the grove. And the horses are there. That's my home, and I want you to live there with me."

"I know that's where your work is, Ben. But there are no rules that say you have to live where you work. I don't live where I work. You can go to work at the grove everyday and take care of the horses while you're there. It's only three miles away."

"Don't you like the house out there? We can change it anyway you want."

"It's a lovely house, Ben. But it was the home you and Katy chose. I want this house to be ours." Ben was a bit confused. The thought of moving from his house in the country had never crossed his mind. He loved living in the country. And it was a man's job to provide a home for his wife.

"I don't know. Leah. I don't think Sam would like leaving his home. And John and Linda are close by to watch the kids. They love being able to get on the golf cart and riding over to see them whenever they want to."

"Ben, I know it would be a huge change for all of you. But I really think it would be a good change. I just feel like we could start our own life better, if we were here." Ben was feeling confused and conflicted.

"Are you afraid Katy's family will be intrusive? They won't be. They usually only come over when they're invited. And I love that they can come to the orchard and feel close to Katy." Ben was struggling with what Leah was asking him to do. The grove was his home.

"I can tell Katy's family is wonderful, Ben. And I'm glad they can come and remember Katy being so happy there. They can still do that. I'm not asking you to give up the grove. I'm just asking you to change your residence."

"And what would I do with my house?"

"You could rent it out."

"Rent it?" Ben heard his voice rise, even though he was trying to be open minded to what she was proposing. "I can't do that. I don't want strangers living in my home, Leah. I mean, who could I trust to live there?"

"Abby." She said it so softly, Ben was unsure what she said.

"Did you say Abby?" As much as he loved Leah, sometimes she had some unusual ideas.

"Think about it, Ben. It's perfect. No matter where I see her in the house, I feel like she belongs there. It was her sister's house and I think that must be a comfort to her—living where Katy was happiest. Maybe the two of you could come up with a deal that would work for both of you. She could do the bookwork for the charter business and the grove, and some babysitting, in return for her living in the house."

"Wow, you've put some thought into this, haven't you?"

"I have. You like this house, don't you?"

"I love it, and I really love the lady who lives in it. But I'm still worried about Sam. The grove is the only home he knows."

"I'm pretty sure that home for Sam is where his dad is. Besides, if Abby lived there, he could go visit anytime he wants. And someday, maybe he'll get married and want to live there himself."

"But do you think Abby would want to do it? She may not want to be a bookkeeper for me."

"I think she would. She isn't having much luck finding a job, is she? And even if she does find one, who's going to watch her kids while she works? This way she gets to be a stay-at-home mom, and she'll have a job that provides a home for her kids too."

"I must say…you've thought about all the details. Just one more thing. Do you think this house is big enough for me and the kids?"

"Of course it is. I have three bedrooms, one for us and one for each of the kids. But I was thinking, if this is something we can do, maybe we could build on another bedroom for us. The empty lot next to this one is mine. Did I ever tell you that?"

"No. You never told me that. You are just full of surprises, aren't you?"

He pulled her close again, just to kiss her.

"But why would we need to build on a new bedroom?"

"The bedroom I have now could be a den, and our new bedroom could be bigger. Big enough for two twin beds." She grinned at him. "Or a huge king size one."

"Don't mess with me, girl. There will be only one bed." And yes, he had to kiss her again, just so she knew he was serious. "But building on could be costly."

"Which brings up another issue. Finances. We need to talk about that someday too."

"And do you have that all figured out too?"

"No. But I think we can figure it out together. You do need to know that I believe in sharing resources. What's mine is yours, and vice versa."

"There's one really important thing you do need to know about that. The grove isn't mine. It belongs to Sam. His mom bought it for him. I'm just managing it for him until he gets old enough to take care of it himself."

"Well...that makes things even easier. I assume you keep separate business records for the grove?"

"I do. And Katy's dad is the overseer of it for Sam. Between him and Abby doing the books and managing it, I wouldn't even have to be involved, except during harvest. Sam and I spend a lot of quality time together during harvest."

"Oh, Ben. I think this is going to work. You'll have your flying business, I'll have my medical practice, and between the two of us, we'll have two amazing kids and this house that we both love."

"Leah... I have to tell you. What you're proposing is something I never dreamed of doing. I'm going to need some time to think about all of this. If I can't see it working, are you open to moving to the grove?"

It took her a few second to answer. "There were a few good things I brought from my Amish home, Ben. One of them is the idea that the husband is the head of the home. I want your leadership in our home. And if this wouldn't work for you, I understand and am willing to compromise. I'm just asking you to consider it."

*****

Sam's birthday was on July 20th. Ben had taken him to Disney for his birthday every year since he was two. It was Katy's idea. She loved Disney and wanted Sam to love it too, and he did.

When they went on his third birthday, Sam didn't know it would be the last year his mother would be with him. Ben did though, and took hundreds of pictures. On his fourth birthday, Sam wanted his cousins to go with them, so Abby, Brett and the kids went along.

But last year, Ben and Sam had gone alone. It had been a special day for both of them. It had been the day that Ben finally realized Katy wasn't coming back, and he needed to do what she had asked him to do. He needed to move on. To Ben, that had meant trying to be content with their family of two or finding someone else who could add joy to their existing family. Soon after that he started to see Jan.

But this year was going to be different. When asked, Sam still wanted to go to Disney, but he wanted to take his whole family with him.

"Who is your whole family, Sam?"

"All the people who live in our house. That's a family, right?"

How could Ben argue with that?

"Okay. That sounds good. There for a minute I was afraid you were going to ask to take all your grandparents and cousins. That would be too many people." Although he had always been closest to Abby's kids, Sam was able to get together, on special occasions with Katy's three brother's kids too. There were five of them, but all of them were younger than Sam. And three of them lived in Philadelphia.

"No. Those cousins are too little to go to Disney. They can go with Molly on her birthday. But Dr. Leah can come if she wants to."

"Yeah?"

"She's fun. And I know you like her, Dad."

Ben had to smile. "How can you tell I like her?"

"Cause when she's here visiting us, you're always real nice to her."

"Hey! I'm nice to everyone."

"Yeah. But you're extra nice to her."

"So, do you like her, Sam?"

"Yep. Her and Aunt Abby are my favorite girls. Plus I like my two Grandmas."

"Molly and Lexie are girls. You like them too, don't you?"

"Yeah. But they're kinda too young to talk to and play with. So can we all go to Disney, Dad?" Ben was doing some figuring in his head. If they all went, there would be eight of them.

"I think we can manage it Sam. But we better make a two day trip out of it. We can stay in one of those hotels at Disney for a night. That way if Molly and Lexie get tired during the day, they'll have someplace to take a rest."

"Two days at Disney? This is going to be the best birthday ever!"

*****

When Ben looked back on that two-day trip to Disney, he had to smile. That trip redefined the word family for him. It took three adults to manage all five kids. When Molly got tired, it was Leah who offered to take her back to the villa so she could rest. Ben had reserved the two bedroom villa for the night. The four "girls" bunked together in one room, while Ben took the three boys into his room.

By the end of the day, the kids were so exhausted they were sound asleep within minutes of going to bed. They had stayed at the park for the electric parade at the end of the day. Sam and Ben had never stayed late enough for it before.

With the kids all tucked in and asleep, Ben, Leah and Abby collapsed in the small living area.

"Thanks for inviting me to come, Ben. I didn't tell you, but this is my first trip to Disney." Leah's cheeks were flushed, and he wondered if it was from the sun or the experience.

"A pediatrician who's never been to Disney? It seems to me like that should be a mandatory class for doctors who take care of kids."

"I definitely have a new appreciation for parents after today. The two of you have your hands full with these five kids, don't you?"

Abby and Ben grinned at each other. "Actually, it's Abby who is amazing at managing all five of them at the same time. I think mothers should be given a degree in management after raising kids."

"That reminds me, Abby. I've been meaning to ask, how's the job search going?"

"Not so good. I may end up here at Disney sweeping up trash." Her smile was a weak one.

Leah looked at Ben and raised her eyebrows. The two of them had talked again about Abby taking over Ben's book work and management of the grove, and he knew it was a good idea. If…no, when he and Leah got married, he was going to need more help. He wanted to be able to spend the evenings with her and the kids.

"Something will work out, Abby. We'll just keep praying about it. In the meantime, I'm so grateful for what you're doing for me."

"We're helping each other, Ben." Talking about her not being able to find a job must have been painful because she changed the subject. "Hey, if the two of you want to take a walk, I'll be here with the kids."

"You want to go? We could even take a swim in the pool if you want." Ben was ready for some one-on-one time with Leah.

"That sounds wonderful. You sure you don't mind, Abby?"

"Not at all. I'll probably be asleep when you get back though."

"I'll be quiet when I come in. And if Molly wakes up during the night, I'll take care of her. You just stay in bed."

Ben was thrilled that Leah and Molly were bonding so well. He wondered if it would be a problem with Abby being her primary caretaker, but it didn't seem like it was going to be. His little girl had started life with no mother, and now she had an abundance of women who wanted to mother her.

Ben took Leah's hand as they walked toward the pool. "Thank you for coming along. I know it wasn't easy for you to get the time off, but Sam really wanted you to come."

"Are you sure you didn't talk him into inviting me?"

"Nope. He was the one who made up the invitation list. I'm really glad you were on it though. When I asked him why he wanted you to come, he said it was because he knows I really like you."

"Perceptive little guy, isn't he?"

"Yep. I think he knows a good thing when he sees it. He's a chip of the old block for sure." Ben stopped walking and pulled her into his arms. "Thank you for coming for me. I love having you here with the family." She was so short, he found it easier to pick her up when he wanted to kiss her.

"It's my pleasure..." He was sure she had something else to say, but he wanted to kiss her before she said anything else. And he knew he wanted to hold her in his arms forever.

Pulling away, she looked at him. "Ben, I think you better get in the pool and cool off."

He slipped her cover-up off her shoulders, picked her up, and carried her to the pool, where he dropped her in. "I'm thinking you need cooled off too, sweet lady."

They swam, talked and cooled off for a half hour. Ben couldn't think of a time when he was happier. And he knew Katy would be happy for him too.

Chapter 34

The next Sunday afternoon, while Molly was sleeping, and the kids were in their separate rooms for quiet time, Ben asked Abby to join him on the deck.

"What's going on, big brother?" She handed him a glass of iced tea.

"I need to talk to you about a couple of things." He stopped and watched as she settled into a lounge chair. Leah was right. She looked like she belonged here. "First, I need to know what you want to do when summer is over." The look of distress that came over her face was almost more than Ben could bear to watch.

"I guess I'm going to move back to Mom and Dad's house. I'm ready to take any job I can get, and they'll be available to help me with the kids."

"I have an idea that might be better for you." He took a sip of the tea. She definitely knew how to make southern sweet tea.

"Yeah? And what would that be?"

"First of all, you should know that I'm shopping for diamonds this week, and I'm going to ask Leah to marry me." She reached over and squeezed his hand.

"Oh, Ben. I'm so happy for you. And I know Katy would be happy for you too. You do know that, don't you?"

"I know she would. And I'm glad her family is so supportive." Ben kept her hand in his. He loved this sister of Katy's and was so happy she had become an important person in his life. "Anyways...Leah and I have been talking about it already, and she wants me and the kids to move into her house with her."

"What?" There was a look of shock and doubt on her face. "You'd leave the grove? She wants you to leave your home? That doesn't sound fair to you, Ben."

"Actually, that's what I thought at first, too. And you know how proud I am about being the provider for my family. But I've put a lot of thought and prayer into it, and I think it's a good idea."

"Why?"

"I don't ever want Leah to feel like she has to live in Katy's shadow. Asking her to move into the home Katy picked out may make her feel that way. She knows my work is here, and she's okay with that, but I think I want to start my new married life with her in a new place."

"Is that what you want, or is that what she wants? Ben, I love Leah too, but it worries me that you have had to give up your dreams of more children for her, and now you're giving up your home for her."

"But look what I get for the sacrifices. I get a woman who I know will love me and the kids I have with all her heart. I get a woman who I can pour all my love into. The fact that she has a career she's passionate about, and a beautiful home she wants to share with me, are just icing on the cake of who she is."

"Are you going to be happy living in town? I thought you loved the openness of the grove."

"I'll only live three miles away, Abby. I'll be here everyday to work the grove and ride the horses. And I still have the openness of the skies when I fly. By the time the day is over, I won't mind going home to an amazing wife, who just happens to come with a beautiful house in town."

"And Sam? How's he going to feel about it?"

"I'm going to talk to him about that. But I think he'll be okay with it if I tell him you and the kids will still live here, and he can visit anytime he wants." Ben watched her face closely as he said the words.

"Me and the kids? Why would we still be here?"

"Because after I'm married, I want to give up some of my work so I'll have more time with my family. I need someone to help me with managing the grove, and all the bookwork that goes along with that. I want to hire you to do that. I probably can't pay you as well as another employer, but you'll get this house as part of your pay. And since you'll be working at home, you won't have to pay a babysitter for your kids."

Abby was speechless. Ben was afraid she was going to say no. What if she missed the city and wanted to be closer to her parents. Then he saw the tears run silently down her cheeks.

"Ben…are you doing this out of pity? I don't want you to do this if you're just feeling sorry for me."

"No, Abby. I'm doing this because I need you in my life. I need someone to help me with my businesses. I need someone I can trust to live in this house. It's the house that Katy bought for Sam and there's no one who will take better care of it for him than you. I want you to live here so your family will be able to visit and feel Katy's spirit that will always be here. I want your kids to be a daily part of Sam's life. If he isn't going to have any more siblings, at least he'll have cousins. Do I need to go on? There are other reasons why I want you to stay."

"No. That's enough."

"No. There is one more reason. I want you to be here so I can move on with my life. I want to share my life with Leah. And I want to share with her the family Katy gave me."

"And you know we'd love to have her in our family, right?"

"Of course. So, do you want to go with me to pick out a diamond this week?"

Her squeal of happiness proved to Ben that even though Abby had been burned by love, she still believed in it.

*****

Ben and Abby were able to work out the details of their arrangement. It was going to be profitable for both of them. Now Ben had to talk to Sam. He was only six, but the grove had been his life.

The next Saturday, when Abby took her kids to see their dad, Ben asked Leah to come to the grove to watch Molly, so he and Sam could have some time together. Sam was finally going to be able to ride Jake. His cast was off now, and his arm was in a soft wrap. They were going to go fishing too.

"Dad…this is going to be so much fun. Just you and me today. Did you bring our picnic?"

"It's in the back pack. Are you sure you're going to be able to handle the reins?"

"Sure." Sam reached over and patted his horse's neck. "Me and Jake are a good team."

As the two of them left the barn, Leah and Molly waved goodbye to them. "Have a good time, guys."

"It sure was nice for Leah to come out and watch Molly so the two of us could have some guy-time, wasn't it, Sam?"

"Yeah. She's pretty nice. Maybe if we catch some fish today and clean them, she'll fry them for us. She's a really good cook, isn't she, Dad?" Ben knew Sam was just parroting what he had heard him say several times over the past few weeks.

"She sure is. Let's go through the grove, first, okay?"

As they rode, Ben glanced around him at the only life he had known for the past six years. It had been a good one. That first year was one of such excitement and happiness for him and Katy. He remembered thinking that life couldn't get any better. They had Sam, a home in the country they both loved, and a whole future ahead of them. That part of his life was shattered when Katy got sick. She fought hard for two years, but in the end, she lost her battle. And Ben was left with remnants of what had been.

But God gave Ben a new lease on life when Molly arrived. Sam had the sibling that Katy wanted him to have, and Ben had a connection to the family he was born into. And now, in a summer he would never forget, God had blessed him with Leah. And once again, Ben remembered what Katy had whispered to him that last day she was awake. "Don't forget, Ben. It's always darkest before the dawn."

Ben looked toward the heavens, "Thank you, Lord. You've blessed me far more than I deserve."

"What did you say, Dad?" They were now in the lane and were riding side by side.

"I was just thanking God for His goodness to us, Sam."

"Yeah. In children's church, we sing a song called "God is so Good."

"That's a great song. You wanna fish over by the bench again?"

"Yeah. That's where we catch the big ones." Sam was already jumping off Jake. "Should I give him a drink first, Dad?"

"Of course. It's hot out here. Then we can let then graze under the trees."

With bait on their hooks, Ben and his son sat down to wait. "Hey, Sam?

"Yeah?"

"I need to ask you something."

"What?"

"What would you think about Leah and me getting married?" A huge grin began to cover Sam's face.

"I knew it. I knew you liked her, Dad. I like her too. Does that mean she would be my new mom?"

"It means she'd be your second mom. The mom that gave birth to you will always be your first mom. But there are lots of people who have two moms. Your mom had two moms, remember?"

As gently and simply as Ben could, he explained what getting a second mom would mean to Sam. When he got to the part about moving into Leah's house, Sam looked doubtful. But when Ben explained that it was the only way his cousins could stay at the grove, he was ecstatic.

"So, I can still come out here every day after school?"

"Yep. On the days I'm flying, you can ride the bus out here with your cousins because Leah will be at work. And on the days I'm not flying, we'll come here when you get home from school. And maybe Leah can come sometimes too. She wants to buy a horse so she can ride too."

"That would be so cool. And maybe we can get a couple more horses for Kyle and Konnor?" Ben had to laugh. Sam was determined to get horses for his cousins.

"Maybe some day when all of you are old enough to take care of them yourselves."

Chapter 35

When Ben asked Katy to marry him, he flew her to the mountains for a romantic get-away. But he wanted to do something completely different with Leah. He wanted to take her back to Ohio. He wanted to see where her life started, and he hoped it could be a special time for her. From what she'd told him, she never really said goodbye to her family and her old way of life. He felt like she needed to do that before they could start a new one together.

It was the first of October before he was able to approach the subject with her.

September had been a crazy month. Abby had accepted his job offer and was still at the grove house with him. When the kids all went back to school, he sat down with her, Linda, and John to plan the future of the grove. Except for helping with the harvest, he wanted to turn the daily operations of it over to the three of them. He knew they would do a good job for Sam. And they were more than happy to see Katy's dream for her son come true.

John and Linda were as surprised as the rest of the family about his decision to move to town after he and Leah were married. But when they heard his reasons, they were understanding. He was hoping once they were married, and the grove was being taken care of, he could increase his chartering service.

It was Leah's day off, and she was flying a charter with him again. She'd been flying with him on her days off for a couple months. With their busy schedules, it was a good time for them to spend quality time together. They were flying one of his clients to Miami and waiting there to fly him back again.

"So, you've never been to Miami?"

"I told you. The only two places I've been in my life is Ohio and Laurelville, Florida. You can take me any place beside those two places, and it will be new to me."

"Poor deprived girl. Tell you what. After we're married, I'll take you anywhere you want to go, okay?"

"You still haven't asked me."

"I will. Be patient. I've had a few loose ends to tie up." Once again they had taken a taxi from the airport to the nearest beach. They were holding hands as they walked. October was a good month to go to the beach and walk. It was a little cooler.

"I'd wait for you forever, Ben." He, of course, had to stop right there and kiss her.

"It won't be long now. I'm not going to be able to wait much longer for you." She squeezed his hand. "You know where I've never been?"

"Where? I thought you'd been everywhere."

"Nope. I've never been to Ohio."

"Well, you haven't missed much." Her voice was soft, but he heard a catch in it.

"I want to go anyways." She stopped walking and looked up at him in confusion.

"Why?"

"I want to see where you grew up. I've never been to an Amish community and I want to see what it looks like. Actually, I've never been north when the leaves have changed color, and I've never been to an apple orchard. If it's possible, I'd like to meet your family."

"I don't know, Ben. The last time I went to see my family, they were civil, but I could tell they had already written me out of their lives. I broke their hearts when I left, I don't think they want to see me." He heard the hurt in her voice. "I would like for them to meet you though. If they still love me at all, I think they'd be happy that I've found someone to share my life with."

"Why don't we take a weekend off and fly up there? Don't the leaves change colors at the end of the month?"

"You really want to do this?"

"I do."

*****

Linda was more than happy to watch Molly and Sam for him. She was helping Abby with Molly part of the time, but was missing Sam. Since he had cousins to play with at the grove, he didn't spend time with her like he once did.

Ben picked Leah up at her house at six in the morning on the last Saturday in October. "Are you sure you want to do this, Ben? You might be disappointed when we get there."

"Being with you is never disappointing." He took her in his arms and held her close. The thought crossed his mind that they could put his car in her garage, and they could just stay at her house all weekend. No one would even know they were there, and a whole weekend of just the two of them sounded like heaven. But he also knew that would lead to things Leah wasn't ready for yet.

He kissed the top of her head and squeezed her a little tighter before he let go of her. "Let's go, my dear. We're off on a new adventure."

The flight into Akron was beautiful. As he was landing, Ben could see the beauty of the fall leaves around him. He knew it was going to be a wonderful weekend.

They rented a car at the airport and headed south.

"It's going to get a little bit hilly pretty soon. It's beautiful to see all the colors on the sides of the hills." She was looking out her window. Ben reached over and took her hand.

"Where we grow up is always beautiful, don't you think?"

"I suppose, especially if you've left a piece of your heart there." He heard her sigh. "Where did you say we're staying tonight?"

"I reserved two rooms at the Mohican state park lodge near here. It looked beautiful when I found it online. I thought maybe we could check in then go exploring. I'll let you be the tour guide if you want."

"I know where that is. Margie took me there once. It is beautiful. But we might as well go home first. It's on the way. That way I won't feel so anxious for the rest of our time here. I can get it out of the way."

"I'm sorry, Leah. We don't have to go if you don't want to. I don't have to meet your parents."

"No. It's okay. My mother used to sell baked goods out of our home, to the English. Maybe we'll just stop in, and see if she'll sell some to us."

"Lead the way, my dear."

An hour later they were at the end of the driveway of her childhood home. The all white, two story home was plain to look at, but was settled between two hills that were covered with fall foliage. There was green pasture on each side of the lane leading up to the house. Several beautiful horses were lazily grazing. A huge white barn sat away from the house, and Ben saw several black buggies sitting between the house and barn.

"Stay right here for a minute, Ben. I'm nervous."

"I'm right here with you, Leah. Look, there's a sign that says we can buy baked goods here." He took her hand and smiled at her. "They won't refuse to sell to us, will they?"

"No. Of course not. And because I was never baptized in the church, they'll treat me just like any other English person they come into contact with. They'll be polite, but reserved. Actually, they probably won't even recognize me. Go ahead. Drive on up to the house."

Ben drove slowly up to the house. As he got closer, they saw three small children playing with some puppies near a windmill. There were two women in the garden next to the windmill. All of them stopped and looked at the car. Ben heard Leah take in a deep breath.

"Who are they, Leah?"

"It looks like two of my sisters. I don't know, Ben. I haven't seen them for a long time. The children are probably my nieces and nephews."

Ben got out of the car and went around it to open the door for Leah. He took her hand and tugged on it. "Come on, Baby. It'll be okay." As she slid from the seat, Ben heard the creaking of the back door of the house. Turning around, he saw an older woman come out onto the steps, and he heard Leah inhale sharply. She pulled her hand out of his and began to walk ahead of him toward the lady.

"Can I help you?" The woman looked closely at the two of them. "Are you here for baked goods?"

"Maemm?" Her voice was soft. "It's me. Leah."

A look of shock crossed the lined face of the lady. She backed up to lean against the door.

"Leah. What are you doing here?" Ben and Leah were now on the bottom step of the porch.

"I've come home to introduce you to the man I'm going to marry. This is Benjamin." Ben smiled. Leah never called him Benjamin.

Ben held out his hand, but pulled it back quickly. He had forgotten what Leah told him. He wasn't supposed to offer to shake hands with an Amish woman. "It's very nice to meet you, Mrs. Miller."

"Benjamin. It's good to meet you, too. Would you like to come in, Leah? I have pie if you are hungry." Ben noticed there was no hugging between mother and daughter, but there were tears in the eyes of both.

"Thank you, Maemm. Ben, would you like a piece of Mother's pie? It's the best."

"I would love a piece." He followed Leah up the steps into the home that had once been hers.

"Sit. Both of you…at the table." Ben could tell Leah's mother was a no-nonsense kind of lady, so he did as she told him to do and sat down on one of the benches next to the large table. He watched her as she bustled efficiently around her kitchen. It was a beautiful kitchen with oak floors and cupboards. There was a sink and faucet on the counter, but in one corner there was also a water bucket under a hand pump. There was heat radiating from a large wood stove in the other corner. The table was huge with benches on both sides. Leah sat down on the one opposite him.

"I see you have refrigeration now, Maemm. That's nice."

"With the gas generator, I have a hot water heater too."

Ben noticed the Amish dialect. It was strong, and he wondered how difficult it must have been for Leah to learn to speak without it.

"That's nice for you. Maybe some day you can get a gas stove too. Then you won't have to use the wood one."

"I like my wood stove. Your sisters have more modern kitchens."

As she sat a plate down in front of Ben, the back door opened, and the two women and children from the garden came in.

Leah's mother stopped what she was doing. "Anna…Elizabeth…your sister is here."

Both women stopped as if they had been struck. Leah and Ben stood up. Ben did it out of respect. Leah did it out of her desire to reach out to them.

"Anna, Elizabeth. It's good to see you again." Leah moved towards them, and unlike their mother, both women moved towards Leah and pulled her into their arms.

"Leah. You are coming back?"

"Not to stay, Anna. I just wanted you to meet my future husband. This is Ben." Both women nodded at Ben. "We came up so Ben could meet all of you and see where I grew up."

"Are you still living in Florida with Margie?"

"I don't live with her, but I see her every week. She is well and told me to tell you hello."

"Are you still a doctor?"

"Yes. I am. I take care of children who are sick. I love what I do. But tell me about all of you. How many nieces and nephews do I have now?"

Elizabeth put her hand on her stomach. "It will soon be sixteen, and David will marry soon, so there will be more." The three sisters laughed together, and Ben wondered if these three had been best friends when they were younger.

"Maemm? Is Daett in the fields?"

"No. Today he is at a barn raising. He will be sad that he did not see you. Can you come back tomorrow? We will tell all the children to come home after worship so you can see them."

Leah looked at Ben. Her eyes were bright with unshed tears. "Ben? Would that be okay?"

"Of course. But we'll need to leave by four."

"Girls…sit. I will get you some pie too." The sisters sat down on the same bench that Leah sat on. Ben was aware of all three children watching him closely as he finished his pie and the sisters chattered. He was sure the oldest boy was about Sam's age, and smiled when he thought about how much fun Sam would have on this farm playing with children his own age.

Leah picked up hers and Ben's plates, and took them to the sink.

"What time should we come tomorrow?"

"One o'clock will be good."

"Okay. We'll see you then." Leah turned to Ben. "Are you ready?"

When he tried to take her hand, she pulled away from him. And he remembered a saying his grandmother used to say. Something about when in Rome, you should do as the Romans do.

*****

When the two of them left her old home, Leah was almost giddy. "Oh, Ben. Thank you for bringing me back home. It was wonderful to see my mother and sisters. And tomorrow I get to see the rest of my family. They still love me, Ben. I could feel it."

"Of course they do. Time has a way of healing wounds, Leah. You should know that. You're a doctor." Ben knew it because he had experienced it.

After the two of them checked into the lodge, they went for a walk. The view was breathtaking.

"I thought you said there was nothing spectacular about Ohio."

"I guess I forgot about this spot." They appeared to be on the highest spot in Ohio, and as they looked around them they could see a beautiful lake surrounded by hills glowing with autumn colors.

"It's beautiful here. I'd love to bring Sam and Molly here some day to walk on the trails. You don't find beauty like this in Florida. In fact, I've seen a lot of places, and there are only a few that are nicer than this."

"Maybe you like it because it's unlike Texas and Florida. Didn't you tell me once that people are more appreciative of beauty they haven't grown accustomed to?"

"I did, didn't I? It's kind of sad, isn't it?"

"I think it's the same way with people who fall in love. After the newness wears off, they tend to lose the attraction. That won't happen to us, will it Ben?"

"Never, Leah. If that ever starts to happen we need to come right back to this spot so it can remind us of how we feel right now. Maybe we could come here on our anniversary every year."

"We're getting married? I didn't know that." She bumped his shoulder with hers. "Maybe because you haven't asked me yet?" He could hear the laughter in her voice.

"Patience, my dear, the moment is getting close."

*****

Ben had done his homework. He knew what time the sun was going to set, and he knew exactly where they should be so they could see the reflection of it on the water.

The hotel dining room was beautiful. One whole wall, the one next to the water was glass. He specifically asked for a table in the middle of that wall, and he wanted it a half hour before sunset.

When he knocked on Leah's door at the designated time, she opened it immediately.

"You knocked, sir?" There was a hint of humor in her voice.

Ben was speechless. It wasn't just that she was the most beautiful woman he had ever seen. There was an aura around her that was almost magnetic. Her hair was down, and it looked like she had done something to curl the ends of it. He wanted to touch it.

Her dress was rose colored, and if Ben had known anything about the style of dresses, he would have recognized that it was a vintage style she wore. She had a delicate cream colored sweater on her arm. Her only jewelry was a cameo necklace. It looked like something his grandmother had once worn. But on Leah, the whole outfit looked classy, not old.

"Ben? Are you okay?"

"Oh, Leah. You are beautiful. When I told you to bring something nice so we could go out to eat, I never thought you would look like this. You're perfect." He put his arms around her and pulled her close. When she put her arms around his neck and pulled his face down to hers, he knew what her lips would taste like before he even touched them. They would taste like Leah.

When he finally let go of her, so he could breathe, he knew it was a good thing they had a dinner reservation. He wanted to stay right there with her for the rest of their lives.

"Ben?"

"Hmm?" He didn't trust his voice.

"You look nice too. The blue tie matches your eyes." It was the only time that day he thought of Katy. She had told him he should always wear blue.

"Thank you. We need to go. We have reservations."

The dining room was full when they arrived. He had read that the park was a favorite tourist attraction during the fall colors. The waiter led them to their table. The candle Ben had requested was lit and the sun was very close to setting. The colors of sunset and fall reflected on the water.

"Ben. Look. Isn't it beautiful?"

"It is. I've always loved sunrise and sunset. Do you remember me telling you how my mom and dad used to get on their horses and ride side by side into the Texas sunset?"

"Yes. That's a good memory for you, isn't it?"

"Yeah. But now it's our turn, Leah. I want you at my side for the rest of my life. Will you marry me?" He pulled the small white box from his pocket. His eyes were on her when he opened it, and he saw the tears of joy that flooded her eyes. He already knew what her answer would be.

"Oh, Ben. It's beautiful. And of course I'll marry you."

"When?" He sounded so desperate, she had to laugh.

"When would you like to get married, Ben?" Her voice was as smooth as honey again.

"Tomorrow. Do you think your dad would give you away?"

"I don't think he has a choice. I took that privilege away from him years ago, remember? But I'm sure if he had time to get to know you he could love you like a son. But you'd have to turn Amish to get his blessing."

They laughed at that. Her Amish life had given her some extraordinary values and knowledge, but if she had not left, they wouldn't be together now.

Chapter 36

After breakfast the next morning, the two of them had time to walk one of the shorter trails that led away from the lodge. Ben was glad Leah told him to bring a warm jacket. The morning autumn air was nippy, but invigorating. The musty smell of fallen leaves filled the air.

"I think I like Ohio." They were at the edge of the lake and Ben was watching a flock of geese rise from it. Within seconds they were in a V-shaped formation and headed south. He wondered how they knew to do that.

"It is beautiful, especially in the fall. When I lived on the farm, I always liked this time of the year best. The difficult work of the hot summer was over, and harvest was fun. In our community, couples get married in November when harvest is over and there's more leisure time."

"Does that mean we're getting married next month?"

"You're ready to turn Amish already?"

"No. But I'm ready to marry an Amish girl. Do you think you'd like to get married here?

"No. My home is in Florida with you now. But, I'm wondering... if I can talk Anna and Elizabeth into coming down for the wedding, would you be willing to fly back up here and get them? I'd like for my mother to be there too, but I'm sure she won't make the trip."

"Leah, if it will make you happy, I'd fly to China to pick them up."

*****

By the time Leah and Ben were ready to leave the park, the air had warmed and they were able to shed their warm jackets. On the way back to the farm they talked about getting married. They had both known, almost since their first date, that the day would eventually come, but now that Ben had asked her they wanted it to happen as soon as possible.

They agreed that the Saturday before Thanksgiving would be perfect. It would be Leah's weekend off and she felt certain she could get a few days off that week if she took call the weekend after Thanksgiving. "So, if my sisters want to come, can you fly up here and get them?"

"I can. But do you think they would be okay with flying home commercial? I don't think I'm going to want to leave you after the wedding." He glanced over at her and saw the blush.

"I'm sure Momma Beth and Alex would take them to the airport in Tampa after the wedding and help them find their flights. We can get them a direct flight so they won't have to change planes."

"I think that would work. I'll ask them today. That's all they'd have to do is find someone to pick them up at the airport in Akron or Columbus."

"Who would do that?"

"They have English neighbors who actually have a taxi service for the Amish. When my little brother was in the hospital my parents were so dependent on them."

"I think that's the part I don't understand about the Amish. They don't want to be involved with the outside world, yet they take advantage of the very things they shun."

"The Amish have had to adapt some as the world has changed, Ben. Just like all the rest of us have had to. Anna told me yesterday that some of the Amish teenagers even have cell phones now. I wonder how they charge them with no electricity? I'll have to ask today."

They had reached the farm and Ben was shocked when he saw how many buggies were lined up on both sides of the lane.

"Leah! How many people are in your family?"

"A lot! Besides my eight siblings, I have many aunts, uncles, and cousins. I was sure they would be here. Anna told me that my dad's mother is still alive too. She'll be here. I'm glad. I've missed her more than anyone, I think. When my mother and father were at the hospital with my little brother, Grandmother Miller came and stayed at our house. We call her Grohs-mammi. I'm glad you get to meet her."

Ben parked the car in the grass out by the road. It was a little distance from the house, but he felt like he needed a little bit of time and distance to walk before meeting the crowd of people that would soon be family to him. When he opened the car door for Leah and pulled her to her feet, he held onto her for just a few seconds. "I'm feeling a little bit nervous, Baby."

"You'll be okay, Ben. Talk horses and you'll have them eating out of the palm of your hand." She reached up and pulled his face to hers. "They'll love you." The quick little kiss she gave him was reassuring. And she even held his hand as they walked up the lane. When they reached the yard, Leah stopped. Ben watched her as she took in the sight before her.

Since the weather had warmed a little, tables and benches had been placed outside under giant oak and maple trees. Ben could see the men sitting in groups, away from the beehive of activity that was created by a number of children, running and playing. The women were scurrying from the house to the tables, arranging food, and occasionally scolding a child that got underfoot.

It was the children who saw them first.

"She's here, she's here!" Ben heard them squealing as they ran toward their parents.

Ben would never forget the next few minutes. It seemed to go in slow motion. Leah let go of his hand and walked ahead of him. She had on the same dress she'd worn to dinner last night and her hair hung down her back. Within seconds he lost sight of her in the sea of blue and black dresses. He stopped, and the thought crossed his mind that perhaps he had lost her for good. These were her people, her family, and he knew if she could be a doctor for them she would still be here.

Then she was back. "Ben. Come, they all want to meet you." She took his hand and led him toward a man who was now standing next to her mother.

"Daett."

"Leah. You've come home." And unlike her mother the previous day, the big man reached out and embraced his little girl. Ben watched his face. It appeared to be a mixture of pain, relief, and pure joy.

"Daett. I want you to meet Benjamin." She pulled away from him, and the first man who had ever loved Leah held his hand out to the second one who loved her.

"Benjamin. Welcome to our home." And Ben knew that bringing Leah home was the best thing he could have ever done. Her family may have been hurt by her desire to follow her heart, but they still loved her. Their future would be blessed because she had made peace with her past.

*****

After a lunch like Ben had never had before, he was taken on a tour of the farm. The beautiful simplicity of the lives of Leah's family was so evident in everything. There were rows of apple and peach trees, and arbors of grape vines. The barn was a haven for cows, pigs and chickens. The land, newly plowed, looked fertile.

In a precious moment when Ben and Leah were able to get away from the crush of the family, she took him inside the house so he could see where she had lived with her family. He was especially fascinated with the basement. She said it was where the family spent a lot of their time in the winter. There were several clothes lines that stretched from one wall to another. She told him it was where they hung their clothes to dry in the winter when it was too cold outside.

The massive area under the house was also where children were sent to play. One whole end of it held shelves where hundreds of canned fruits and vegetables were stored. Ben could see how these people could live without outside assistance or interference.

When they returned to the yard, Ben found a seat with the men and listened to them talk about their community. He could tell from their conversation that they were there for each other in the bad times, and in the good ones.

But what he enjoyed most about his afternoon was watching Leah. He could tell she had been the older, much respected, and much loved sister. After her young nieces and nephews lost their initial shyness, her lap became a favorite resting spot for them. And Ben thought again about her decision not to have children of her own. He knew it was right for her. This way, they all belonged to her, just like her young patients did at home.

Ben didn't realize it was time to go until one of the men said it was time to go home to do the chores. It was like they all had an internal watch, or perhaps they had been watching the shadows of the huge oak trees lengthen in the afternoon sun.

The women began to pick up their dishes, and the older children began to round up the little ones. Quietly, they began to slip away, one family at a time. There was no slamming of car doors and no revving motors. Their departure was noted by the whinny of a horse and the clopping of their hooves on the packed dirt lane.

The only ones that remained to see Ben and Leah off were her parents, the grandmother she loved, and the two sisters and their families.

On their trip back up the lane, Leah stopped just once and looked behind her. The family she loved was watching her leave once again. But this time, Leah was leaving with the knowledge that they still loved her.

Chapter 37

Ben and Leah were married on the Saturday before
Thanksgiving, at sunset, in their new home. Leah had it decorated
with fall colors, and their vows included a prayer of thanksgiving to
the God who brought them together.

Leah's two sisters, Anna and Elizabeth, were the only
members of her Amish family present, but she insisted on some of
the customs she'd grown up with. She wanted to be married in
November because that was the month Amish couples traditionally
married, and after the ceremony she had a large meal for the family
who celebrated with them.

She had planned to have it catered, but with her two sisters in
the house for four days before the wedding, it was all home cooked.

Leah told Ben that Amish weddings and the reception that
followed usually included the whole community. Because her
community in Ohio was so large, there could have been close to five
hundred people to feed. Ben was extremely happy they didn't have
to celebrate their wedding in Ohio.

They were both happy with the few that came to witness their
vows and celebrate with them. Besides Ben's immediate family that
included his sisters, Abby and Carly, and his two sets of parents,
they were joined by Margie, the woman who had been instrumental
in making Leah's dreams to be a doctor, come true.

Their only attendants were Sam who carried the rings for his
dad, and Lexie who was thrilled to hold Leah's bouquet during the
ceremony.

After dinner, Momma Beth and Alex took Leah's sisters back to Tampa with them. They would leave the next morning to return to the family that would be waiting to hear about Leah's new life.

And because Leah still had some Amish in her heart, she wanted to spend their wedding night in their home. It was the Amish way, and Ben really didn't need to take his bride away to show her how much he loved her.

Ben woke early on the Sunday morning after their wedding. When he reached for Leah, she was there. His spirit soared, and he breathed a sigh of contentment. And he knew, in his heart, that this was the love he would grow old with.

Slipping out of bed, he went to the kitchen to make their coffee. When it was finished, he took his cup and went out to the patio. The beauty of the garden Leah had created around their pool was alive with the music of the night. His eyes went to the water, and in it he saw the reflection of the brightest star in the sky. It twinkled for a few seconds before the light of the coming day hid it from his view. But the reflection of dawn remained.

Epilogue

One Year Later

"Hey, Miss Molly. You better finish your breakfast if you wanna go ride Beauty." Ben was picking up the breakfast dishes left behind when Leah and Sam hurried away from the house fifteen minutes earlier in a flurry of activity. She was going to drop him off at school before she went to the office.

"Booty…ride Booty?" Ben turned from the sink when he heard the clapping of little hands. Molly's blue eyes were shining and the curly blond pony tails Leah put in her hair that morning were sticking straight out from the sides of her head like little appendages. The blue ribbons that held them matched her eyes.

"We'll go as soon as you finish your milk." Molly picked up her sippy cup and looked at it.

"Kitty milk?" She held the cup out to Ben.

"Oh no you don't. That's Molly's milk. Kitty has her own. Now drink it. Beauty's waiting for us."

He smiled when he saw her begin to suck on the straw, and turned back to the sink. With-in seconds he heard the cup hit the floor.

"All gone. See Booty."

Even though she'd be two years old this week, Molly had just started to talk. In September, Ben had been worried about her lack of a vocabulary, but Leah had reassured him that she was okay. "Kids will talk when they're ready. Stop fretting about her." And she was so right.

It was like Molly went to bed mute one night, and the next morning she woke up talking in complete sentences. After Ben thought about it, he realized that the older kids had been doing her talking for her all summer, and when they went to school she knew she had to do it herself.

Her vocabulary had gone from about ten words to at least a hundred in a matter of a couple weeks. It was like she had known the words all along, but never had any reason to use them as long as she had an older brother and three older cousins around who would talk for her.

When Ben leaned over to retrieve the empty cup off the floor, he felt her sticky little hands patting his head. He'd fixed pancakes for breakfast.

"Oh, yuck, Sis. Now I have to wash my hair. I'll have bugs swarming me at the grove if I don't."

"Uck!" Ben couldn't help but smile. Now she had a hundred and one words in her vocabulary. He finished the dishes then washed the maple syrup out of his hair, and hers, before he picked the little girl up from her highchair. "Okay, let's go ride Beauty, then you're off to Grandma's house today while Daddy goes to work."

The trip to the grove took all of five minutes. When Ben arrived, he noticed that his father-in-law's golf cart was already parked next to the office door. The orange harvest was at its peak this month, and every one involved was trying to get an early start in the day. Christmas orders from up north had doubled this year. Walking into the office, he was greeted by the sound of the phone ringing and the smell of fresh brewed coffee.

"Hey, Ben. Did you oversleep this morning?" Abby looked up from the computer and grinned at him. It was a standing joke between the two of them and she just wouldn't let it go.

"Wouldn't you like to know?" He smirked at her and waved at his mother-in-law who was on the phone. "Where's John?"

"He's already out in the grove with the pickers. They all showed up on time today."

"Good. We should be almost done with that southwest corner, shouldn't we?"

"Yep, and the harvest is looking real good. You gonna have time to sit down with us and look over the numbers after…" The phone rang again and Abby stopped mid sentence to pick up the second line. "Browning Family Farm. Can I help you?"

Ben looked around him. *Katy-girl…your dream is a reality. You would love it.* The thought was cut short by the wiggling baby in his arms. "Booty?"

"Okay, Sis. Let's get you on that horse so Grandma can take you home and I can get to work." Leaving the office, he traveled across the gravel driveway to the horse barn. The main doors were wide open, and when he went in, he noticed that all six stalls were empty except for the last one. He'd seen his and Sam's horses in the pasture when he drove in. The two horses he'd bought for Abby's boys were grazing under the oak trees on the far side of the house.

"Booty," Molly began to wiggle again and looked at her dad. "Down."

"Okay. Go see your Beauty." As soon has her feet hit the floor, she was across it to where her horse's stall was. Beauty had her head hanging over the side and when Molly reached her hand up to touch her, the horse nuzzled it.

Beauty was an older Arabian mare Ben bought for Molly on her first birthday last year. Since he'd bought a horse for Sam on his first birthday, it only seemed fair that Molly would get one too. When he bought Beauty, he also bought a two year old Arabian for Leah. It was his wedding gift to her. Both his girls had fallen in love with their gifts and the whole family went riding on Sunday afternoons as often as they could. Molly always rode with him on those rides, but loved it when Ben would put her on the back of Beauty and lead her around the pasture field.

"Okay. Up you go. Hang on tight to her mane." As Molly hung on to the horse and Ben hung on to her, he thought again about how lucky he'd been to find just the right horse for her. He chose Beauty because she was small and had a mild disposition.

Three times around the corral and Molly was still yelling "more."

"I'm sorry, Sis. We have to stop so daddy can go to work." Ben took his daughter off the horse and set her down on the ground where she proceeded to throw a full-blown temper tantrum. Ben sighed. *Sorry, little girl. Daddy's going to win this one today.* He slapped Beauty on the rump and sent her running before he picked the tearful girl up off the ground.

"Don't you want to go home with Grandma, Molly?" He knew she did, but right now she was asserting her two year old will. He was relieved when he saw Linda coming across the driveway.

"Hey. What's wrong with my girl?" As soon as Molly saw her grandmother, she turned the tears off, wiggled out of Ben's arms again, and ran towards her grandmother with arms outstretched. Ben watched as Katy's mom picked the little girl up and swung her around.

"Wanna go swimming with Grandma today?" And just like that, Beauty was forgotten with the promise of a swim in Grandma's pool.

"Hey, Linda. Thanks for taking her again today. Abby said things should slow down after the holidays and she can start watching her again."

"Don't be silly, Ben. Abby and the rest of you are going to be busy for the next couple months. I'll just plan on keeping her until things calm down here. And tell Leah if she needs any help getting ready for this angel's birthday party on Saturday, to let me know. I can bake the cake if she wants me to."

"I think she has it all planned out. You just get to come and have fun this time."

"Okay. I'll keep this one busy until you come and get her tonight."

"I'll be there about six. I'm going to pick Sam and Abby's kids up from school so we can clean the stalls out before supper. Then I'll be over to get her."

"Sounds good. You still doing that charter tomorrow?"

"Yeah. So I'll have to bring her out at seven. But Leah is only working till noon so she'll come and get her then." Ben leaned over and gave Molly a kiss. "Have fun with Grandma, Molly. Daddy loves you."

"Lub oo." Linda had set the little girl down and the two of them walked toward the golf cart, hand in hand. Gratitude flooded Ben's heart again as he watched them walk away.

*****

The past year had been a busy one for Ben, but one that had made him stop several times to just recognized God's goodness to him. After years of almost unbearable grief, his heart was healing and joy had resurfaced. His and Leah's wedding had been the beginning. Every day this past year he got up loving her more than he loved her the day before. She was so easy to love, and to live with.

When he, Sam and Molly moved into her house the week after the wedding, they instantly became a family. He often wondered if her years of growing up in an Amish home made her so adaptable and easy going. The extra work that went along with an instant family didn't seem to phase her. Even the building project to make their home bigger, to accommodate all of them better, went smoothly.

The highlight of their year though had been the two week honeymoon they took in June. It may have been late, but it was perfect for both of them. They had flown into Las Vegas before traveling on to Zion National Park and the Grand Canyon. Neither of them had been there before, and the Amish girl from Ohio and the Texas cowboy fell in love with the west.

That trip also ended with the two of them becoming the official parents of Molly.

Soon after they married, Ben's lawyer began the process of finding Sage. She was still in Las Vegas where she'd given birth to Molly, and she agreed to meet with Ben before he and Leah returned to Florida. Ben hadn't seen her for almost thirty years and was shocked at what the years had done to her. But the shock didn't diminish the love that flooded his heart when he took her into his arms. She was his big sister, his only sibling, and she gave him an amazing gift when she asked him to take Molly.

She signed the papers that gave Ben and Leah full custody of Molly. When Ben asked her if she wanted a picture of her little girl, she accepted it with tears in her eyes. "Thank you, Ben, for giving her a good life, and lots of love." When he asked her to come and see them sometime, she whispered, "maybe someday. Until then, can you tell her I couldn't take care of her?" Ben gave his sister another hug and reassured her he would.

Two days ago, Molly received a birthday card in the mail from her "Aunt Sage." Ben slipped it into her baby book and knew he would use it someday to tell his little girl about her biological mother. Until that day arrived though, Molly had the best mother a little girl could have. She adored Leah and the feeling was mutual. They even looked alike with their blond hair. But Molly had the same midnight blue eyes that her dad and brother had.

*****

Molly's second birthday party on Saturday was a festive one. Leah said it should be special since it was the first one she was able to plan for her one and only daughter. She even took Friday off so she could get ready.

Since their home was right beside the park, it was a perfect place for a party that would include many children. Besides her brother, all of Molly's extended family was there. None of them were related to her by blood, but all were connected by a bond of love.

As Ben and Leah sat together, holding hands, and watching the kids play, his eyes were drawn to the figure in the middle of the group of laughing children. "Look at Momma Beth, Leah. She looks like she's having more fun than the kids."

"I know. Isn't she a beautiful grandmother? Thank you for sharing her and Katy's story with me. Just think, if she hadn't walked out of that abortion clinic almost forty years ago, none of this would be happening today. When she gave birth to Katy, she gave life to Sam's mother. When you needed a doctor for Sam, I was the lucky one who was chosen to treat him and his little sister. And now, I get to be their mother and your wife. I think I'm going to thank her today for having the courage to choose life for her child. It's because of that one loving choice that all of us are together today."

Ben squeezed Leah's hand. Years ago, Momma Beth had promised Katy that the darkness of any night would always be followed by dawn. Katy had passed that promise on to Ben. And now that it had been proven true in his own life, Ben knew he and Leah would pass it on to Molly and Sam. Some promises are true for all generations.

About the Author

Brenda Young writes under the name of B.J.Young. After retiring from a rewarding career in nursing, she continued to feel a need to nurture those who were hurting. She started to help others by writing devotionals and short stories. Her prayer is that every thing she writes will inspire and encourage others to make the best of the life given to them.

She now writes short stories and devotionals for two magazines published by Front Porch Publishing. She has been a contributing author to anthologies and devotional books, including Gary Chapman's *Love is a Verb Devotions*. She has been published by *Guideposts*, *Angels on Earth* magazines and *The Huffington Post*.

This book is the last book of her Dawn Trilogy. Her debut novel, *A Portrait of Dawn* was a semi-finalist in the ACFW Genesis contest. *Dawn's New Day, A Love Story* is the second of the Dawn Trilogy.

She and her husband live in Northwest Ohio, where she enjoys her children and grandchildren. She is presently working on a fourth novel.

She is a member of ACFW and Northwest Ohio Christian Writers.

She blogs at http://www.bjyoung28.blogspot.com/